# MAIDEN

## BOOK ONE IN THE MAIDEN TRILOGY

## CHRIS SORENSEN

POND
PUBLISHING

www.maidentrilogy.com

ISBN-10: 0971942331
ISBN-13: 978-0-9719423-3-2

To ALEXIS, my first maiden.

Always remember that true royalty
cannot be bought or plundered.

It is already inside you.

*I am not afraid;*
*I was born to do this.*

- Joan of Arc

# CHAPTER 1

Jeanette knew it was wrong to be out after dark, away from the village, heading to the one place girls were forbidden to be, yet she kept moving forward. One last outing with Addy before the royal caravan came to festival, that is all she wanted.

"I can't see where I'm going," Addy whispered. "Slow down."

"Stop dragging your feet and you'll be able to keep up," Jeanette replied, her trim frame and long, black hair gliding between the trees. Of all the excursions she had talked Addy into over the years, this one took top prize.

"Why did I let you convince me this was a good idea?" Addy asked between breaths, her plump cheeks red from exertion, and her long, wool frock clinging to her from the humidity.

"I didn't talk you into anything you didn't want to do. It was your idea in the first place."

"My idea?"

"You are the one who wanted to see Rendall, remember?" Jeanette said. Addy groaned and wiped the back of her hand across her brow, attempting to move the sweaty, burgundy curls from her face.

"Get down," Jeanette said, the dancing light of a fire coming into view.

"What do you see?" Addy asked, kneeling next to Jeanette in the brush.

Jeanette raised her head to get a better look. "There's lots of tents...and it looks like a bunch of boys around the fire."

"What are they doing?"

"Oh, Addy" Jeanette said with a hint of amusement," even under the noblest of missions - such as training to protect the kingdom - if you put a bunch of juvenile boys together what do you expect they would be doing?" She pulled Addy up to see the young soldiers in their undergarments, holding drinks, dancing around a bonfire.

"They look like a bunch of imbeciles," Addy said.

"I don't know how we're going to pick Rendall out of the crowd."

"This was a bad idea, Jeanette," Addy said, squirming. "There is no way we'll find him. Please Jeanette, let's just go."

"Maybe we just need to call out to him," Jeanette said with a grin. "Oh, Rendall, we have come to call on you," she cried out, fluttering her eyelashes, imitating Addy's voice.

"Are you out of your gourd? Stop it!"

"I hope you are ready to hold me in your big, manly arms and make me blush."

"Enough, Jeanette. Please!"

"All right, all right," Jeanette said, turning her attention back to the camp. "But we're not going yet. Let's see if we can find him." She was happy to help Addy pick out Rendall, but Jeanette personally had little use for boys. She comprehended that boys and girls were supposed to be attracted to each other. In fleeting moments, she would admit that maybe some of the boys in town noticed her. Perhaps one day they would not be so immature and she would be willing to notice them, too. If Addy wanted to fantasize over potential husbands, like the rest of the girls in town, that was her business. If there were someone for Jeanette, he wouldn't be a boy dressed in his undergarments dancing around a campfire.

"Come on, let's go back home."

"We already made it this far and our parents don't know. We are perfectly safe, unless you are worried about being attacked by Red Eyes?"

Addy gasped.

Jeanette had meant to be flippant, but as she surveyed the surroundings – alone, in the woods, the middle of the night – she realized her words were poorly timed. She did not believe in the Red Eyes, or Rogues, the savages that supposedly lived in the forests and scavenged village after village to stay alive. Everyone knew the stories, but she had never heard of them coming near Emerleigh. Old folk tales to keep the children minding their elders; that is all they were.

"Everything is fine," Jeanette promised. "Besides, we made it this far and I want the full tour." Jumping up, she grabbed Addy's hand and began running, the leaves and brush rustling underneath their feet. Jeanette's pace quickened as she entered a small clearing. On the next step the earth beneath her instantly gave. Still holding tight to Addy's hand, they fell through a hidden barrier of limbs and leaves.

Jeanette landed flat on her stomach, knocking the wind out of her. She drew quick, short breaths and rolled onto her back. They were at the bottom of a pit.

"Are you okay?" Jeanette asked, wiping dirt off her face.

Addy rolled to one side. "I don't know," she said wincing, grabbing her leg through the skirts of her dress. "I landed on my knee."

Jeanette stood and jumped a couple of times, trying to reach the top of the hole. It was just out of reach. She looked down at Addy and could see the fear welling up in her face.

"There's nothing to grab for me to climb out," Jeanette said. She tried jumping one more time to no avail. She paced for a moment and then kicked the tomb of dirt in frustration. How was there a pit in the middle of the forest? Who would have dug it?

Jeanette stopped in place, ears perked, listening. It was quieter. "Do you hear that?"

Addy listened. "Hear what?"

After a few more seconds, fear building, Jeanette said, "I don't hear anything...that's the problem."

Both girls craned their necks. The sounds of the young soldiers reveling at the camp had ceased.

"We can't just sit here," Jeanette said, "we have to try to get out. If I stand on your shoulders, can you lift me up?"

Addy massaged her knee. "I don't know if I can put any weight on it."

"Well let's find out," Jeanette said, helping Addy up. "The only other option is to stay here all night and have our parents not find us in the morning and send everyone looking for us. Or wait to see if...something else shows up."

Addy limped over and crouched down, placing her back against the earthen wall.

"Do you think you can stand?"

"I think so," Addy said, bracing as Jeanette stepped up on her good leg and then onto her shoulders. When Jeanette tried to stand to full height, Addy's knee gave out and Jeanette fell down beside her.

"What do we do now?" Addy asked.

"You don't have to do anything," a male voice responded from outside the pit. Addy cowered to the corner. Jeanette crouched next to her.

"If you try to hurt us we'll scream," Jeanette proclaimed. "The men from that camp are from our village and they will protect us."

A silhouette appeared at the top of the pit. Jeanette searched the face, trying to see the eye color, but the figure remained in the shadows. Her fists tightened.

"Well, you can scream if you like, but I don't think you want more men over here. And I use the term *men* loosely." The voice was familiar. Jeanette stepped away from the corner to get a different angle. The light from the moon brought the young man's face into view.

"Corwin!" she yelled, relief and anger somehow coexisting inside.

"Really, Jeanette, you pay them far too high a compliment by referring to them as *men*." Corwin paused for a response and when there wasn't one, he laughed.

"Get us out of here, now!"

Corwin looked behind him, "What do you think Rendall, should we get them out?"

A towering figure appeared behind Corwin, chuckling. "Hmm, I don't know. Looks like they are in quite a mess. But at least we know our trap worked. We'll get points for that with the boys, won't we? Oh, I'm sorry, points with the *men*." They both laughed.

Jeanette wanted to curse them, but she knew it would only feed their immaturity.

"Ah, there are so many questions, Jeanette, so many questions," Corwin said, his shoulder length, dirty-blond hair messy from days at camp. Sometimes the young men would hold drill in town and she would see him in his fighting tunic, with the dark green colors of Amarin and the kingdom's seal in gold. Tonight, he wore a simple work shirt and breeches.

More than any other boy in the village, Corwin always seemed to be nearby. Wherever Jeanette was Corwin would be in her peripheral with a gleam in his eye, as if he knew something about her. Something he wouldn't share.

"Yes, Corwin, we fell in your big, manly, secret trap! You got us good. Now can you please get us out of here?"

"I guess," Corwin said, "but you're spoiling all my fun." He nodded to Rendall who left for a short time and came back with a ladder. "Move out of the way," Corwin said. "I've already hurt your pride; I don't want to hurt anything else."

Jeanette groaned in frustration. "Why are they all alike?" she mumbled to herself, turning to Addy. "Is your knee feeling better? Will you be able to climb up the ladder?"

"Yes, I think so," she said, walking over to start her ascent. As she put her foot on the first step, she looked straight up to see Rendall's outstretched hand waiting for her.

"Don't worry, Miss Addy, I'll help you if it gets shaky." There was a pause. Addy started to wobble and then fell backward onto Jeanette. They both hit the ground, again.

"What'd you do?" Corwin asked.

"I didn't do nothing!" Rendall answered. "She just...fell."

Corwin looked down and saw Addy sprawled out, unconscious. "I think she's fainted."

"Addy...Addy, wake up," Jeanette said, gently tapping her on her cheek.

"I don't think this could get any better," Corwin continued, almost cheerfully. "But, unfortunately we need to leave before the camp sends scouts. Rendall, get in there and get her up." Rendall climbed down to get Addy.

"Be careful of her knee," Jeanette warned.

"I will, Miss Jeanette," Rendall said, lifting Addy off the ground and over his shoulder with a heave. He looked at Jeanette, pointing to the ladder, "After you."

Jeanette made her way up the ladder and out of the pit, happy to breathe the fresh air of the night again. She stood straight up to see Corwin in front of her. He almost spoke, but she turned around before he could say anything.

"I'm coming up...a little help...with the ladder...please!"

Rendall begged from below, trying to carry Addy and balance on the rickety rungs.

Jeanette and Corwin each grabbed a side of the ladder to steady it. Corwin looked at Jeanette. "Are you okay?" he asked, speaking sincerely for the first time.

"I think so."

He smiled. "No more night trips to the training camp?"

"We would have been fine if it wasn't for your ruddy pit."

At the top of the ladder, Corwin and Jeanette carefully took hold of Addy and laid her on the ground. Rendall knelt beside her and took his water pouch off his belt. Pouring some onto his hand, he sprinkled Addy's face. "Miss Addy, wake up now."

She started to groan a little, her head wavering back and forth. Slowly, her eyes opened. "Oh good, you're here with us again," Rendall said. "You fell down, Miss Addy." She remained perfectly still on the ground, frozen. "Aw, it's just the nerves. Fainting is never much fun."

"Are you feeling okay, Addy?" Jeanette asked.

"I...I think I'm okay. How did I get out of the hole?"

Corwin grinned. "Rendall was kind enough to help you out."

Addy turned and stared at Jeanette. Jeanette shrugged. "Can we please go now?" Addy asked, slowly getting to her feet.

"Are you sure you can walk?" Jeanette asked.

Addy took a few steps, favoring her healthy leg. "I think so."

Jeanette turned to Corwin. "Thanks for making the pit for us to fall in and thanks for getting us out, but we're going to be on our way."

"We can't just let them go back by themselves Corwin, can we?" Rendall asked. "The festival is coming up soon; there's more traffic than normal and what about the..." he paused.

"Other dangers. It's not safe."

Corwin looked at Jeanette. "You will head straight back to the village?"

"Yes, of course."

Corwin pondered for a moment. "They found their way here; they can find their way back." Jeanette sensed Rendall wanted to argue, but Corwin's tone did not invite debate. Addy turned and started walking towards home.

Jeanette looked at Corwin. Her body moved forward, slightly, as if propelling her to speak; to say something else. He cut her off before she could. "Please be safe. If you make good time you should be back before dawn."

"Are there any other secret traps we need to know about?"

"No. That was the only one," he answered with a smile, then motioned for Rendall to help him start covering the pit again.

Jeanette walked as quickly as she could to catch up to Addy, who was moving briskly, albeit with a small limp. With each step, the night seemed more still.

"I am so sorry, Addy. I should have never brought us out here."

Addy sighed. "If I didn't have you to push me into trouble, my life would be pretty boring."

"Oh my dear Addalynn, what would I do without you?"

"You would have gotten yourself killed a long time ago."

Jeanette grinned and added, "True. And in the case of my demise, I am more confident than ever that if I'm not around to push you, it looks like Rendall is certainly able to carry you wherever you need to go."

Addy reached out to push Jeanette. Jeanette lunged out of the way, laughing, as they moved farther from the camp and closer to Emerleigh.

After a while, Addy spoke. "Corwin seemed happy to see you."

"Don't you ever say that again," Jeanette said. There was a warm feeling in her cheeks. It was the last thing she wanted; one of the boys in the village having feelings for her. Or worse, having the boy think that she had feelings for him. But with Corwin, avoiding that kind of trouble was just a waiting game. The festival started in a couple of days and all of the boys Corwin's age who had been training locally would be sent to the Royal Academy, their last stop before seeing the battlefield.

She would not see him again for years.

"We certainly didn't have to worry about finding Rendall," Jeanette said, changing the subject.

"Did you hear what he said?" Addy asked. "He didn't want us to be by ourselves! Do you think he'll ask me to dance at festival?" Jeanette shook her head and kept her gaze forward, drowning out Addy's gushing as a strange feeling came over her.

Guilt.

Guilt because she had not told her best friend that, regardless of what happened at festival, they would not see each other for a very long time.

# CHAPTER 2

Later that morning, all the young women in the town of Emerleigh aged fourteen to nineteen sat in the town hall waiting for instructions. Wooden benches lined row after row on the packed dirt floor. Like the town itself it was old, but sturdy.

Around the room, Jeanette saw fear, hope, and uncertainty in most of the wide, gray eyes around her. But more than anything, she saw excitement.

Festival was a day away and there had never been a festival like the one planned this year. Prince Braxton was searching for a bride and personally making stops at each of the four major towns in Amarin to find one.

Jeanette was also excited, but it had nothing to do with the festival, the caravan, or the prince. After years of hoping and dreaming, she had finally decided that when festival was over, she was leaving, running away. A trip away from farm life, away from her crazy mother, and away from everything she had ever known. She had everything planned; except for how to tell Addy.

"Can you believe it? It's festival!" Addy exclaimed, sitting next to her. Brandy, Addy's younger sister, was at her side.

"How can you be so perky with no sleep?" Jeanette asked, trying to keep her eyes open. Even though Addy remained quiet, Jeanette knew the answer.

*Addy's dream of serving at the castle will come true in the next few days.*

Every two years at festival, the Royal Caravan would seek out new servants to help keep the castle running smoothly. This year, the citizens of Emerleigh were asked to submit their finest works of art, sewing, and baking for consideration. Addy was formidably known as one of the best bakers in town. Jeanette had no doubt she would be leaving with the caravan.

Jeanette wanted nothing more than for Addy to be chosen; it would make her choice to run away that much easier. It felt selfish to think it, but Jeanette knew it was the only way for both of them to get what they truly wanted.

Elizabeth, the matron of Emerleigh and wife of the mayor, stood before the crowd of girls and called them to order. Behind her, attached from the ceiling, hung a long, dark green banner with the symbol of Amarin: a bail of hay with a sickle on each side.

"The first day of festival," Elizabeth started, "will be the same as usual; lots of fun and games for everyone. The only difference, of course, is that..." she paused for affect, "the prince will be among us."

Chatter, giggling and feigned swoons rippled through the room. Jeanette rolled her eyes. She had no use for giggling or swooning.

"There are two ways that you may be called to go to the castle," Elizabeth continued, describing how the judging would take place and what it meant to serve at the castle. Elizabeth herself had served in the castle - as a seamstress - when she was younger and recounted her experience.

Jeanette had no intention of entering anything for judging. She couldn't bake, sew, or sing. She felt no connection to the female traits that all girls were supposed to have as they prepared for a married life on the farm. Though she respected it, the thought of being shackled to the land made her anxious. It made her angry.

"The second opportunity to leave with the caravan," Elizabeth continued, "is specifically for the seventeen to nineteen year olds. The advisers to the king and queen feel they have created a special formula, a serum, which can help bring out the true eye color. There will be a special ceremony to see if any girl's eyes will change."

Prince Braxton had never brought his rumored good looks and natural born green eyes to Emerleigh before - not to enjoy a holiday, not to pay his respects as prince, and certainly not to look for a bride. How in the heavens will they find a girl with green eyes? The only person - ever - that Jeanette had seen with true green eyes was Elizabeth's husband, Alden, the mayor. He was one of only six people in the kingdom who still had the true color and gift.

More than a half-century ago, a baby had been born with gray eyes, not the natural green that was accustomed to the citizens of Amarin. People brushed it off as a fluke, the result of a sickness with the mother or child. But when baby after baby, all throughout the kingdom, began to be born with gray eyes, there was panic. As the true eye color died out, Amarin's gift of growth and harvest slowly dwindled. Year after year, more and more crops failed and hopes faltered.

The change was devastating and the Kingdom of Tamir - their brown eyed cousins to the northeast - soon took notice. With a lust for power and a gift for battle, Tamir decided it was a sign that Amarin was week and ready to be overtaken. The war had taken land, materials, food, and most important, numerous lives, including Jeanette's older brother, Jaren.

It felt like people in the kingdom ignored the reality of the situation. Jeanette could not see a scenario where Amarin could win the war, but she felt as if she was the only one. Any mention of the dire situation and those around her ignored it. The last time there was any positive outlook was twenty-three years ago, when Prince Braxton was the first baby since the change to be born with green eyes. There was a short spike in morale after his birth. Maybe fate had won its way back and the gift would return? But the celebrating did not last long and nothing else changed.

Until now.

The queen hoped that if the prince could find, or create, a girl with true color, marry her, and produce offspring with green eyes, it would be the catalyst needed for the country to finally regain control and start anew.

"Is it true that no girl's eyes have changed yet?" came a high pitched, determined voice from behind. The hair on the back of Jeanette's neck bristled.

*Lorelei.*

"That is correct," Elizabeth answered. "So far, the special serum has not had any effect on the girls in Lynnhaven or Crespin." More murmuring ensued in the crowd.

This was no surprise to Jeanette. How could it work? Eye color was not something to be forced. Either you had it or you didn't. Someone's eye color should not determine privilege or status.

"And what about Miss Emerleigh?" Lorelei continued. "Is it true that the girl named Miss Emerleigh at last year's festival gets the first dance with the prince at the closing ceremony?"

Jeanette loathed Lorelei and everything about her: the hair, the clothes, the winy sing-song voice, and most importantly, her status as the most two-faced shrew to ever live. Addy turned to Jeanette and gave a patient nod, encouraging her to stay calm.

"That is correct, Lorelei," Elizabeth said. "With the Royal Caravan coming, we will not hold a pageant, so you, as the winner from last year, will have first dance with the prince."

Jeanette did not turn around, but she had a perfect picture of Lorelei's face and the pretentious grin she wore.

"Do you think any of our eyes will change?" somebody whispered from behind.

"Well, from what my father said this morning, it has to be somebody special," Lorelei replied. "In order for the serum to work, the girl has to make herself worthy."

Jeanette looked at Addy and pretended to gag.

"My father also said," Lorelei continued, "that there is another person at the castle who has green eyes. He tried the serum personally to see if it would work and his eyes turned." Jeanette had not heard that before.

"What a dream come true it will be to dance with Prince Braxton." Soft approvals followed from the gaggle of girls hanging on Lorelei's every word.

Jeanette lost her patience. Turning around, face firm, she asked, "If it's not too much trouble, could you please save your dreaminess for the dance and quiet down so the rest of us can listen?"

A smile and giggle ran across Brandy's face. Addy bumped her sister with her elbow. "Shush, Brandy. You will only make it worse."

The girls sitting around Lorelei looked at each other and then back at Lorelei. Lorelei corrected her posture and ignored Jeanette.

Elizabeth continued, "All entries should be in judge's tent before the opening ceremony and all of the girls preparing to take the serum need to be in their best dress, looking presentable."

Lorelei leaned forward, right between Jeanette and Addy and said, loud enough for only them to hear, "I wouldn't be

14

too worried about either of you being chosen. They say Prince Braxton is looking for a woman, not a dirty, crop digging little girl."

Turning, standing, and stepping over the bench, Jeanette got right in Lorelei's face. Lorelei and the other girls on her bench went tumbling backwards. Every lock of long hair in the room swung toward the commotion.

"Why can't you just keep your big mouth shut!" Jeanette yelled, leaning closer. There was fear and panic in Lorelei's eyes. All the girls that had been sitting around her crawled away to safety. Whether out of shock, complacency, or enjoyment all the other girls in the room were completely still.

"Jeanette! Jeanette!" Elizabeth said, finally pushing her way through the crowd and grabbing hold of Jeanette. Some of the girls around Lorelei came to her aid and helped her up.

Elizabeth plopped Jeanette down in one of the chairs at the front of the room. She regained her composure and turned to the rest of the girls. "I think that's enough excitement for today. Everyone is excused...except for you Lorelei. Up here, please."

The crowd slowly exited. After everyone left, Elizabeth stood between them. "Now you two, what is the trouble?"

Lorelei started, "Miss Elizabeth, in all fairness to Jeanette, I was probably talking more than I should have been and I'm sure that upset her. I know everyone is excited and nervous about the festival and I should have been more respectful."

Elizabeth looked at Jeanette, as if to ask if she wanted to respond. Jeanette glared at Lorelei who, now that Elizabeth was not looking at her, wore a smirk. Jeanette held her tongue, complacent in the fact that she would only have to deal with Lorelei for a few more days.

"Very well. Lorelei you are excused." Lorelei gave a curtsy and walked out, her red satin gown prancing with her.

Elizabeth waited for Lorelei to leave and as the door

closed behind her asked, "Is she always like that?"

Jeanette looked at Elizabeth, shocked by the honesty in her voice. "Always," Jeanette answered.

"Do any of the girls like her?"

Jeanette let out a small laugh. "There must be some who do, because there are always girls fawning over her. But for the life of me I don't know why."

"Do you think she wants to get out of Emerleigh?"

The sun was starting to set. The shadows bounced off the walls and dust danced off the light. Jeanette's tension eased at Elizabeth's soft, approachable manner.

"Sure she wants to leave, but only if it means on the coat tails of some royal carriage."

"What about you?"

Jeanette laughed again, harder. "Me? Some royal snob? Can you imagine, me all fancy and...?"

"That's not what I meant Jeanette. Do you want to be somewhere other than here?"

The feeling that came over Jeanette did not come easy. It was new. From the young girl who always was outspoken and stood her ground, the one that never needed any help and was always tough, there was a feeling of longing.

As the seconds passed, Jeanette could feel the warmth in her cheeks and the knot in her throat. "Yes. One day."

Elizabeth smiled. "But why would you want to leave? What's wrong with what we have here?"

"I don't know, it's just not me," she answered. "It seems useless. Each year more and more crops fail and we sink deeper into war. Eye color is supposed to be so important and that's all anyone is worried about. But even the handful who still have it...what difference does it seem to make?" she asked, quickly wishing she hadn't. The only person in town *with* eye color was Elizabeth's husband. "I didn't mean any offense to Alden."

"I know you didn't."

"But seriously, what difference does his eye color make?" she continued, Elizabeth's demeanor inviting honesty. "Does he actually feel a difference? I mean, has he ever felt like he can manipulate the outcome?"

Elizabeth nodded, as if she understood Jeanette's frustration. "He struggles. I think Alden wishes it was as simple as manipulating the plants or the seeds. But that is not how it works. It's more of a...it's more of a relationship. A partnership."

Jeanette tried to understand, but a relationship with nature is not what was needed. Wheat, potatoes, fruits and vegetables...that's what was needed. If there was no control with having the true eye color, then what was the point?

"As bad as things are, imagine what would happen if we had nobody with the gift. Imagine how much worse things would be."

*I don't think it could be any worse.*

The people of Amarin clung to the only thing they had left, hope. But Jeanette saw nothing in the emotions or the actions of her people that gave her hope. She wanted hope and was determined to find it, somewhere else.

"What about you?" Jeanette asked. "Have you ever been outside of the kingdom?"

"Only once."

"And I bet it was wonderful."

Elizabeth smiled, "It was exciting. It was years ago, when I was at the castle. When our market town, Enzion, was having a hard time getting traders from Bandar to come and trade with us, the kingdom asked a delegation of servants from the castle to attend a special council. It was held up north, in Bandar. What a beautiful country," Elizabeth said, her face glazed over with remembrance. "Every time I see your cousin, Tristyn, I think of that trip, and the beautiful people I met."

Jeanette nodded, trying to hide the place inside her that Elizabeth had touched. To hear somebody else talk about Tristyn in a positive way meant a lot.

"But what if...what if this never goes away?" Jeanette said, pointing to her eyes that, unlike her cousin, were both dull and gray.

"I don't know if we'll ever get color back. All we can ask for is that maybe, one day, the war will end."

"Do you think anything will happen at the festival? I mean, do you think they really have a serum that can bring the color back?"

"I honestly don't know."

Jeanette sat quietly, realizing she didn't care whether anybody's eye color changed or not. She wanted the hours to move faster so the festival would be over.

# CHAPTER 3

Jeanette stood in front of the door to her house; a one-story wood and mud home, just like most of the homes in Emerleigh. This was the only home she knew, at least physically. Emotionally, much had changed over the years.

Elizabeth had calmed her senses and given her plenty to think about on the walk from the town hall. It felt good to talk to a woman who was calm, thoughtful, and seemingly caring. Outside of Addy's mother - Rhilynn - Jeanette did not have someone in her life like that. Not anymore.

She took a deep breath and opened the door slowly.

Her mother was where she expected her to be, in the kitchen preparing lunch. A pot boiled over slightly in the fire. Chopping sounds echoed off the wood table as her mother cut carrots.

Standing in the doorway, unnoticed, Jeanette studied her mother. Disheveled hair, fraught with nerves. Sullen face with baggy eyes. A small frame that once was more robust, full of life. Her mother had been a pleasant, attractive lady. It had been five years since her brother, Jaren, was killed in battle.

Her mother had not been the same since.

*Jaren.*

She avoided any sustained thoughts of him because they brought emotions that she could not control. She liked being in control, which is one reason she had grown to hate being around her mother. Isabelle was not in control...of anything. Jeanette tried to understand her, but it usually ended in feeling pity. There was no conflict or companionship in their relationship, it just was.

Jeanette tried to close the door without being heard. A soft creak echoed.

"You're back a little late, aren't you?" her mother asked, putting a handful of carrots in the pot. "Most of the other girls are already home."

"Miss Elizabeth wanted to talk to me after the meeting," Jeanette answered, quickly heading to her room.

"I'm assuming she wanted to talk to you because you were tormenting poor Lorelei."

Jeanette stopped. Her pulse quickened. Turning around, she glared at her mother. How did she know already?

"Lorelei stopped by to apologize if she had caused any harm," Isabelle started, wiping her hands on her apron. "That's right...she had the decency to stop by here and apologize for my daughter's horrifying behavior to her."

Jeanette felt an even stronger urge to punch Lorelei.

"That's what we need," Isabelle continued, "you getting into it with one of the nicest, most well respected girls in the village. Why do you always feel you need to show off and be so hateful?"

Jeanette wanted to scream, to curse her mother. She had been so close, so many times, but the thought of Jaren always made her stop. He loved their mother. She respected his memory enough to try and at least be civil.

As Jeanette stood, thinking of what to say, Isabelle turned

her attention back to lunch and said, almost to herself, "As much as you might want to, try not to embarrass this family anymore, especially during festival. I don't think my nerves can take it."

Fury.

Maybe her mother *wanted* her to confront her, to get her to fight back and lose grasp of her emotions. Her mother was miserable and she wanted Jeanette to feel the same. She swore she would never give her the pleasure. Her mother didn't know anything about her, about her life, the constant backstabbing from Lorelei.

Her plan to leave.

Jeanette was ready to give in, to truly tell her mother her thoughts. She felt the words pushing up from her heart out her throat. As she opened her mouth to scream, the front door opened and her lips came back together.

Her father, Jacob, walked in with a scowl across his face. Jeanette knew he had heard about the incident. Behind him stood her fourteen-year-old cousin, Tristyn. He wore a smirk of approval below his dual colored eyes.

Isabelle left her cooking and ran over to Jacob. Jeanette's father was a little taller than her mother, and much broader. He was in good shape for his age and still healthy. A full head of dark black hair lay on his head, above the stern eyes and stiff jaw she had always known. He was not a hurtful man, but she had always felt intimidated by him. That changed a few years ago when she started taking the frustrations against her mother out on him.

"Jacob," Isabelle said, "did you hear what happened? How can she do something like that to us?"

"You don't even know what happened," Jeanette snapped back. Her father gave her his look. His unhappy, 'I'm disinterested in your opinion', look.

With an audience, Isabelle became more and more

hysterical. "I can only imagine what went through her mind as she did it? Why!? And so close to festival."

Isabelle had been more on edge than usual the past few weeks. She was always like this around festival time. Though it was never spoken, Jeanette assumed it was the sight of all the young men who had reached fighting age heading off to battle.

Her father continued to console her mother, seemingly oblivious to Jeanette's desire to explain the situation. Tristyn finally moved from behind Jacob, closer to her.

"Did you really almost punch Lorelei?" he asked softly, unbelief across his face.

Jeanette peered at him; into his blue eye. She tried to avoid singling it out, knowing how he felt about being different. But with her temper broiling, instinct drew her gaze to it. "Not now, Tristyn!"

He hung his head and backed away. Jeanette turned back to her parents and met her father's eyes. His face was not angered, but begging. Begging her not to push her mother. Begging her to be patient and understanding. Begging her to let it go.

*How can you love her? Don't you know she's crazy?*

Jeanette's lungs ached to empty what was running through her veins. She wanted to weep, but she would not give her mother or father the satisfaction. Nothing left to say, she let out a scream of despair aimed at whoever was willing to accept it and ran into her room, slamming the door behind her.

Tears started forming, but she stopped them, allowing the anger to overtake the sadness, as usual. She paced, thinking of all that was wrong with her life.

*Jaren gone. My crazy mother. My uninterested father. Stifled village life. The stupid festival. Corwin.*

She stopped, heart still pounding. Why would Corwin come to her mind?

*Corwin.*

Shaking her head in frustration she reared to the side and swung her fist into the air. There was nothing to hit. She swung again and again, and then stopped. Her head low, breathing deep, perspiration rolled down her back. Lifting her head slowly, she saw herself in the mirror.

Catching her breath, she stood taller, moving her hair behind her ears to get a better view. Jeanette was trim and fit. Her long dark black hair hung below her shoulders, straight and coarse; her face was thin and tight, like her father's.

*As long as I'm not like her.*

She continued to stare, moving closer and closer to the mirror, focusing on her eyes. Her serious, focused gray eyes. Gray, just like everybody else. Why all the fuss about it? Why the power struggle, the war, the death?

*Jaren.*

She often heard girls in town talk about how they hated their brothers. She could never have anything but love for Jaren. Heat built in her cheeks. She watched as her eyes transformed from defiant to sorrowful. She let the tears continue to come with the realization that she was not a child anymore. This was not her home anymore.

After festival, she had every intention of going to Bandar, and taking her cousin, Tristyn, with her.

# CHAPTER 4

The next morning, Jeanette made her way to Addy's house amid a blue, warm sky. A hesitant Tristyn walked next to her. The feelings from the night before were still present, but suspended.

She looked back at Tristyn. "Are you doing okay?" He wore a cautious look, hiding behind his long, disheveled, brown hair.

"I'm fine...I promise," he replied.

Though her cousin, for the last six years he felt more like a younger brother, having moved in with the family after his mother died. Now fourteen years old, he was almost as tall as her and was the only male that Jeanette did not mind being around; and next to Addy, her only friend. She knew Tristyn felt the same way.

Tristyn's life was hard, as hard as anyone she knew, but he never complained. Even as the boys in town considered him an outsider - *half-caste, mixer, wet-head* - all because he had one blue eye and one gray eye. His father - Jacob's brother - was from Emerleigh and his mother from Bandar. All of the kingdoms frowned on inter-kingdom relationships, the end result being a child with two eye colors having no true gift from either kingdom.

He had always talked of returning back to 'his people', feeling a semblance of origin and acceptance. Jeanette knew he respected her parents, and was grateful to have a roof over his head, but like Jeanette, it didn't feel like home. Jeanette did not think Bandar would necessarily feel like home, but it would be different.

"They really went all out for festival this year," Tristyn said, breaking his silence.

Jeanette nodded. The streets were filling with people making their way to the opening ceremony. Over the last few days, Emerleigh had transformed. No expense spared to impress the royal visitors. Green banners and ribbons lined the streets. The main grounds behind the town hall were a true spectacle; booth after booth of performers, trinkets, and food.

Jeanette knocked on Addy's door and Addy's mother, Rhilynn, answered. "It's about time," she said, pulling Jeanette and Tristyn inside. "It's been chaos all morning. I need somebody to help restore my sanity."

Rhilynn pointed toward a room off to the side. "If it's not out of your realm of ability, would you help my youngest daughter find something to wear? She thinks she is attending a royal ball." Jeanette picked out the sarcasm in her voice and smiled.

"Yes, it's very funny, mother," Brandy chided from the room, "as long as you don't care that I will be the only girl at the festival naked..." Brandy stuck her head out to finish, "because I have nothing to wear!" Saying the final words, she noticed Tristyn, yelped, and ran back into the room.

Jeanette let out a laugh and Tristyn stood, mouth agape. Rhilynn put her hand on Jeanette's shoulder. "Then, if you could be so kind as to teach my middle daughter how to clean up after herself." Addy was fidgeting over the cooking fire, a mess surrounding her. As she tried to carry a pot to the wash bin, it fell to the floor and a loud echo went through the house.

Suddenly there came bursting, loud cries of baby Drury from a different room. Addy didn't move a muscle. "Sorry," she mouthed.

The door flung open and Kaitlynn, Addy's older sister, appeared, hair matted, face tired and eyes glossed over. She looked around accusingly and then walked directly to Addy, who had not moved an inch.

Kaitlynn, trembling from nerves, held up her finger, and with waves of baby screams wafting in the background, whispered to Addy through clinched teeth, "Please! Stop!"

Addy, wide eyed, stared at the humble mess of a sister before her, as if expecting more, but that's all that came. Kaitlynn did not wait for a response, but turned and walked back towards the room. When she got to the door her husband, Pearce, stood in the frame rubbing the sleep out of his eyes.

Kaitlynn looked up at his muddled hair and goofy grin. "Morning sweetie, how was your night?" he asked lovingly, with a half yawn. She pushed him into the room and slammed the door.

"And finally," Rhilynn continued, "I will bless you forever if you could find room and board for my oldest daughter, her caring, but not so bright husband, and my handsome, yet overly loud grandchild."

Jeanette didn't try to hide her amusement. She took in another view of the room in what seemed like slow motion: Addy wiping her brow, leaving a mark of flour; Brandy huffing about; the closed door behind which Kaitlynn was arguing with Pearce, and finally back to Rhilynn. Widowed, strong, but not bitter. Fun, but sensible. The matriarch to a crazy, busy, loving family. Jeanette felt comfortable here. It felt like a home. A real home.

"How is your mother doing?" Rhilynn asked.

The comfortable feeling left. "She's okay, I guess." Rhilynn nodded knowingly. "She wasn't too excited about my ruckus with Lorelei yesterday," Jeanette added.

"Tell her that I'm thinking of her," Rhilynn said, "and I did hear that you were quite the show at the town hall yesterday, giving Lorelei a black eye."

"I didn't punch her!" Jeanette responded, wondering how the circumstances of the event continued to be embellished. Brandy stuck her head out from around the corner, still trying on dresses. "You should have seen it, mum. Lorelei looked like she was going to soil herself."

Rhilynn and Jeanette both laughed. Addy was nearby, but focused on her cooking. "It wasn't that bad," Jeanette said, trying to downplay the situation.

"Well, maybe that's what she needs, to be put in her place," Rhilynn added.

"Mother, that's not nice," Addy responded, rolling dough.

"Well that's easy for you to say, Addy. She doesn't mess with you like she does with Jeanette. I'm sure you would think different if she had her claws in your back."

The door opened again and Pearce emerged fully dressed.

"Did Drury finally go back to sleep?" Rhilynn asked.

"Seems so," he said, peering back into the bedroom. He walked out into the kitchen, rubbing his chest and stretching, "Everyone seems to be scampering about this morning? Why all the hurry?"

Brandy emerged, wearing yet another dress. "Are you really that dense?" Pearce looked at Addy, arms out, as if asking for more information.

"Pearce, today is festival," Jeanette finally said matter-of-factly. "And aren't you supposed to be..."

"Crunch! I'm supposed to be helping Jacob with the

platform!" Pearce said, eyes widening with the realization that he was late. "He's going to kill me."

He rushed back into the bedroom, slamming the door behind him. Everyone in the kitchen cringed and waited for the inevitable. The seconds ticked until Drury's voice, which had been silent, bellowed through the air again. The door opened and Pearce ran out the front door with his tools in hand. Kaitlynn's yells followed close behind.

Rhilynn shook her head and walked into the bedroom to help Kaitlynn with Drury. Addy and Brandy ignored it while Jeanette sat on the table, still smiling.

***

As soon as Addy finished her baking, Jeanette found herself weighed down with pies and cakes and on her way to the festival.

"I wish you had entered at least one of the contests," Addy said.

"You know better than that, Addy. I could think of a barnful of things I would rather do than cook, or sew, or sing. Besides, I am not very good at any of them."

"But it wouldn't have hurt," Addy replied, a slight pause to her step, "especially this year. We could have even worked on it together."

"Would you stop fretting and just keep walking," Jeanette said, kicking Addy gently in the back side while trying to balance the dishes.

After a brief stop to enter Addy's goods into the judge's tent, they made their way to the center fairgrounds. The air was still damp and the sun had not yet removed the dew from the field. Throngs of people stood, facing the grandstand, waiting for the opening ceremony. Everything was green: the banners, the tents, even the trees that nestled the outskirts of the large field seemed more lush than usual.

"There they are," Jeanette said, pointing. Jeanette and Addy's families were in the middle of the crowd. As the girls approached, Jacob and Pearce were having a disagreement.

"But you said the posts needed to be six feet high," Pearce said.

"Pearce," Jacob responded, his face growing impatient, as if he had already moved on from the conversation, "I told you that Alden wanted the *stage* six feet high. So you needed the posts to be cut smaller to account for the flooring on top. Now, the steps are not flush." Jacob put his hands together trying to help Pearce visualize how his error affected the scaffolding for the stage. Pearce's long stare showed his apparent lack of understanding.

"Oh forget about it," Isabelle said. "You did the best you could Pearce, right?"

Pearce nodded, still moving his hands around, measuring in the air. Addy, Jeanette, Tristyn and Brandy laughed. Kaitlynn stood close by trying to coo Drury, unamused.

"Do you think it's true what everyone is saying? About the prince and the eyes changing?" Rhilynn asked.

"I don't know what everyone is so up in a fuss about," Isabelle answered. "It doesn't make any sense, getting everyone's hopes up. We lost the true eye color so long ago and it's not like they know what took it away or what's going to bring it back."

Jeanette agreed with her mother, but didn't dare say it. Rhilynn gave a polite nod to Isabelle and then looked at Jacob.

"All I know is what I hear," Jacob said, "and the kingdom seems set on Prince Braxton getting married this year, but only if it is to a girl of true eye color. I've said all along, I don't know if it will work, but the town leaders in Emerleigh claim that someone has created a serum that works. The man tried it on himself to prove it worked. I guess we'll see."

"If it did happen though, would the prince marry one of the girls from our village?" Rhilynn asked.

"We can only hope," came a voice from behind.

Everyone turned to see Jonathan, Lorelei's father, wearing a wide smile. The same fake smile that Lorelei carried. Next to him were Lorelei and her mother, Miranda. Miranda was the spitting image of an older Lorelei, only with maturity and more tact.

"What's the use of raising young girls with manners and dreams if it can't take them somewhere truly special? Isn't that right Jacob?" Jonathan asked, putting his hand around Lorelei's shoulder as if she were a prize. "I also heard you talking about Cadmus - the one who found the serum. Eyes as green as jade. I got to know him a little when he came through last month prepping for the festivals. He's a very important man in the kingdom."

Jacob turned his head to cough, ignoring the question. Jeanette knew her father had no use for Jonathan and his ability to talk out of both sides of his mouth.

"What are you entering into the festival?" Lorelei asked Jeanette.

"I'm not entering anything."

Lorelei raised her brow. "Hmm?" she said, her parasol spinning in the breeze. She turned to Addy. "And what about you? You always enter something." Before Addy could answer, Jonathan and Miranda motioned for Lorelei that it was time to go. Lorelei turned to Addy, out of the earshot of the adults, and said, "Good. A part of me hopes you win. It will be nice to have some familiar faces waiting on me at the castle." She turned and followed her parents.

Brandy piped up, "Don't worry about her, Addy," she said, nose up, tip-toeing around, imitating Lorelei. Drury gave a chuckle as she pranced.

"I hate her blonde hair and stupid fancy dresses," Jeanette

added.

"There is nothing wrong with having a nice dress," Brandy corrected, "as long as you don't have the attitude to go with it."

Tristyn looked at Brandy. "I think your dress looks nice." Jeanette and Addy looked at each other with knowing grins. Brandy's cheeks reddened and she kicked around in the dirt in the long, unsure pause. Tristyn let out a nervous chuckle. A long horn blast brought everyone's attention back to the stage.

Alden was standing, ready to speak, his green eyes bright off the reflection of the morning sun. Elizabeth's words came back to her...

*He says it's more of a relationship.*

The same feeling of futility and wasted energy gnawed at her. She admired Alden, but his words about tradition, sacrifice, honor, and hope were meaningless. The crowd cheered and reveled in his optimism. On their faces were worn prayers that this last ditch effort by the queen to find the prince a bride would work.

She wanted no part of it.

# CHAPTER 5

After Alden's speech, Jeanette and Addy roamed the festival, the smells and sounds heavy in the air. The city itself was a maze of people and carts: baked goods, fresh meats, and every custard imaginable. At first thought, it didn't seem right that if the kingdom truly was struggling to feed itself, then why all the gluttony. But Jeanette ignored her rational thinking and threw another handful of maple roasted nuts into her mouth.

"What do you want to see first?" Addy asked between bites of a honey glazed apple.

"There's archery, stone throwing...like that takes any skill," Jeanette said.

"Don't be so harsh," Addy cut in, "it's good to have people around that can...throw heavy things."

"Ah, yes it is," Jeanette said, smirking, "especially when his name is Rendall."

"Don't make fun! It's probably the only game he entered. At least give me the chance to watch him compete."

Jeanette ignored her and continued, "Then there are the foot races, swords, and grappling." She looked at Addy as if to ask her preference. She tried to be nonchalant. Deep down Jeanette already had her preference, but there was no way that she would admit out loud that she wanted to see Corwin compete in grappling.

"Did Tristyn enter the foot races?" Addy asked.

"I wish he would, but he won't."

"Then I'm not interested in that," Addy said. "Archery is nice, but it's the same thing every year...and it's slow. How about swords and then stone throwing and then grappling? We should be able to watch a little bit of each."

"Perfect," Jeanette replied. "Swords will be right up here," she added, pointing up towards the top of the dell and then throwing a few more nuts into her mouth.

A large crowd had already gathered around the arena, more so than usual for one event. Jeanette and Addy squeezed their way through to find Tristyn and Brandy already waiting, chatter in the air.

Jeanette looked into the ring and saw Thomas, one of the boys her age. She didn't like most of the boys in town, but she especially disliked Thomas. Clumsy, condescending, and clueless. He was suiting up with padding.

"Is that..." Jeanette started, peering into the ring, "Thomas' father in the ring?"

"Everybody's been talking about it," Brandy said. "Dalen is royally upset with him for setting the family barn on fire."

"Didn't Thomas accidentally set the house on fire a couple of years ago?" Addy asked.

"Yep," Tristyn answered. "Thankfully it didn't do much damage. But then to have him do it again, even if it was an accident...Dalen wants to teach him a lesson."

The crowd continued to grow as word spread of the match. Tradition was that it was only the younger men who competed in the games, those who were part of the training camp and had not gone off to war yet. But there was no official rule on age.

"Looks like somebody made sure they would contend against each other," Brandy continued.

"I'm assuming it was not coincidence," Jeanette added, a sense of glee building. To see Thomas get his comeuppance would truly be a treat.

The judge checked the padding of both men and placed the wooden swords in their hands. Thomas looked as if he would throw up.

"Points are scored when you strike the arms, legs, chest or back," the judge said. "The first one to five points is the winner. Begin!"

"Get him, Dalen!" Jeanette bellowed, supporting Thomas' father with fervent approval.

"You have no heart," Addy said.

"Nope," Jeanette answered. "Strike him hard!"

Thomas moved around the dirt ring, avoiding his father. "This is ridiculous," he said. "I will not fight you, father."

"Oh, yes you will," Dalen replied, lunging in for a hard hit to the chest. Thomas fell back, shaken.

"Stop it!" Thomas pleaded.

"Make me," his father egged on. The crowd continued to cheer and taunt.

"Come on, Thomas. Lay into him!" came a loud, recognizable voice behind Jeanette. She turned to see Corwin.

"Oh, hello Jeanette," he said with a wry smile. "I noticed you cheering for Thomas' father. Interesting." Corwin looked ready for the day, energetic and excited.

"What's so interesting about it? Thomas is an inept buffoon who needs to learn a lesson. I'm all for it."

The crowd continued to cheer and push in, jostling Corwin closer. Jeanette was standing right next to him, arm to arm. Corwin leaned across her, in the middle of the noise, and said, "Good morning Addy. Are you enjoying the first day of the festival?" A breeze blew and Jeanette smelled leather and musk off of Corwin. The scent was not overpowering, but just enough to prick her senses.

Addy nodded and then looked around, searching. "Is Rendall with you today?"

"He's getting ready over at the stone field."

Jeanette sighed. "If you are quite done, I'm trying to watch the match." Corwin held up his hands in apology.

Thomas was less apprehensive as his father continued to taunt him. "Come on you pansy boy, fight like a man," his father shouted, taking another hard lunge at him.

Thomas dodged and said, his face getting red with unease, "I don't want to fight you father, but I will if you don't stop this nonsense."

His father smiled and parried a blow to the arm, winning another point. The crowd cheered.

"Ah!" Thomas shrieked, charging his father.

Jeanette laughed at the site. Corwin tapped her on the shoulder.

"If you don't mind," she scolded, "I would like to watch this match." He just stood, smiling, almost ignoring her rebuttal. Any other boy she would have left standing there, but she knew he did it just to watch her get riled up, and that forced her, oddly, to try and stay calm.

"I don't know if you were aware, but I'm going to be competing in grappling later this morning. What do you think my chances are?"

"About as good as Thomas'."

"Just because you want Thomas to lose doesn't mean he will."

"Didn't you say you had somewhere else to be?"

"You are right, I do. But before I go, are you *sure* that Thomas will lose to his father?"

"Yes!" Jeanette yelled.

"What if I told you I am sure Thomas will win and am willing to bet on it."

He was reeling her in, and she knew it, but she couldn't stop herself. "I will bet you whatever you want. There is no way Thomas wins this match."

"Shall we shake on it?"

"Will you go away if I do?"

Corwin laughed. "Yes, of course."

She turned and reached out her hand. He gently placed his palm next to hers, their fingers sliding by each other. He gave a small squeeze of confidence and asked, "So what are we betting?"

Jeanette considered for a moment. "If Dalen wins then you will leave me alone for the rest of the festival."

"Agreed. And if Thomas wins," Corwin continued, "you have to give me one turn at the dance tomorrow night."

Shocked, Jeanette stood, trying to think of something to say. Nobody said anything about dancing. Why would she submit herself to the public speculation that would come from it? But she had seen enough of the match to know there was no way Thomas could win.

"Fine," she said flatly.

"Thank you for your time, Miss Jeanette," he said with a bow and left. Jeanette tried to turn her concentration back to the match, but couldn't.

Addy squealed. "Did you just say you will dance with him?"

"Yes, now leave me alone so I can watch Thomas lose."

While Corwin had diverted her attention, the match became tied and the momentum was very much in Thomas' favor.

"Come on, Dalen!" Jeanette cheered, louder than before.

Dalen and Thomas were facing each other, walking in circles, defending carefully to avoid the final blow. Suddenly,

Dalen lunged and Thomas parried the blow awkwardly, but kept from being struck. Thomas had trouble regaining his footing and Dalen turned around quickly and went for an arm blow. Thomas blocked and swung his sword around, going for the leg. Dalen jumped to avoid the hit, but Thomas had continued his momentum, spinning around and jabbing his sword forward, directly into Dalen's chest as he hung in midair.

Half of the crowd let out moans of frustration as the other half reveled in the victory. Jeanette stood silent while Thomas danced around the ring in victory.

"Thomas is the winner!" the judge proclaimed, holding up the young soldier's hand.

Addy looked at Jeanette and grinned. A scowl formed on Jeanette's face as she walked away. "I hate festival!"

# CHAPTER 6

There was a bang on Jeanette's bedroom door.

"Wakey, wakey girls," Tristyn yelled. "Prince Braxton is here to make sure you have all your toes and teeth before he hauls you off to the castle."

Jeanette moaned, her eyes slowly opening. "Oh, go away!" Tristyn laughed, making his way back down the hall.

Addy sat up from her makeshift bed on the floor, her thick, curly hair out of control. "Are you ready for today?"

Jeanette could feel the apprehension in Addy's voice. They had talked about everything during the night - the music, the food, the games - but Jeanette could not bring up the thought of Addy, or herself, leaving.

"I think so," Jeanette answered, lying. "If nothing else, it will be fun watching Corwin get his arse walloped." After the bet, she avoided the grappling matches just to spite him. But she knew he won his rounds and would be in the finals today.

There had been plenty of talk of Corwin during the night as well. "He has to have feelings for you; you know that right?" Addy had said. Jeanette tried to brush it off and turn the discussion back to Addy's infatuation with Rendall and his throwing of large rocks, but deep down she knew Addy was right.

It was a confusing realization as she allowed her heart to probe the unknown. What if? Is Corwin really that bad? But then her thoughts turned realistic. Why now? Right before festival when he was about to leave for the Royal Academy? What good did it do?

*None!*

It did no good to ponder on hypotheticals. She would own up her loss and give him his dance, but that was it. He would be on his way to prepare for war, Addy would be on her way to the castle, and Jeanette would be on her way to Bandar with Tristyn. Everybody moving on with their life.

After getting dressed, the girls made their way into the kitchen. "Thanks so much for letting me stay over," Addy said, pulling up a chair for breakfast.

"You know you are always welcome, Addy," Jacob answered. They sat down and began to eat. Jeanette eyed her mother, who was focused on her plate. Isabelle seemed less anxious, subdued.

The table was quiet at first, but it was not long before Tristyn asked, "So did you hear what they are saying?"

Everyone stopped to look at him. He did not answer. "Well?" Jeanette prodded.

"Lorelei is going to make sure she leaves tomorrow with her eyes changed, one way or another. Her parents already got it taken care of."

Jeanette scoffed, "Don't be ridiculous. I know she wants the highest chair in the first royal carriage out of here, but there is no way they can fake it. If they knew how, they would have already done it. Her daddy would have made sure her eyes were sparkling green long ago."

"That's enough," Jacob interjected. There was silence and

everyone went back to eating.

"Are you nervous about today at all?" Tristyn asked Addy.

"About what?"

"I mean, I saw all the things people were taking into the judging tent yesterday. I think you've got just as much chance as anyone to find a place at the castle."

Addy smiled nervously. "Thank you, Tristyn. I guess we'll find out today, won't we?"

"It's not right," Isabelle said. "The castle has no business coming around and taking the young people from their homes. Everyone is all excited...for what?" she said poking her sausage with a fork.

Even when Jeanette agreed with what her mother said, she found it hard to support her. She never knew if what her mom said and what her mom believed were one and the same. Jeanette was not willing to peel back all the layers that her mother would wrap herself in.

Jacob eyed Jeanette. She could see in his eyes patience, asking her to be still. Her mother's head was moving slightly, back and forth, as if the conversation had carried on without anybody else. Eventually, Isabelle continued. "Regardless of what I think, there is a good chance Addy will be chosen. She is too talented not to be. I don't know if you two girls have talked about life without each other yet, but this could be the last day you see each other for a long time," Isabelle said, finally taking a bite.

Jeanette's mouth clinched and her foot started tapping the floor. Addy and Tristyn stared at their plates. Jacob stopped chewing and said in a calm, patient voice, "I'm sure they have discussed the possibilities, Isabelle."

Jacob moved his hand over, close enough to touch Jeanette's, and left it resting next to hers.

"Well, if you do get chosen," Isabelle said, "we will sure miss you, Addy. You seem to be the only one who can keep

Jeanette under control."

Her plate still full, Jeanette stood up, drawing the glances of everyone at the table, except for Isabelle. But Jeanette stared at her as if everybody else in the room had vanished.

"Can you once think about others before you speak? Can you think of anybody but yourself?" Jeanette asked, not completely angry, but with truth. Jacob reached for Jeanette's hand. She avoided his touch and walked around her father to be closer to her mother.

Isabelle bowed her head as sobs started to come.

"You've said your piece, Jeanette...enough," Jacob said, looking at her, a pleading in his eyes. She knew the only reason he was still calm was because he knew that she was right.

"When I leave one day mother, you don't have to worry about blaming the war or the castle," Jeanette said, walking over to the door. "I will leave of my own choice and you can just blame me." Jeanette waited for a moment to see if her mother would look up. She didn't.

Jeanette walked out the door ready to get through the second day of festival and on with her life.

*** 

Still recovering from the celebrations the night before, the townspeople were starting the day a little later and slower. The event finals were taking place in the main arena, one after another. Archery had already passed. Grappling was about to begin.

"I thought you didn't want to see Corwin fight?" Addy asked with a knowing smirk. Jeanette's pulse quickened.

"Normally I wouldn't care about guys sweating all over and grabbing each other who knows where," Jeanette answered, "but I'll let it slide to watch Corwin get pinned."

"Okay, but I still think you are looking forward to the

dance tonight, you just don't know it yet."

Jeanette ignored her and turned her attention to the match. Corwin entered the ring, smiling and shirtless.

"Come on Corwin, you can do it!" Addy yelled. Jeanette gave her a stare, a plea to quiet down. "You should be cheering for him, too."

"She is right," came a voice behind them. "You should be cheering for him."

Lorelei.

"I've heard about the little bet you two have made," Lorelei said, glancing at Corwin with raised eyebrows. "Are there some harbored feelings you haven't shared?"

"If there were, would you be jealous?"

Lorelei thought for a moment. "Corwin?" she considered, tapping her folded fan on her chin. "Interesting thought. He's worthy enough, but I am saving myself for someone a little more..."

A bustling crowd came down the road, interrupting Lorelei's statement. In the middle of the moving throng marched a circle of soldiers. Inside the secure circle walked two men. One was bald, tall, with a regal air. Lorelei's dad said his name was Cadmus. The other had a youthful face and dark, curly black hair covered with the royal crown. Prince Braxton.

"I'm saving myself for *him*!" Lorelei finished, practically molesting the prince with her eyes. The crowd grew and the guard's formation around the prince tightened. She had never seen anything like it. Two pairs of green eyes; right next to each other. It was surreal.

The prince stopped and the crowd quieted. He requested the soldiers make an opening and he stepped closer to Jeanette. His gaze briefly turned to Lorelei, who gave a perfect curtsy. His eyes then fixed on Jeanette's and he reached out his hand, smiling.

A rare feeling of vulnerability came over her. Without a

curtsy, she reached out her hand.

"Are you enjoying festival?" Prince Braxton asked. He stood with his hands behind his back. Next to him, the taller gentleman smiled politely, impatience in his eyes.

"Um, yes...sir," Jeanette fumbled. All around her everything had stopped.

The prince nodded and then started down the street again. After the prince's entourage passed and the noise abated, heads turned back to Jeanette. She ignored the onlookers and turned to find Lorelei standing perfectly still in the glow of her own self-righteousness.

"I hope you enjoyed that moment of glory," Lorelei said, a new fierceness in her eyes, "because starting tonight he won't care about anything but me." She turned and walked away.

*Fine...you can have him!*

Addy grabbed Jeanette's shoulders. "What was that?"

Jeanette opened her mouth to speak, but nothing came out. Focusing her attention back on the grappling ring, she found Corwin was staring like everyone else.

"That was the prince...the royal prince!" exclaimed Addy.

"Don't you think I know that!?" Jeanette snapped back. Around her the crowd was dispersing and the match started again.

*Why would the prince want to talk to me?*

Corwin was pinned on his side, contorting, twisting and grunting, trying to break free.

"Did you see Lorelei's face? It was priceless." Addy said.

To see Lorelei's expression was the only positive thing about the interaction. Jeanette tried to block it from her mind and focused on the match. Breaking out of a hold, Corwin found leverage and flipped his opponent, pinning him and winning the match. The crowd cheered. As the referee lifted Corwin's arm, he caught Jeanette's eyes and gave her a wink before his comrades tackled him to the ground and rolled around in the mud, celebrating.

Jeanette cursed and stormed off.

\*\*\*

At midday, everyone gathered at the grandstand. Anticipation ran through Jeanette. Her mother's words this morning, the prince's random interaction, and Corwin's wink were all behind her. She was now facing the stark reality of what had only been hinted at; whether Addy would actually be picked to go to the castle. In a few minutes, Elizabeth would share the results of the judging.

"It's the man that was walking with the prince," Addy said, pointing on stage. "The one that has made the formula." Elizabeth and Alden were on stage, holding hands. Next to them stood Cadmus, wearing a dark green robe down to the floor. His presence was demanding, though he seemed reflective, calm, despite the fact that his eyes were not the same color as everyone else present. Jeanette still did not understand the importance of the eye color, nor how some concocted serum could help bring it back, but she was gazing at the proof.

"Alden introduced him to Jacob earlier," Pearce said, holding Drury awkwardly on this hip. All of Addy's family was standing next to Jeanette. "He is an advisor to the castle."

"Shh... they are getting ready to announce," Rhilynn said.

Elizabeth stepped forward. "We would like to thank all those who submitted entries this year. As you know, there is the potential for representatives from the caravan to choose some among you to serve in the castle for a space of two years."

A collective murmur bristled the crowd. Jeanette glanced at Addy, who was biting her lip and seemed to be hanging on Elizabeth's every last word.

The reality of life without Addy turned Jeanette's stomach.

"Having served in the castle many years ago, I can assure you of the wonderful opportunity it is. It is an honor for you and your family. Today, there are four among you that have been chosen to return to the castle with the caravan." Elizabeth named one of the young girls for sewing and needlework, another girl for music, and one for animal tending.

"What about you?" Brandy asked, looking at Addy.

"I said shhh!" Rhilynn snapped.

"And the last of our girls chosen will help in the kitchen. To nobody's surprise, that honor goes to Addalynn." Addy covered her mouth.

"Woo-hoo!" Brandy yelled, along with cheers that came from the crowd.

"If your name was called, please meet me on stage right away for more instructions. Everybody else, we will enjoy a break in the festival for a few hours and then meet back here again this afternoon for the final ceremony."

Addy gave hugs to her family while others came to give support. She then turned to Jeanette.

"I spit in the pie yesterday morning, but I guess I'll have to try harder next time," Jeanette joked.

Addy started to laugh, but it suddenly choked into tears. She reached out and hugged Jeanette. "It's going to be okay," Jeanette said as a tear ran down her cheek. "Everything is going to be okay."

"I really didn't think it would happen."

"I know you didn't; that's what makes you so special."

"I'm going to miss you so much."

After the embrace, Addy was surrounded again with family and friends. Jeanette took a deep breath, trying to fight back the guilt for not telling Addy her plan. Would she actually run away if Addy had not been picked to serve at the castle? She didn't know, but she didn't have to worry about it anymore.

The only thing left to worry about was the dance with Corwin.

# CHAPTER 7

As the afternoon sun began to fall, the festival horn again cut through the breeze. The entire village stood shoulder to shoulder to witness the final ceremony. All went quiet.

There were thirteen girls between the ages of seventeen and nineteen lined up, waiting to be called on stage. They stood in a row, youngest to oldest. Lorelei, as the youngest, would be the first girl on stage, but the last to receive the serum. There was one girl between Lorelei and Jeanette. Addy stood in the middle of the line.

In front of the girls were all the eighteen year old boys from the village, dressed in their battle uniform: long black pants tied into calf high boots, and a white long sleeve shirt underneath a heavy cloth tunic bearing the ensign of Amarin. Shields in their left hand and swords in their right, there stood a total of six, Corwin and Rendall among them, ready to be recognized and report to the Royal Academy.

At the bottom of the platform, Cadmus stood next to Prince Braxton. Alden stopped briefly to talk with Cadmus before walking onto the stage. Alden lifted his hands and said,

"We gather together towards the end of another festival to enjoy and remember the many blessings we share; our freedoms, our friends, our land. But, as we know, they come with a price. As with every festival, we prepare to send more of our sons off to battle." He motioned for the soldiers to come on stage. In unison, their backs stiffened and they walked in single file on stage and stood behind Alden. Cheers and calls of support came from the crowd.

Jeanette quickly glanced over Corwin. He looked the part of soldier, proud to help the cause, ready to go to war.

*Ready to die.*

Alden continued. "They will train, they will fight, and all things willing, they will return to us." He turned toward the young men behind him and yelled proudly, "To the sons of Emerleigh!"

The townspeople erupted behind Jeanette. She wanted to feel gratitude, to feel positive for their departure. But she only felt sorry for them. Did their parents, or the boys themselves, have any idea what awaited them? It was a continuous cycle of honor, fighting, and death. The same sacrifice required of her family, of her brother.

Alden turned and gave the soldiers a nod to exit the stage. Jeanette looked up and down the line of girls; shuffling feet, fidgety fingers, and heads turning, seeking confidence. It was time.

"Today, we have in our presence Prince Braxton, heir to the throne of Emerleigh," Alden said, motioning to the prince, who was now sitting on the stage. Braxton stood and gave a simple bow. Next to him Cadmus stood, looking regal and pleased.

"He has graced us with his presence to help oversee the ceremony tonight." Alden looked down at the row of girls and motioned for them to come on stage. The girls turned and walked to the bottom of the steps. Royal Guards held their positions around the structure.

Alden continued, "People of Emerleigh, news has traveled about the festivals at Lynnhaven and Crespin and how no eyes were changed. If today, Master Cadmus finds the same results, there is no need to think any less of our great village, nor any of these wonderful girls."

The line of girls started up the steps, passing Prince Braxton. Lorelei passed first. The prince bowed, lips tight together, without an exchange of words. The next girl followed.

Curtsy.

Bow.

No words.

Jeanette headed up the steps and tried not to make eye contact with the prince, but it was hard. She noticed his eyes were a darker hue than Alden's, more sullen.

"What is your name?" the prince asked, wearing the same smile he had flashed earlier, his hands still behind his back.

"I'm sorry?" Jeanette responded. The flow of girls entering the stage was interrupted, causing a noted pause in the line movement.

"Your name," he whispered again, "what is it?"

"Jeanette," she finally answered.

His grin widened slightly and he bowed. Jeanette moved forward, taking her place in line. She scanned the crowd before her. Everyone she had ever known or interacted with was now staring back in bewilderment. Why her? Why did the prince seem to be focusing on her?

Jeanette tried to make eye contact with Addy as she came on stage.

*She is already going to the castle, why make her go through this?*

Jeanette looked to her left. Even Lorelei, with all her pretense and posture, appeared a little smaller standing in front of the crowd. After all the girls lined up, Alden glanced at

Cadmus to see if he was ready. Cadmus spoke to the prince and nodded back. The crowd was still gazing, waiting.

Cadmus walked to the center and removed a tiny glass vile from a belt that he wore. He walked to the first girl, Gabriella, the youngest. She looked ready to cry. He placed a reassuring hand on her shoulder and took the vile of green liquid and turned, holding it up to the audience.

"It is true what Mayor Alden says; there is no guarantee that today neither you nor I will see what we have hoped for all these years. I have had the good fortune to daily sit with Prince Braxton and I can tell you that when I look into his eyes, I see the future of this kingdom. He and the good queen have allowed me to use my knowledge and experience to try and find a way to bring about that change. I stand before you as a testimony that change can come, perhaps even today."

Cadmus had already uncorked the vial. Gabriella's hands could barely hold it. She looked up at Cadmus. "There is nothing to fear," he reassured. "If it *does* take effect, the change will be quick."

In the audience, some of the attention had turned to Gabriella's family. They had made their way closer to the front. "Come on Gaby...drink up...quick, quick! That a girl!" her father encouraged, half-shouting, with an almost fanatic grin on his face. Gabriella's mother stood by with her hand covering her face.

The girls on stage watched, mouths open, as Gaby finally put the glass to her lips and swallowed in one gulp. After drinking, she kept her head tilted back.

"Is there a change? We can't see," her father cried out. She finally lowered her head. Cadmus was still smiling at her.

"No change," he said simply, removing the vial from her hand. Jeanette could feel a collective sigh across the crowd as her own pulse continued to rise. Gabriella exhaled, tears slowly falling on her cheek.

Cadmus stepped to the next girl. The crowd drew a breath as she quickly took the vial and drank.

No change.

Cadmus moved down the line with efficiency and purpose, but for one girl after another the green liquid went in and only gray eyes remained.

Jeanette tugged at the sleeves and waist of her dress, the afternoon sun starting to take its toll. She wanted to move, to be free. She looked out over the crowd for familiar faces.

She found Tristyn. With his blue eye he was always easy to spot. He gave a classic shrug. Isabelle stood next to him. Even though she knew her mother hated the whole production, she still had a look on her face of curiosity, wanting to know what happened next. Her father stood behind her, expressionless, stoic as usual.

Jeanette continued to scan the crowd. Every eye focused on the next girl in line, as if they were all watching the sun set to nothing but a speck. As she looked, she met Corwin's eyes. He still stood next to his fellow soldiers that would be leaving. He wasn't watching Cadmus move down the line like the others in the crowd. He was looking at her. She held his view for a moment, long enough for him give her a friendly smile, as if he was trying to prepare her for the outcome. Jeanette turned away, embarrassed.

She looked back to find Cadmus standing in front of Addy. He handed Addy a vial and she drank the liquid. Seconds later, still no change. But it didn't matter, the caravan was still taking her to the castle, away from Jeanette.

*It will be over soon and Tristyn and I will be gone.*

Down the line Cadmus continued, girl after girl, all with the same result. When he stopped in front of Jeanette, she tensed, set her jaw, and extended her hand. She was ready to drink a liquid she knew would make no difference.

Impatiently she waited. Cadmus's head tilted slightly to the side, an interested look on his face. He handed her the vial, but did not let go, and asked, "What is your name young miss?"

*Why is everyone from the castle so concerned with my name?*

"Jeanette," she answered, taking the glass between her fingers and trying to pull away. Cadmus held his grip. She tensed her brow and looked him straight in the eyes. The green that reflected back was like a fascinating forgery. It defied all rational sense of what she knew eyes should look like, yet it was beautiful and right before her.

Murmuring began in the audience as the seconds ticked by. Cadmus held his smile and finally let go. Quickly she uncorked the vile and sucked down the liquid. The amount was minuscule, but it was noticeable. The taste wasn't unpleasant, but hit her tongue bitterly and settled down the back of her throat.

A few seconds ticked by and Cadmus turned to the crowd and replied, "No change."

*Of course there is no change.*

"Ouch!" Jeanette exclaimed suddenly, reaching over to rub her left arm. The girl next to her, Margaret, had let the vial slip out of her hands and flailed about trying to catch it, elbowing Jeanette in the process.

"Sorry," Margaret mouthed, reaching down to pick up the vial. While Margaret knelt, Jeanette caught a glimpse of Lorelei in full profile. Her satin dress was far beyond the quality of the wool and cloth the other girls wore. Her posture was that of a true princess and - as much as Jeanette hated to admit it - if ever there was a girl who looked the part of a prince's bride, it was Lorelei.

"No change," Cadmus said, leaving Margaret and moving on to Lorelei. Jeanette couldn't stomach the possibility that a change could come over Lorelei that would make her even more loathsome. Was this charade what made somebody deserving of a kingdom?

Jeanette averted her eyes as Lorelei took the vial. She turned back to her right and caught eyes with Addy. Jeanette sensed a disappointed reality in Addy's expression. Yet there was still a smile. Addy's smile. It was the most peaceful sight she knew.

Without reason, Addy's smile and reassuring gesture quickly turned to astonishment. As if in slow motion, each girl in line seemed to conjure up the exact same expression, arms raising to point past Jeanette. Jeanette turned around, catching the amazed look of the crowd as she did so. Finally, she saw Lorelei's profile again. Her right eye blazed like emerald an emerald. The liquid worked.

Lorelei stood, tall and erect, chin out. The crowd's cheering continued to escalate and intensify. Cadmus kept his composure, took Lorelei by the hand and encouraged her to step forward. She did not hesitate.

The commotion swelled. Cadmus raised his hands, asking for silence. A hush went over the crowd. He spoke, loud and clear, with Lorelei proudly preening next to him, "People of Emerleigh, I give you the first Jewel of Amarin!"

He stepped to the side and the people let loose with all the emotion they could muster. As soon as they did, Jeanette's mind went blank. Her ears went deaf and her vision went black. Her stomach heaved and she felt like retching. She did everything she could to stay balanced and keep standing, but ended up on her knees, her arms wrapped around her stomach.

In the next moment, the nausea in her stomach left and there was a warm, bright tug that started at the back of her neck and rippled along the top of her scalp. She cupped her hands over her face, the pain unbearable.

As the feeling traveled over to the front of her forehead, flashes of light filled her mind rapidly. There were images; faint, but discernible. They were moving quickly, as if she was looking through them underwater, carried with the current.

*A castle in flames, a lone figure hanging out of a window.*
*An old sign hanging over a merchant shop.*
*A soldier standing across a body of water.*

The images kept flowing until she could not see them anymore. And as quick as they came, they left. She could hear again and sense her surroundings.

Jacob pushed through the guards and emerged from the crowd on stage. "Jeanette, snap out of it. Jeanette!" he said, trying to rouse her. He turned to Cadmus. "What did you give my daughter?"

"You have the kingdom's pledge, the liquid is safe," Cadmus answered, though his face held a look of concern. "It must be nerves."

Finally, aware, alert and covered with sweat, Jeanette let down one hand to steady herself on the floor. She wiped the sting of perspiration out of her eyes with the other.

"Take your time," Jacob said, holding on to her.

"I think I'm okay. I don't know what happened," she said, looking up.

Jacob gasped and Cadmus took a step back, clutching his robe. Curious, the other girls on stage slowly arched around to see what was going on.

Jeanette rose to her feet and looked out over the crowd before her. Gasps filled the air.

Cadmus reacted quickly, grabbing her hand and bringing her forward. Lifting her hand high in the air he exclaimed, "Our second Jewel of Amarin!"

# CHAPTER 8

As far back as Jeanette could remember, all she ever wanted was to be in control and one day leave. Standing under the large tent arranged for the dance, the reality set in that one of her dreams was coming true.

Just not the way she wanted.

After the ceremony, everything happened quickly. An armed escort to the main hall. Her father coming to make sure she was okay. Aides and servants shouting orders and bustling about. Her head pounding and her thoughts racing. Lorelei standing on the other side of the hall in similar commotion, but on her face Jeanette saw excitement and peace. Her eyes, shining.

A lady named Emilia had been assigned by Cadmus to be Jeanette and Lorelei's transition coordinator to the castle. The green satin gown she wore was Emilia's choosing, and prettier than anything Jeanette had ever adorned. Her long black hair was put into a bun, bringing out the detail in her face and cheeks.

*I now have something in common with Lorelei.*

The thought came in an instant and she shuddered. What else did she have in common with Lorelei? The visions she had seen after her eyes changed...did Lorelei see them too?

On a makeshift stage, slightly higher than the ground, Jeanette now sat to the right of Prince Braxton. Lorelei was on his left. Multiple guards stood around them.

Cadmus stood at the front of the stage and the musicians at the other end of the tent stopped playing the soft, welcoming music. The crowd was larger than any other celebration crowd Jeanette had ever seen, and they were all looking in her direction. Her mom and dad were present, but not Tristyn. He was old enough now to have provision duty and take food and supplies to the older boys at their posts. Especially with the prince in town, security was amplified.

*Addy.*

That is whom she wanted to find. Addy had been chosen as a servant for the castle. Jeanette had also been chosen, but not as a servant. A possession.

"Friends of Emerleigh," Cadmus started. "Welcome tonight as we celebrate a glorious day in the Kingdom of Amarin. Not one, but two, of your fair daughters has been found worthy to bring back the true eye color." Everyone in attendance clapped and cheered. "As was planned, the prince will lead the first dance of the night," Cadmus said, motioning to the prince.

*Finally, Lorelei can get what she wants and take the spotlight off of me.*

Jeanette wanted time to clear her mind and think. Tristyn would be devastated. He had waited so patiently for her to lead him to Bandar, back to his people. Would he be able to forgive her? What was going to happen to her at the castle? Would she be able to see Addy? The prince would *have* to choose Lorelei as his bride, wouldn't he? What happens to the 'Jewel of Amarin' not chosen to be princess?

The prince stood and bowed to the crowd. Then turning to Jeanette he extended his hand. "May I have the first dance?" He looked at Jeanette through his dark, curly bangs. He had a pleasant face, thick eyebrows, and cheeks that looked tight from lack of laughter. In some ways, he seemed about the same age as Jeanette, not the four years older that he really was.

*Me?*

Jeanette turned to Lorelei. She had seen Lorelei angry, petulant, nasty and cruel – even this afternoon she sensed Lorelei's jealousy - but she had never seen her murderous.

"Yes," Jeanette answered, a little less nervous knowing Lorelei was dying inside.

She took the prince's hand and walked out onto the floor. The crowd parted as the chatter increased. The musicians started playing and the music built slowly. Braxton positioned his hand on her waist, she followed suit. Holding her other hand out to the side, he asked, meekly, "Do you know how to dance?"

She nodded, hesitantly. Even though she avoided it, she knew the basics. All youth in Emerleigh took dance classes leading up to festival, even though she had not planned on needing it.

He smiled a youthful, giddy smile and started to sway with the music. The crowd formed a wall around them. "I'm assuming you were not expecting all this," he said.

"No."

"To be honest, neither did I. I know Cadmus was able to change his own eyes, but the idea of using that method to find a bride didn't seem right."

Jeanette cocked her head slightly. This didn't sound like the prince she had heard about. "I thought the ceremonies were your idea?"

He laughed as they continued to gently turn to the music. "I can assure you, it was not. There was a time when I had no desire to take part in the festivals."

"So why go along with it in the first place?"

"You have never met my mother have you?" he asked jokingly. Jeanette smiled for the first time. "This fall is her and father's twenty-five year anniversary of taking over the throne. She is insistent that the marriage happen this year to align with it, and only to a girl of green eyes. It is what she has worked tirelessly for and hence, it is my lot." There was something familiar in his voice. Something longing for more space, more options. More control. "Have you felt...different...since the change?" he asked. "I mean, everyone talks about the true gift of growth; have you felt that?"

There had certainly been a change, but not in the way that he was speaking. Outside of the strange visions, she felt no different. "I haven't. Everyone talks about those with true eye color having a gift. I don't really know what that means, but the whole town practically worships Alden because of it."

"He seems like a good man. We are very lucky that we have some of the original ones left. I think it does make a difference."

"What about you? You have the true eye color. Have you felt...different?"

Braxton lowered his head slightly, contemplating. "Let's just say I'm still working on it."

Jeanette did not understand the hesitancy to answer, so she changed the subject. "What about your father? You mentioned your mother and Cadmus; what does your father think?"

Braxton laughed to himself, "My father has his own issues."

Everyone in Amarin knew the King was half mad, but no one ever spoke of it publicly. She heard that the king suffered a horrible fever when Braxton was young and it permanently affected his mind. Since then, Queen Devony had been the real leader of the kingdom, her husband by her side only in name.

The music slowed as the dance came to a close. As much as it pained her to admit, she felt a connection with him, and even some empathy. It was a strange feeling.

"Why did you pick me out of the crowd today?"

"You," he started, searching for the words, "intrigued me. Maybe it was not a coincidence you were standing next to Lorelei. I envision her as the epitome of what a princess should be. But you...I could sense you are different. It was in your face. You don't seem like someone that is easily controlled. I guess I found that attractive. Interesting."

That was not the answer she wanted. "So what is going to happen to us...me and Lorelei I mean?"

"I will be honest, I don't know exactly," he answered, the music dying down. "But I do know one thing," he continued. The music stopped and they stood, still connected, the crowd around clapping gently. He leaned in closer, "I will pick you even if it is to spite my mother."

He placed a kiss on the top of her hand and a chill ran down her back. The warm, welcoming demeanor she felt quickly turned cold and cocky. Where once was a pleasant smile now was a sneer on the prince's lips, as if he had won a bet. Her body tensed as he walked her back to her seat. The music started again and he took Lorelei out to the floor.

Jeanette felt tied to the chair. She wanted to scream, to run, but there were guards all around her. This is not what she planned. She was not ready for it.

Addy emerged out of the crowd, coming toward her. The guards bristled and stood at arms. Addy stopped in her tracks and looked to Jeanette.

"It's okay, she's my friend," Jeanette said. The guards looked at Cadmus who still stood nearby. He nodded and motioned for them to relax. Addy came up to Jeanette and grabbed her hands. Her presence grounded her, made sense. Jeanette wanted to cry, laugh, and run in terror, all at once.

"Look at your eyes," Addy said with awe, staring. If it had been anybody else, she would have slapped them. "Does it feel different?"

"Not really. They are still just my eyes, just a different color," Jeanette said, even though she had not seen them yet.

"What happened to you on the stage? It certainly looked like something happened."

*The visions.*

How could she ever explain it to Addy? She wanted to tell someone she could trust, to help her make sense of it. Addy would believe her. "I have something I need to talk to you about."

"That's an understatement. Green eyes, dancing with the prince, and..." Addy said, getting more excited with each word, "we will be at the castle together!" There was true joy in her words.

Jeanette wanted to feel that joy, that excitement, but she couldn't. The thought of going to the castle had never crossed Jeanette's mind, ever. She had already prepared for life with Tristyn, roaming free in Bandar, living by the great sea. The current outlook made her scared. She felt the sting of the vision, of the castle in flames with someone hanging out of a window.

*I am not supposed to go to the castle.*

The thought came clear and powerful. Taking a deep breath, Jeanette tried to stay in the moment. "Yes, we will both be at the castle." The music stopped and the prince brought Lorelei back to her chair. As soon as she sat down, she looked at Jeanette and the smile faded, very briefly. The dagger in Lorelei's eyes told Jeanette their relationship had just reached a whole new level.

The prince sat down and tried to get Jeanette's attention, but she had suddenly turned her focus to the crowd.

Corwin.

He still had his military uniform on and looked like a real soldier. He looked older and taller and...handsome. He walked up close to the stage and again the guards stiffened. Corwin bowed to the prince and then spoke directly to Jeanette. "I believe you owe me a dance," he said, holding out his hand.

Braxton's jaw tightened. He looked Corwin up and down and then turned to Cadmus. Again, Cadmus nodded his approval. "You have good taste, soldier. What is your name?" Prince Braxton asked.

"Corwin, your majesty," he said, with another bow.

Reaching over, the prince took Jeanette's hand and held it out for Corwin. "One dance is fine." Corwin took Jeanette's hand and led her out to the floor.

Corwin walked Jeanette to her line and backed away a few feet, facing her. The other men in the group each faced their partners. Jeanette looked across at Corwin, at his smile, but there was a new look. A look of concern. He looked wounded.

The men's line moved closer, reaching out their hands to their partners.

*I would rather dance with you than the prince.*

He took her hand and began leading her through the steps and turns. With each movement, each sway, each hand exchange and touch, he continued to wear a smile.

"Thank you for accepting the dance," he said. "I know I kind of tricked you into it, but I truly did want to share this moment with you before I go."

*Why? You'll be gone tomorrow. Now, so will I. We will probably never even see each other again.*

"It's okay," Jeanette replied, "I will admit I was flustered with you. But a lot has changed since then."

Corwin laughed and then caught his breath. "I needed to dance with you. I wanted to have the chance to share...to try and tell you..."

"It doesn't matter," Jeanette interrupted, afraid of what he might say. "You are going to battle and I am going to the castle." She paused another moment and then repeated, a little less convincingly, "It doesn't matter."

The line turned and Corwin and Jeanette were facing each other again. Corwin looked away.

The lines stepped closer to each other. Corwin looked back again, defeat in his eyes. Jeanette looked away. Another step closer. They held out hands, clasping in the middle. His hands were rough, firm. Her hands felt smaller, smoother, more feminine. She had never thought of her hands, or any other feature on her body, as feminine.

A final step and they were standing close; her nose not far from his chin. He leaned in next to her cheek. "Even if it doesn't matter, I still want it to."

A lump caught in her throat as he pulled away, took a step back and gave a bow. For the first time in her life, she was looking at someone who she was willing to let her guard down for.

*Maybe it does matter.*

Out of nowhere, a long, shrill horn echoed over the music. Jeanette looked at Corwin, who held the same confused expression as she did. Another blast came rumbling over the tent. It only meant one thing...

"Red Eye attack!" Alden shouted. "Everyone find shelter, quickly!"

Panic enveloped the mass. Jeanette felt her heart plunge and her pulse rise. She stepped closer to Corwin. He put his arm around her and tried to push through the screaming crowd. In an instant, she felt safer.

"Hold on," he said, a look of battle in his eyes. Before they reached the edge of the tent, the royal guards stepped in and pulled Jeanette away from Corwin. He reached out for her.

"Corwin!" she yelled out, unsure what would happen. His image got farther and farther away as the guards carried her out of the tent.

# CHAPTER 9

A few minutes later Jeanette found herself inside the town hall, dozens of the Royal Guard surrounding the building. Veins pumping, she looked around.

Lorelei was in the corner, hyperventilating. Braxton paced nervously, returning to the window often. Two guards stood at the main entrance and additional ones at each window. When the prince went back for a peak outside, the soldier motioned for him to back away.

Cadmus and Alden were talking near the door when it quickly opened. Jacob and Tristyn were ushered in.

"Tristyn!" Jeanette screamed and ran to meet him. As she hugged him, his arms stayed limp by his side. She pulled back and saw fear. "What happened?"

Jacob wiped his brow and answered the question, though he was speaking to Alden. "Tristyn saw the Rogue. He's the one that made the report." Cadmus and Braxton came closer to listen.

"Are you sure you saw a Red Eye, Tristyn?" Alden asked.

Jacob prodded Tristyn, who shared his events of the night.

He was on his normal route, checking in with the posts. He decided to take a shortcut back to the main village through Hampton Woods. There was a light in the forest, off the trail. He moved closer and saw it was a campfire. Not hearing anyone, he drew closer.

"In the middle of the fire, was a...was a Red Eye," Tristyn said. "He was lying on his back, with his head, arms and legs sticking out of the pit. His torso was completely burnt. His eyes were wide open. They were still red."

"Were there any others?" Cadmus asked.

"I didn't see any. I ran straight here and told the soldier on alarm duty," he said, his eyes turning doubtful as the circle of leaders around him glanced at each other. "I promise, I saw it."

"We know you did," Alden said. "Can you remember where you saw it?"

Tristyn nodded. "I can take you there."

"That won't be necessary," Alden assured.

"I need you to go home and look after your Aunt Isabelle while I stay here and help," Jacob said.

Tristyn turned to Jeanette, a different look of fear in his eyes. "You aren't leaving tonight, are you?"

She didn't know. Hesitation crept up inside her. She had no idea what exactly was going to happen to her. Cadmus put a hand on Tristyn's shoulder. "Assuming everything is safe, she will be home tonight my young friend. The caravan is not leaving until morning." A measure of peace came across Tristyn's face. He recounted the exact location of the body and then left.

"Mayor, we need that body," Cadmus started. "We still don't know where they came from or what their motives are. It is very rare that we have an actual corpse to study, regardless of its state."

"Jacob, go and dispatch a unit to the location to bring the body back," Alden commanded. "Tell them to keep an eye out for any other Rogue activity."

"Of course," Jacob replied and then looked at Jeanette. "Stay here, you will be safe." With the building surrounded by soldiers, she didn't think there was an option to go anywhere else.

***

"Your cousin lives with your family?" Cadmus asked, sitting down next to Jeanette. It had been almost thirty minutes and there was no word on the Red Eye. During that time, Cadmus traded time consulting with Alden and the prince. When not talking to Cadmus, Braxton seemed to be doing everything he could to avoid Lorelei. So far, the prince had made no notion to be the least bit interested in her.

*I wonder if he will get sick of her before tomorrow morning and just leave her here.*

Jeanette laughed a little to herself and then realized it wasn't funny.

*I cannot go to the castle!*

"Lady Jeanette?"

"I'm sorry...my mind is elsewhere."

"I think we all understand that tonight."

"Tristyn...yes, his mother died a few years back and my father's brother - Tristyn's father - well, he left a while ago and we haven't heard from him since."

"I don't know how it is in all the villages, but I'm assuming your cousin struggles with the other boys making fun of him because of the heterochromia."

"The what?"

"Heterochromia," Cadmus replied, pointing one finger at each eye. "It's the name for someone with two eye colors. Though, more often than not, they are called by...less formal names."

"Yes, he does struggle."

Cadmus nodded, as if he understood. "One day, we will overcome our loss of eye color. No more war, no more fighting, everybody living in peace."

"Your eyes haven't always been green, have they?"

"No."

"If your eyes changed, why can't you just give the serum to anyone and have there eyes change. Wouldn't that bring just as much hope," Jeanette asked.

"I wish I knew the answer, Jeanette. I didn't know if it would work on me. I have tried it on, well, far too many to count. It is very, very difficult to make and the queen is adamant that we find a bride for the prince. So I made enough for the festivals and it will be a while before anymore is available."

Braxton approached and interrupted. "I do apologize for the security measures keeping you from your family."

Before Jeanette could answer, Lorelei swooped in. "Please do not apologize, your majesty. With the heightened level of danger we are much better protected here."

Cadmus nodded his agreement. "Lady Lorelei is correct. For the time being this is the most secure location in the village."

"What happens next?" Jeanette asked.

"There are a few logistics to take care of," Cadmus started. "The first is to make sure there are no more Rogues still in the vicinity. Once we confirm that, then you two will be escorted home to spend the last night with your family. Royal Guards will be stationed at your homes for protection.

"But before you go home, you each need to pick someone - a young lady - that you trust dearly to be your handmaiden. She will attend you at the castle."

Lorelei and Jeanette shared a surprise look. Cadmus continued, "The good queen has allowed this, knowing that your transition to the court will be complicated and time consuming. Having a familiar face will help you make that transition."

Addy was the first person that came to Jeanette's mind, but her dream of serving in the castle had finally come true. She could not take that from her. Jeanette considered the options silently as Cadmus continued, "As soon as we know the area is clear, we will send a messenger to the castle to make the queen aware of your arrival. I know her majesty will be excited to hear the news."

"Excuse me, Master Cadmus," Lorelei interjected, "is there a necessity to head to the final festival in Pembrooke? With everything that has happened and the commotion that the caravan will bring, is it not more efficient and safer to go straight to the castle?"

"I discussed that option with Prince Braxton," Cadmus said, giving the prince a glance. Braxton appeared less than enthused about attending another festival. "I think it is best that we stick with the intended schedule. We will have the safety needed as we travel and, if necessary, we can add reinforcements in Pembrooke."

*I cannot go to the castle!*

Jeanette was not sure where the feeling came from. Her desire to avoid the castle was more than her own selfish desires. It felt like a pull, forcing her to act, regardless of her personal intent.

The door to the town hall opened.

"The scouting party is back, Your Majesty," the guard said.

"Bring the Rogue's body in here, immediately," Cadmus ordered.

Everyone in the room other than Cadmus, took a step back. Jeanette was unsure about being close to a Red Eye. They were things of bad dreams, make believe.

Seconds later Corwin and Rendall walked through the

door, struggling with the weight of a tarp holding a heavy load. They each had a cloth wrapped around the lower half of their head, covering their mouth and nose. As soon as they entered the room, a putrid smell followed.

"That's far enough," Cadmus said, moving forward, eyes transfixed. Everyone in the room moved closer, except for Lorelei, who stepped back in shock. Jeanette put her hand over her mouth and pinched her nose, trying to evade the scent. She caught eyes with Corwin. He was breathing hard and covered in sweat.

Cadmus knelt down, and with a flick of his wrists, removed the cloth.

Jeanette's insides lurched. The smell set in. The odor was a blend of blood, feces, and raw meat. She heaved, fluids entering her mouth, but not forcing their way out. Patches of hair on the Rogue's head remained. What few items of clothing left were intermingled with flesh. A knife protruded from it's chest.

Its eyes were still open.

Red.

She found herself staring into them. They were void, but a feeling of surprise came over her. There wasn't any evil, like the horror stories she had heard. It wasn't a thing, a monster; it was a person, it was a man - lifeless - but a man.

Cadmus, holding part of his shirt to his face, reached down and extended the hands of the body out to the side. He examined the wrists, looking for what, Jeanette did not know. She glanced at her father. The look of awe and confusion was one she had not seen before. Deep down, she knew he had never truly believed the tales either.

"Did you see any others?" the prince asked.

"When we found the body, sir," Corwin started, "it was already dead. His whole torso and some of his head were in the fire, with his legs practically untouched by the flames. On his left wrist is a small marking, but it's not discernible. There is a tan line on his right wrists. Looks like he may have had some jewelry on, but whoever did this to him must have taken it," he said, pointing to the obvious tan lines around the Red Eye's wrist, where a bracelet once sat.

"That's what they do; desecrate their bodies with markings, plunder, and kill," the prince said. "Were there any others?" he asked again. Cadmus covered the body.

"No sir," Corwin answered. "The other troops have canvassed the village perimeter and haven't seen any sign, Whoever killed it must have fled."

"We must destroy it," Braxton exclaimed. "These things have no place among us. We need to finish the job and obliterate it."

Cadmus stood, calm and stately, and put his hand on the prince's shoulder. "This is a rare occurrence that would allow us to study and learn more about them, your highness. I understand your feeling, but we should not let this opportunity pass us by."

There was silence in the room. During the seconds that passed, Jeanette focused on Braxton. He looked concerned, wanting to make the right decision. Who was really in charge? What kind of studying would be done on the body?

"Of course, Cadmus," Braxton said, nodding, as if convincing himself. "Under normal circumstances we would eliminate the threat, but this is a very unique opportunity."

"Mayor Alden," Cadmus gestured, "could you please have the Rogue appropriately covered and stowed to accompany us on the caravan back to the castle?"

"Certainly," Alden answered. "Corwin, Rendall, would you please take the body to the infirmary and get the medic to help you prepare it for transport? And then get back with your group; you have a big day tomorrow."

"Yes, sir," they said in unison. Braxton started a private

discussion with Cadmus while Alden and Jacob walked outside. Jeanette had not moved, standing close to the body. Corwin walked around the Rogue to her side.

"Are you doing okay?" he asked.

Was she okay? Green eyes. Going to the castle. Seeing a Rogue face to face.

"I think so," she lied.

He smiled at her; the uneven, sincere, knowing smile she had learned to expect. Bending over, he grabbed one side of the cloth casing covering the body as Rendall grabbed the other. They lifted the body and exited the door.

Her body stiffened. In the morning, he would be leaving for the Royal Academy and she would be leaving on the caravan. Would she see him again? Did they just share their final words together?

After the body was gone, the smell still lingered, but not as strong. Lorelei emerged from her corner, shock still in her eyes. "Can you believe they are going to bring that *thing* on the caravan with us?" she asked, still trying to wave the smell away.

"I'm sorry, were you asking *me* a question?" Jeanette asked, confused at Lorelei's close proximity. Realization of Jeanette's sarcasm came to Lorelei's eyes. She huffed and walked closer to the prince.

Jacob and Alden walked back through the door as a horn sounded, long and loud. "All of the scouts are back and the area appears safe," Alden said. "We have given the all clear signal."

"Jeanette and Lorelei will be able to spend time with their family tonight, is that correct?" Jacob asked Cadmus.

"Of course, though we will have members of the Royal Guard surrounding the homes, just in case." Cadmus turned to Jeanette and Lorelei. "Tomorrow morning you will need to report here by dawn prepared to leave. You may bring one trunk of belongings with you." How Lorelei could make that work was beyond understanding.

Cadmus said, more somber, "I can't even imagine what you two are going through right now. It is a lot of change. But I assure you, you will be taken care of and you will be safe." His eyes were strong and his tone truthful. Jeanette felt comfortable around him.

Cadmus motioned for everyone to exit the building. Jeanette's father was by her side, heading toward the door. The prince stepped in front of them. "Sir," he said, speaking to Jacob, "as Master Cadmus said, we will take very good care of your daughter." He gave a formal bow of respect to Jeanette.

Her insides tumbled. She didn't want to be taken care of. She wanted her freedom. Jacob returned a bow and thanked the prince. As soon as they walked outside a group of six guards encircled them.

The villagers had come out of their homes at the all-clear and watched in awe and whispers. Jacob put his arm around Jeanette's shoulders, pulling her a little closer. She looked at his profile, trying to get a reading of his thoughts or feelings.

Did he want her to go? Was he worried about her? Did he really think she would make it at the castle? There was no answer to her silent concerns, from him or within. The questions disappeared as her thoughts shifted to seeing her mother.

As they reached home, one of the guards opened the door and motioned them in.

"Is there anything else you need, my lady?"

Never in her life had anybody addressed her as lady.

# CHAPTER 10

"I told you all this would come to no good," Isabelle screamed. "Look at her! What have they done to her?" Standing in the middle of her living room, nobody answered.

The voice building up inside Jeanette came out as tears.

"She's hated it here long enough; she's probably excited to leave. It's what she's always wanted!"

Jeanette wiped her cheek. "You are right...it is what I have always wanted," she said softly and quietly walked to her room and slammed the door.

She cursed under her breath and started pacing. She stopped in the middle of the room, closed her eyes for a moment, and took a deep breath. She opened them slowly. Staring back at her in the window was a face that looked like hers, but wasn't.

Her breathing calmed. She reached her hand up to touch the side of her eye, her new eye, with color. It *was* her. She walked closer to the window, closer to reality.

She moved past the reflection and could see faintly into the night. So many times she had looked out the window, wondering when she would have the courage to leave. Now she didn't have to. She was leaving whether she liked it or not.

Her nose not far from the pane, she saw three guards facing the crowd around them, keeping watch, protecting her. An asset. There was a knock at the door. She shook the thoughts from her head. "It's me," Tristyn said softly.

She took a deep breath and sat down on her bed, crossing her legs, and taking her hair out of the bun. Pressure released down the back of her head and neck as her hair fell down. "Come in."

Tristyn opened the door. Jeanette could sense his apprehension as the door closed. "I'm fine Tristyn, I promise," she said, calming him. He stood a little straighter.

They waited for each other to speak.

"I am so sorry Tristyn," she started. "I know this is not what we planned. More than anything I wanted to go to Bandar with you." Tristyn would have to stay here, in Emerleigh, an outsider. "One day we'll make it work, I promise," she said, searching for a way to not feel guilty. "And I know my father has every intention of taking you. I'm sure you will get to go much sooner than you think."

"I don't want to go with Uncle Jacob, I want to go with you," he finally said, voice breaking. She almost choked on his sincerity and had to take a breath. "Do you really have to go?"

The guilt was unbearable.

"Come here," she said, motioning for him to sit down next to her. He walked over and sat down, resting his head on her shoulder. She tilted her head sideways to rest on his. They sat there, silent, comforting each other.

"I know it's not your fault," he said and then leaned forward and put his elbows on his knees and turned, looking into her eyes again. "Besides, it's not like we would have probably left anyway, right?"

The words hurt. She *had* planned on leaving with him. She

wanted to run away, live free, explore Bandar and give him the opportunity to find himself. Would she have followed through with it?

"Did it hurt?" he asked, pointing to her eyes.

"No. I didn't feel anything," she said, not wanting him to worry.

"It sure looked like you felt something. You looked like you were going to pass out on the stage."

Jeanette scratched her temple. She did not have an answer and she hadn't taken the time to try and think it through.

*A castle in flames, a lone figure hanging out of a window.*

*An old sign hanging over a merchant shop.*

*A soldier standing across a body of water.*

Tristyn was waiting for a response.

"I don't know what it was...fatigue, boredom," she paused, "showmanship." A grin slid across her face. Usually, Tristyn appreciated her sense of humor, but he did not laugh.

"I don't know what it was," she continued. "One minute I'm me, and have regular non-fun eyes like everybody else and the next second I'm a 'Jewel of Amarin', whatever that means. Now I have something in common with Lorelei, do you think that's what I wanted?"

She could tell he wanted to smile, but he didn't. "Can I show you something?" Tristyn asked.

"Of course."

He reached up to the top of his shirt and pulled his necklace all the way out. She had given it to him on his twelfth birthday. Attached to the end of it was a beaded bracelet. Jeanette knew he wore a necklace, but she had never seen the beads before.

"Where did you get that?"

He held them out in front of him, the string pulling on his neck, and ran them across his fingers. "I got it from the Rogue."

"He had a tan line on his wrist," Jeanette said, remembering. "You really took it off the Red Eye?"

Tristyn grinned. "Yeah," he responded, as if still surprised he was able to do it. "I just couldn't believe I was actually seeing one in real life. His arm was sticking out of the fire and the stones were shining off the light." He pondered for a moment. "Was it wrong to take it?"

"Of course not," Jeanette said, wondering if she would have done the same thing. "It's something you get to keep to help you remember. Have you shown it to any of the other boys?"

"No," he said, stuffing it back down the opening of his shirt. "You are the first. I didn't want them to tell anybody and then have to give it back."

"Do you think the other boys have heard about you finding the Red Eye?" Such a story would probably elevate Tristyn in the eyes of his peers.

"I haven't talked to any yet. I've been here ever since. And honestly, it's not like anything really changed. All I did was find a body lying in the forest. It could have been any one of us."

"But it was you," Jeanette said, trying to build him up. She grasped for anything positive, knowing that she would be leaving him here, alone. "I don't think it was an accident."

Tristyn reached up and touched the bracelet through his shirt, then stood and walked to the other side of the room. "Have you thought about what will happen if Prince Braxton chooses you?"

Jeanette's thoughts exploded and she searched for words. "What are you talking about? Of course I haven't thought about it yet. A couple of hours ago I was an ordinary girl from Emerleigh and now I have green eyes and will be on a caravan tomorrow that will take me to the castle. Sorry, I haven't thought the whole thing through quite yet!" she shrilled, rolling over on her bed and pulling the pillow over her head.

Under her pillow she heard Tristyn finally let out a small laugh. She moved the pillow over slightly to see him better "What's so funny?"

"Do you honestly think the prince would pick you over Lorelei?"

Jeanette gave him a hard stare, the memories of the last two days replaying. A smile. The first dance. The possessive attitude. She sat up again and put the pillow in her lap. "Why *would* he pick me over Lorelei?" she asked, still trying to decipher the answer.

"So then don't go," Tristyn begged. "What's the point if you don't want to be there and he can have Lorelei? Do you even know what will happen to the one that doesn't get chosen?"

"Would you stop with the questions? I told you I don't know, okay," she said, throwing the pillow at him. Tristyn caught it. She put her head in her hands and ran her fingers through her hair. Did she want to go? Was it better to leave on the caravan with Addy than try to leave on her own?

"I guess I'm just jealous. I would give anything to come with you," Tristyn continued.

"I know."

"You should try and get some sleep. I'll see you in the morning," he said, walking to the door. She searched for something, anything to say that would give him more confidence. "I love you...it's all going to work out."

He nodded again.

She was still sitting on her bed, thinking about what she had said.

*Maybe the castle won't be that bad.*

And as quickly as the thought came, the image of the castle on fire, a figure hanging out of the window came to her mind again.

*I cannot go to the castle!*

*If I go, someone I love will get hurt.*

She heard the feeling deep in her heart. It made no sense, but it was true, she knew it. Intuition? Nerves? Whatever it was trying to get through to her, it was real.

She started pacing again, glancing at the guards outside her home. She now belonged to Amarin and had no other option but to go to the castle.

# CHAPTER 11

Clouds cluttered the sky ominously as a breeze ruffled the dark banners that still hung from festival. It would take two or three days to clean.

Jeanette would not be here.

"Bless you, Jeanette. Bless you!" came a call from the crowd that was gathering. The Royal Guard had roped off a section to keep the spectators away from the carriages. There were thirteen carriages in all.

"Jeanette!" Addy called out, walking right past the guards. The new green sash on her waist signified her place in the caravan. Everything Jeanette wanted to share was bubbling up inside, ready to come out. More than anything, Jeanette wanted a few minutes of quiet to talk to her best friend.

"Have you lost your crackling mind?" Addy snapped.

"What?"

"Brandy. My sister! Are you crazy?"

Jeanette looked past Addy to see Brandy following behind, dragging a trunk. After Cadmus' invitation for Jeanette to pick a hand-maiden, Brandy was the only girl that came to mind that Jeanette knew would not get on her nerves.

Jeanette tripped over her words trying to answer. The look on Brandy's face was one of sheer joy. "What's wrong with Brandy?" Jeanette started. "We get along fine."

Addy took a few breaths and tried to remain calm, her tone quieter. "*You* may get along with her fine, Jeanette," she exclaimed. Then in a heartbeat she was pleading, "but you don't know what it's like. Last night was one of the happiest nights of my life. Realizing that we were both going to be at the castle together. And then this morning finding out..."

Jeanette grabbed Addy by the arm and moved her out of Brandy's earshot. Addy continued to let out her frustrations. Jeanette looked back over her shoulder to make sure Brandy was okay. Brandy gave a patient nod, as if to say she understood her sister's feelings, but didn't care.

Jeanette finally interrupted, changing the subject. "I would have given anything to talk to you last night. I don't understand any of this...any of it at all." Now that Addy was with her, she felt more confident, more excited. "There's something that happened yesterday, something I haven't told anyone about."

A trumpet sounded and the royal procession seemed to swell in numbers. Members of the Royal Guard made a circle around them, protecting the newest assets of Amarin. The prince walked by, spoke a few words quickly to Lorelei and then bowed. Then he was in front of Jeanette, a broad smile on his lips. Cadmus was at his side.

"I very much look forward to getting to know you more at the castle," he said with bow.

"Thank you," she said, with a small curtsy and a fear in her stomach.

Lorelei inched closer to Jeanette and Addy. "I'm so sorry Addy," she said, "but this area is restricted for us and our families. I believe anyone else going to the castle will be loading up somewhere else." There was nothing new in the condescending tone Lorelei used, but there was no grin or pleasure. The new look on her face was one of power.

Jeanette reached out and gave Addy the biggest hug they had ever shared and whispered in her ear, "Everything's going to be okay." Addy turned and walked away.

"I honestly don't know why you spend time with her," Lorelei said. "If you wish to continue to associate with others of a lower status, Prince Braxton and I support you fully and without hesitation."

Normally it would have struck a nerve, but with the events of the past day, Jeanette was able to put Lorelei out of her mind. Jeanette walked away, completely ignoring her.

Tristyn approached, carrying Jeanette's trunk. She walked over and punched him in the arm as hard as she could. Wincing in pain, he let go of the trunk and it fell to the ground. Everyone nearby turned to look.

"Have you gone crazy?" he scolded, massaging his arm. Jeanette smiled from ear to ear, trying to hold back the emotion. There was only one regret she had for leaving Emerleigh and he was standing in front of her. She threw her arms around him and started to cry.

"I'm so sorry I have to go, Tristyn," she said softly and they pulled away. Even though she was two and a half years his senior, they stood eye to eye. " I love you very much. You will be okay."

Tristyn could not speak. He wiped his eyes with his sleeve. Isabelle came up behind and put her hand on Tristyn's shoulder.

*I may never see you again mother.*

This is the moment she had dreamed about for years. Oddly, she felt like apologizing. It was a strange feeling.

"Goodbye, mother," was all she could muster.

"Goodbye, Jeanette." Nothing else needed to be said.

"Isabelle," Jacob spoke up, "why don't you and Tristyn

head home and I'll be there in a moment." Tristyn gave Jeanette another hug and then he and Isabelle walked away.

Jacob took a step forward to Jeanette and he reached out his hand to move her hair out of her face. He had done that when she was younger, often.

"Thank you for being kind to your mother," he started. Jeanette did not feel saying goodbye was the same as being kind, but she understood what he meant. "Whether or not you believe it she will miss you."

"Why have you..." Jeanette started and then debated whether to finish. "Why have you stayed with her all this time? Hasn't she made you miserable?"

Jacob sighed and then replied, "No, not miserable. Concerned and frustrated, but not miserable."

Jeanette did not believe him.

"One day you will understand."

She still did not believe him.

They stood together for a moment, watching as the caravan continued to assemble. "Jeanette, I..." Jacob started, low and sincere.

"I know," Jeanette said, cutting him off. Her father could be hard sometimes, but mostly he had been absent, emotionally. She wanted to blame him for not opening up more; for not being the one sane parent she could turn to.

She looked up at him and could see his eyes welling. He didn't take the time to wipe them. It was the first time since her brother died that she had seen her father cry.

"Time to load the caravan!" a loud cry came down the line.

Jacob wiped his cheeks. "Do you have everything you need?"

"I think so. I hope so."

"I know you have looked forward to leaving for a long time," Jacob said, "but just know that everything I have ever done..." She turned away and ran her fingers over the hair above her ear.

Jacob raised his eyebrows and grabbed her lovingly by the shoulders. "I know I have not been there for you like you needed me too. I know it's been hard," he said, looking into her eyes.

More and more people were crowding around as the servants loaded crates and bags onto the carriages. Jeanette kept moving her gaze from her father to the carriages.

"Listen to me," he said, getting her attention. "I have never doubted your potential, only your choices. Don't doubt yourself and the good things you can do."

*Was he just going to let her go? Was he going to let the prince take away his little girl?*

Emilia walked over. "Are you ready?"

She felt the urge to hug him, but couldn't make herself. "I know Tristyn wants you to take him to Bandar. Sooner rather than later," she said. He nodded and finally wiped his eyes. She turned to follow Emilia.

Before ducking into the carriage, she took one last look. She saw Addy and Brandy saying goodbye to their family. Rhilynn was being left with one daughter at home, the castle and Jeanette taking her other two. She saw Alden with his arms around Elizabeth. Jeanette waved at Elizabeth who smiled and waved back.

And then she saw Corwin.

He did not have the usual smile. On his face was sadness. She used to ignore his advances because that is how she dealt with all the boys. But after the dance at the festival, she had opened herself to the idea that *maybe* Corwin was worthy of attention. The feelings she had that night were undeniable. It was a spark of potential.

Corwin tried to push through the crowd to get closer. He lifted his hand and mouthed something she did not understand. She lifted her hand and waved back, swallowing hard.

In the depths of her heart, she was willing to admit that she would miss him. If they were both staying, what would happen? Was there a chance for a relationship? She didn't know, and now wasn't the time to dwell on it.

Jeanette got in the carriage and was greeted by a wide-eyed, grinning Brandy. "Can you believe it?" Brandy asked, hands wedged between her legs trying to contain her excitement. "We are going to the castle!"

# CHAPTER 12

"How much longer do we have to eat this muck?" a soldier muttered, tossing his plate on the ground. The sloppy substance splattered into the dirt and fire. His peers around him continued eating, as if nothing happened.

John walked by and heard the complaint. Lately all he heard was complaining. He should put the soldier in his place. John was good at helping others change their attitudes; it was one of the reasons he moved so quickly up the ranks. But he restrained himself. Morale was low enough already.

At only twenty-one, he was a captain. Currently the youngest in all the Army of Amarin. Like the other boys of Amarin, at the age of eighteen he left home to train at the Royal Academy for six months before getting his first assignment. Two and a half years later, his service paid, he had the option of going home or re-enlisting as an officer. The choice was easy.

He wanted to fight, to help end the war, but the last year had been a steady downhill fall. Defeat after defeat. His ranks that swelled at four hundred a year ago, now held closer to two-hundred and fifty. Lost lives of men he was responsible for that will never return.

Taking slow, deliberate steps, he surveyed the camp. Shoddy tents lined in unison. Men - boys, really - striving to represent the kingdom they loved. Young, clueless, and full of fight in their worried gray eyes. The green uniforms with the symbol of Amarin stitched in gold were now stained with sweat, dirt and blood. The swords and spears, once bright and sharp, were now dull and ragged. Rations were down, the weather warming, and after six days of sitting on the outskirts of the northern town of Samdon with no assignment, the men were getting idle and John's hope waned.

He stopped outside of his tent to pat down Cheswin, his black stallion. Cheswin had been with him all the way up the ranks and was as much a part of the war as any soldier.

"How are you doing today, boy?" John asked, rubbing the white spot in between Cheswin's eyes. Cheswin closed his eyes and seemed to appreciate the affection.

Burleigh, John's personal assistant, bodyguard, and best friend, met him outside of his tent. "Did you eat yet?"

"I had a little bit."

"I think Gordy is getting the hang of it, don't you?" Burleigh asked with a grin. John grimaced.

"It's not like he has a lot to work with," Burleigh continued. "I've heard horror stories about cooks and the stuff they put in a stew. Eck! Remember that one fellow that told us about a stew he had once that had rat meat and tayberries and..."

"Stop, please!" John said, putting his hands over Cheswin's ears. "He doesn't need to hear any of this."

Burleigh laughed. John gave him a smile and continued into the tent as Burleigh kept talking, "But while we're on the subject of making something out of nothing, what are we going to do with the men?" John stopped and turned to listen.

Burleigh spoke in a more serious tone. "We can't keep making things up to keep them busy. They're catching on and getting restless. If this goes on much longer they are going to start to desert."

John glanced over the camp again. He couldn't feel anything. There was no life.

"Is it bad to say I hope they find us soon?" Burleigh asked, talking about the brown eyed army of Tamir, the sworn enemy of the Kingdom of Amarin. "The men need to be ready to fight."

A trumpet sounded from the entrance to camp. John shook his head in disgust.

*Captain Barrett.*

John expected Barrett's arrival, but was not happy about it. "That fool! Why does he have to make his presence known to every Tamir army nearby with that stupid trumpet." Barrett was a career military man known for his opportunism, arrogance and willingness to do anything to get ahead. Presently, John and he shared the same title of Captain, but that is all they shared.

"The men and I are saving up to buy you a trumpet," Burleigh said with a grin. John gave him a tilted stare and shook his head.

The convoy arrived at John's tent at the center of camp. Barrett, from astride his saddle, spoke first. "Captain, I trust you and your men have taken comfort in your new...home?" he asked, glancing around the camp.

"We have made do."

"Well, if nothing else they are well rested," Barrett said, a mocking undertone present.

John's mood was quickly deteriorating. "Shall we begin, Captain?" he asked, motioning toward his tent.

John and Barrett were the only captains in the region. As such, they were ordered to meet periodically to discuss plans and maneuvers. John did not understand why; it seemed all his men were asked to do from the Royal Command was obey. There was never any counsel with the generals or the castle.

Barrett slipped effortlessly from his saddle and made his way into John's tent. Burleigh and one of Barrett's men followed. "I will ask that you remain out here, Hanson," Barrett said to his assistant. "I will not be long." Hanson nodded and took up his post by the front of the door.

Burleigh kept walking, intent on coming inside. "I will talk to Captain Barrett in private, Burleigh," John said. Burleigh snarled a little, but dutifully took his spot outside the door, giving Hanson an intimidating look.

John pointed a finger. "Play nice."

Barrett strode around John's tent with a prideful air, slowly taking off his riding gloves. Barrett was a ten year veteran of the war and had seen far more action than John, but John had become a Captain quicker. John assumed this fact was not lost on Barrett.

A drop of leftover dew from the top of the tent fell on a large map unrolled in the middle of the room. "It's unfortunate you haven't received the new command tent from headquarters," Barrett said, running his fingers along the cloth. "It's lighter, roomier, and much cooler in these warmer areas."

"Thanks for the update; I will be sure to get with the quartermaster. Do you come with any new information?" John asked, getting to the point. He was in no mood for Barrett's showmanship.

Barrett grinned. "You're not one for pleasantries are you, John?"

No response.

"One of the things you'll learn, John, with more training and experience, is just how good you have it."

"What is that supposed to mean?"

"Our position is ideal. You over think it my friend. I watch you, every time we meet, and I see your frustration. You have the desire for victory so completely wound up inside you that there is no other thought." Everything Barrett said, so far, was the truth.

Barrett continued. "It's admirable. Truly it is. But one of the things I have learned over my years of service to the kingdom is that you and I have no reason to concern ourselves with the actual victory. We are the doers - the actors if you will. It is not our job to write the script, only to play out the scenes," Barrett explained. "You need to relax and be more willing to follow where this war takes you, appreciating the good things as they come. Because up until now," Barrett said, reaching out his hand to catch another drop of dew falling from the ceiling, "it does not appear you are taking full advantage of the situation."

"Taking full advantage?" John challenged, his voice raised. "My situation shows me nothing but wasted opportunity after wasted opportunity to fight. And all we do is cower to the enemy while good men die!"

Barrett's face tightened. "That is not our decision to make," he retorted. "We get orders and we follow them. Right now, the orders are for our camps to hold the line and protect. Information shows that the Brown Eyes are heading toward us and we are to make sure they break no further. The longer we hold them off the more time for the festivals; to find the prince a bride. The plan is clear!"

"The plan is wrong!" John did not need a lecture. The more Barrett talked, the more John realized they were on the losing side. Ultimate defeat was inevitable without a strategic change. A change more substantial than the prince getting married.

Barrett's eyes grew sharp, his mouth stern. The small talk was over. "Listen to me, boy. Your idealism may have gotten you through the ranks quickly and won you over with the soldiers, but don't think for a minute it does anything for me. War demands realism. To think that you can go out to meet the army of Tamir, waving your swords, screaming mightily, and win is utter foolishness."

John put his hands on the desk and leaned in, face rigid with disgust. "Get out!"

Barrett pushed by John, going for the door. He paused. "We have our orders and they will be followed," he stated and then left.

Burleigh came in. "From the sound of it that went well?"

"Oh, shut up," John said.

Burleigh chuckled. "Well the tension outside wasn't any better. Hanson? He's a piece of work. Apparently Barrett's attitude rubs off on his subordinates." He made a fist and punched his other hand, "Just one shot to the jaw would have set him straight. Just one."

John wasn't listening; Barrett's comment stuck in his head. *To find the prince a bride.*

"Burleigh, are we honestly holding back a concerted war effort because we think some girl with green eyes getting hitched to the prince will save the kingdom?"

Still muttering to himself about Hanson, Burleigh had to refocus. "I don't know. Word is that the castle has created something that can change some people's eye color." Burleigh held out his hands to explain. "You have a green eyed prince and a green eyed princess, seems to make sense that a baby would have the true color. An event like that would certainly boost morale I would think."

"But wouldn't engaging our men in an offensive and taking this war to the Brown Eyes be more beneficial?"

Burleigh did not answer.

"Maybe Barrett is right, maybe I over think it?"

Burleigh walked closer to John. "I don't know how we're going to win this war. I don't know if any body's eye color is going to change from these festivals. But I do know one thing," he said.

"What's that?"

"I do know that Barrett is a jackass."

John grinned. Burleigh always tried to cheer him up, even if it didn't always work. "Barrett being a jackass doesn't change the fact that I completely disagree with the orders we have from the castle."

"Well, maybe you should take that up with them?"

For now, John didn't have the will power. His men would sit in Samdon and wait for the fight to come to them, at least until new orders arrived.

"Maybe one day I will," John said quietly and ordered Burleigh to call the men together.

# CHAPTER 13

The sun fell as the caravan approached Pembrooke. Two days from Emerleigh and Jeanette was already in a world far from any she had ever known. The previous night the caravan rested at a beautiful clearing on the banks of the Tamblin River.

The first day's journey had taken them from the expansive fields and gardens of Emerleigh north into the rolling forests and less occupied territory of the kingdom. Jeanette and Brandy had shared the long carriage ride. Brandy was still very excited and Jeanette wished she shared the same naïve, youthful curiosity. She could not shake the impressions left by her vision.

*I cannot go to the castle. Someone I love will be hurt.*

Jeanette sensed that with each turn of the carriage wheel she was approaching impending disaster.

"You do realize the whole kingdom is going to be talking about you and Lorelei's eyes, right?" Brandy asked at one point.

Jeanette did not respond. The long ride gave her time to look over the landscape, taking in the view through a new lens.

Did it look different? She couldn't say for sure, but since the change she felt things were closer, more real. They looked the same, but the trees, the river, the fields of grain...she could sense them.

One of the guards rode up on horseback beside the carriage and called out, "We will be at the main gate momentarily."

"If it's anything like they say, Lorelei should fit in perfect," said Brandy.

The city of Pembrooke sat closer to the castle than any of the other towns in Amarin. It was the first choice of holiday and retirement for the privileged. Pembrooke was also close to Enzion, the main market city for the kingdom, and usually had first pick on merchandise. Because of the opulence, Pembrooke had a reputation for turning its nose up to the other villages in Amarin.

"There it is," Jeanette said, the caravan rounding a small bend and Pembrooke coming into view. The wall around the city was ornate and well crafted. Flyer's and flags were abundant, advertising the new Jewels of Amarin. The city gate was open to welcome the caravan and a sea of people lined the streets.

"I've never seen anything like it," Brandy said, face pressed to the window.

Rolling down the main street of Pembrooke, the stones were smooth and polished underneath the carriage wheels. The houses were close together, plastered tight, as if people lived on top of each other. Many of the homes were two stories high.

Doors opened and the noise rose as people lined both sides of the street. "Can you believe all these people?" Brandy asked.

Even though a part of her realized some of the attention was for her, Jeanette didn't want it. But looking out over the crowd it was hard to deny the expression that she kept seeing on the faces of those yelling out and cheering.

*Hope.*

The carriage stopped. The door opened and one of the guards stuck his hand in. "Quickly, my lady."

Before Jeanette could rise, Brandy leaned over and gave her a hug and whispered, "Thank you for picking me." After the incessant questioning and childlike giddiness Brandy had displayed for two days, there was a maturity Jeanette felt in her words.

"Well, go on!" Brandy said, backing away. "Your fans await." Jeanette stepped out, flanked by four guards, Brandy following behind. The walkway led to a house bigger than Jeanette had ever seen. Unlike the other homes that seemed clogged together, this was a manor, situated on a small parcel of land. The yard was meticulously landscaped. Instead of plaster, hewed stone covered the facade. It was beautiful.

Jeanette looked to her left. Lorelei came up the walk followed by Kellan, her handmaiden. They were surrounded by three guards. Cadmus and Emilia waited at the front door to usher the girls inside.

Cadmus spoke to one of the guards directly inside the house. The guard nodded dutifully and disappeared down the long hallway in front of them. As the company stood around waiting for instructions, Cadmus called Jeanette and Lorelei closer.

"This is Mayor Villard's home. We will be dining with him tonight at his invitation. He is honored to have you here. When we meet him don't be surprised if he is a little..." he paused for the word, "eccentric."

Jeanette and Lorelei both looked confused.

Cadmus thought for a second. "You will understand what I mean. Today was the first day of their festival and spirits are high. Just know that he likes to put on a show."

Looking around, it didn't surprise Jeanette. She had never seen furnishings like these. Ornate, thick tapestries over the windows in the sitting room to the left. Wild, colorful rugs and large oil paintings of various animals in the music room to the right.

"Where is Prince Braxton?" Lorelei asked.

Cadmus pondered for a moment. "The prince has had a very busy few days and is skipping dinner this evening to get some much needed rest."

"There they are!"

Jeanette looked past Cadmus and down the end of the hall to see a tall, middle aged man with long blond hair. His bright green cloak with orange outlay wisped on the floor as he came forward to meet them.

Cadmus extended his hand, but Villard walked right past him as if he were invisible. Stopping in front of Jeanette and Lorelei, Villard reached up and placed a hand on each of their cheeks. Jeanette flinched. With great passion, as if tears might ensue, he gushed, "You are the most heavenly creatures I have ever seen!" He closed his eyes and drew in a deep breath.

Confusion covered Jeanette's face. The only mayor she knew was Alden - seasoned, reserved, patriarchal. Villard did not seem like Alden.

Villard snapped his eyes to Cadmus and waived an accusing finger. "And why could you not wait to find such celestial gifts in my city?" he asked, clutching his cloak at the breast. "Now Emerleigh will get all the praise."

"My good friend," Cadmus said, putting his arm around Villard, "you have the distinct honor of being able to say that you, the great Villard, Mayor of Pembrooke, were the first to receive them and pay them honor. The queen, when she hears of this, will be very pleased," Cadmus said, spinning it to satisfy Villard's pride.

Villard stroked his mustache, looking at Jeanette and

Lorelei thoughtfully. Standing behind Cadmus and Villard, Emilia was motioning for Jeanette to stand tall and smile. A huge grin crossed Villard's face, elation in his eyes. Clapping his hands loudly, he exclaimed, "Yes! Why am I making such a fuss? Of course you have come to our lovely city first!" Suddenly, Villard put his hand over his mouth, shocked. "Where is the prince? Is he not here?"

Cadmus gave the same excuse he gave before about the prince needing rest. Watching Villard's theatrics, Jeanette knew perfectly well why the prince was missing dinner. "But rest assured he will be with us for the festival tomorrow. He is looking forward to spending time with you and the people of Pembrooke."

Villard paused, as if debating with himself whether or not to believe Cadmus. "Of course," he finally said, "I am sure the travel has worn him out." Villard took a step in between Lorelei and Jeanette and then spun around, locking one of his arms with each of theirs. "Please come with me, my dears," he said, escorting them down the hall.

Villard led the group to the entrance of a large, lavishly decorated dining room. Two male servants stood at the entrance. Again, Jeanette stood in awe.

The table was long with chairs down the sides and one at each end. The wood on the furniture was dark and polished. A delicate, white cloth covered the length of the table. Brightly cleaned plates and gold utensils were intricately placed at each setting. A large, shiny chandelier hovered over the table with brand new candles twinkling.

Villard paused at the entrance, dropping Jeanette's grasp, and walked Lorelei over to one of the chairs nearest the head of the table. "If you would be so kind as to sit next to me?" he asked, pulling out the chair.

Lorelei gave a curtsy, "I would be honored, Mayor."

"Oh please," Jeanette mumbled, realizing that Villard was

on his way back to escort her to the chair directly across from Lorelei. She had never been escorted in her life, and the thought of sitting across from Lorelei for an entire dinner made her lose her appetite.

Instead of waiting for the frivolous display, Jeanette took the initiative and walked over to the chair, not waiting for Villard. Halfway around the table, Villard stopped and watched in horror as Jeanette started to pull out her own chair. One of the servants standing against the wall rushed over to assist. Emilia, still standing in the entrance, cleared her throat to get Jeanette's attention. Jeanette gave the servant a fierce look, but it did not move him away. She looked at Emilia.

Emilia, with a smile of embarrassment, looked at Villard, still frozen in place. "Jeanette, *after* your chair is pulled out you may be seated," she stated. "She is *so* excited and nervous to be here," Emilia said, speaking to Villard. "There is still much to learn. Aren't they wonderful?"

Villard slowly allowed a smile to come back. Jeanette rolled her eyes and let the servant pull her chair out for her. Villard's smile widened. Jeanette plopped down in the chair and caught a glimpse of Lorelei, grinning proudly.

*What am I doing here? I am not a Princess? All of it is a farce.*

After the initial party sat down, Brandy and Kellan were brought in and told to wait against the wall behind their respective ladies.

"So, tell me," Villard asked with a childlike grin on his face, "what do you think of our city thus far?"

A door opened and servers dressed in dark green uniforms, white stockings, and shiny shoes brought in dinner. Each tray was bright silver, steaming and full of food. For a moment, Jeanette's spirits lifted to think that she might get to see Addy, but she did not appear.

"It is marvelous!" Lorelei answered. "I have always loved Pembrooke for its culture and refinement. My father used to bring me here for...."

Jeanette tuned out as everyone chatted and began to eat. The soup was very good. Some kind of tomato base with chicken and spices she had never tasted. The bread was crispy on the outside and light on the inside. She took a bite and closed her eyes, a sweet, gooey substance hanging on her lips.

"And what about you Jeanette?" Villard asked, bringing her back to the conversation.

Jeanette slurped another sip of soup and cleared her throat. Villard wore an uneasy expression. Emilia looked on, nervously. "Well, we just got here, but so far everything has been fine," she answered simply.

Villard raised his eyebrows, as if waiting for more. Jeanette went back to eating. Cadmus spoke up, "Mayor, how was your first day at festival?"

"It was wonderful! We were already excited at the opportunity to have the royal caravan arrive, but then when we heard that these fine young ladies would be joining us...well...you are the talk of the city. Everyone is on pins and needles with the thought of meeting Jeanette and Lorelei."

Jeanette stopped eating. She had forgotten that Pembrooke was more than a stopover. She was going to have to put on a show.

"I would prefer to not have to be involved," Jeanette said, looking directly at Cadmus, trying to keep her true disdain at bay. Even though Villard was their host, she knew Cadmus was the one who held her reigns. Utensils stopped moving, sips came in awkward silence, and eyes darted back and forth. Cadmus wiped the sides of his mouth with his napkin. "Mayor, dinner has been delicious," Cadmus said calmly. "Thank you so much for your hospitality. It has been a long day and I think it is time for us to retire for the evening."

"Um...yes, well of course," Villard said, unsure. He stood, giving permission for the rest of the table to stand. Everyone did, including Jeanette, thankful it was over.

"I must be going anyway you know," the mayor added, as if the early release was his idea. "The city council is getting together again to make sure everything is on track for the big day tomorrow."

He reached over to Lorelei, took her hand, and kissed it. Lorelei gave another curtsy, and replied, "Dinner was delicious. I can't remember the last time I had better company." Villard brushed the compliment away with a wave of his hand.

He then turned to Jeanette. "It was also a pleasure to meet you," he said, no other courtesies extended. Jeanette rose, gave a semi-polite curtsy, and left the table before anybody else.

She walked past Brandy and whispered, "Let's go." Brandy gave a nervous chuckle and slid along the wall and out the opening behind Jeanette.

When they were down the hall, back in the foyer, Brandy grabbed Jeanette's arm, "Are you crazy? You could have cut that tension with a knife."

"I won't do it! Watching the way Lorelei seeks attention. I can't be like her!" Jeanette said, pacing.

"Nobody said you had to, but you don't have to make everybody hate you in the process of *not* trying to being like her," Brandy added.

After Villard and the guests exchanged pleasantries and said their goodbyes, Emilia and Cadmus made their way toward Jeanette, with Lorelei and Kellan following behind.

Emilia spoke up, "Well that was...interesting, wasn't it?" she asked, eying Cadmus.

"Yes, it was," he said, glaring at Jeanette. Jeanette crossed her arms and looked away. "But no matter; tonight, each of you will be special guests in the manor. I do not think Villard would have it any other way. Emilia will show you to your rooms. Brandy and Kellan, I do not believe that you have eaten yet, is that correct?"

Brandy and Kellan both shook their heads.

"If you wait here, I will go and see about getting some food for you in the kitchen. Then, after you are finished, you will head to your rooms and Emilia will go over the schedule for tomorrow."

Cadmus paused and looked at Jeanette. "I expect everyone to understand the importance of tomorrow and behave accordingly, not only for the festival, but for security as well." His words were calm, but stern, more so than Jeanette had seen from him.

"I'm glad you mentioned security," Lorelei piped in. "When we arrived today, I noticed that the guards on hand were, how can I put this..." she asked, tapping her chin with her finger, "unevenly distributed."

Cadmus looked perplexed. Jeanette rolled her eyes, amazed that Lorelei could be so petty as to bicker over which of them had more guards.

"We got out of the carriage and walked thirty yards into the house...what difference does it make?" Brandy asked.

"Ladies, please be assured that the kingdom has taken every precaution to make sure each of you is safe," Cadmus said. "I imagine Emilia has a few things to go over with you and I need to get these girls some food." He gave a small bow and walked back toward the kitchen.

"If you will follow me ladies," Emilia said, heading up the flight of steps.

Lorelei lingered behind and stopped in front of Jeanette and Brandy. As soon as Emilia was out of earshot, Lorelei swung around, her yellow braid flying over her shoulder like a whip. She was staring at Brandy. "How dare you rebuke me?" Lorelei hissed, her bright, green eyes wide with fury.

Brandy flinched, but stood her ground. "What are you talking about?"

Lorelei took another step closer. "In case you have already

forgotten, you are in the presence of a lady and you," she said, looking down her nose, "are just a servant. Don't you ever address me again without first being spoken to."

Emilia was halfway up the steps and had turned around, looking for the girls. Jeanette stepped in between Brandy and Lorelei and said, "Lorelei, you need to calm down before..."

"Is everything okay ladies?" Emilia asked, starting to come back down the steps.

"Oh yes, everything is fine," Lorelei said in a somber tone. "We're on our way."

Emilia turned and started back up.

Lorelei swung back to Jeanette. "Calm down!?" she said through clenched teeth. "You may not care about anything that is happening, but I do. And if you don't want to be here, trust me, you can go." Lorelei was very close to Jeanette now as Brandy and Kellan watched.

Jaw tightened, Jeanette took a step closer. "Even if I wanted to, I wouldn't give you the pleasure."

Lorelei's face turned blood red.

"You think the prince is all yours," Jeanette continued, "because of who you are, and who your daddy is, and how you dress. Well, in case you haven't noticed, you aren't the only one getting all the attention anymore!" Jeanette said, pointing to her eyes.

"Ladies, if you please," Emilia encouraged again, this time with more eagerness in her voice. "We have a long day tomorrow and there is much to discuss."

Jeanette continued to glare at Lorelei, until over Lorelei's shoulder, down the hall next to the dining room, the kitchen door opened and Addy walked out. It was the first time seeing her since they left Emerleigh.

Forgetting everything around her, Jeanette called out, "Addy!" Not hearing, Addy had already walked into the dining room followed by a slew of other servants. Jeanette's face fell.

Instantly, Lorelei's demeanor changed. "Jeanette, let's just be honest, you are out of your element and misinformed as to what is expected of us. You can treat your servant girl however you like, that's your business. You can even treat the other servants as peers. But I assure you, I am looking forward to having people cater to me. Some of them in particular," she said, looking back to where Addy had just been.

Jeanette wanted to slap her, hard. But before she could react, Lorelei was already walking up the steps. "Sleep well," Lorelei smiled.

Jeanette turned to Brandy and said, "I don't know how long I'm going to last. I'm going to hit her hard enough it will knock the green out of her eyes!"

Brandy took Jeanette by the arm and led her to the second floor. "Just make sure I'm around when you do."

# CHAPTER 14

The light danced off the ceiling in one of the many guest rooms in the mayor's house. Jeanette and Brandy were already down for the night. Brandy tossed a little in her bed, but had been sound asleep for hours.

Even though the bed provided a comfort unlike any she had ever known, Jeanette could not sleep. She sat looking out of the window, down on the street. For such a large city, it was too quiet. She wiped the sweat from her brow and tried to relax. Lying back down on her pillow, she closed her eyes.

*Addy.*

Where was she staying? It had to be close enough to help with the meals. Is this what it would be like at the castle, random sightings in the hall every couple of days?

*Lorelei.*

If today was only a taste of what the future had in store, she did not want to have anything to do with Lorelei. The prince could have her all to himself.

*Braxton.*

Would he really choose her just to spite the queen? He

didn't even know her.

*The visions.*

She had been fighting them, resisting them, but alone in the still of night they felt stronger. The events of the festival replayed in her mind. Watching the other girls drink the liquid. The crowd's faces, hope, then nothing, hope again, then nothing still. The small vile. Green liquid. Nothing. There was no relief, no excitement...no anything.

Lorelei's change. Jeanette never wanted to make it personal, but with Lorelei, it just was and always had been. Just as she knew her eyes were not going to change, it's as if she also knew that Lorelei's would, and when it happened, she hated her even more.

On the stage, that's the last thought that she had before *it* happened. She had never in her life felt anything like it. The piercing pain in her head and the images that came into her mind. She didn't want to forget. Something inside wouldn't let her forget.

*A castle in flames, a lone figure hanging out of a window.*

*An old sign hanging over a merchant shop.*

*A soldier standing across a body of water.*

They were floating, distant, but with each remembrance getting clearer, closer. She knew they were connected; they had to be, but how?

Alone and unsure, Jeanette started to cry. Slow and steady. She looked over at Brandy to see if she was awake. She wasn't.

"You cannot go to the castle. Someone you love will get hurt."

She opened her eyes wide. The voice was as clear and audible as any she had ever heard, yet she was certain that the words were not spoken. The same feeling she had heard a few times already.

Was it really a voice?

She got up and stepped quietly over to Brandy's bed.

Maybe Brandy had whispered it, or vocalized a dream. Jeanette gently nudged her shoulder. "Brandy, are you asleep? Brandy?"

No response.

Jeanette nudged again, but noticed an uncommon warmth radiating from Brandy. She felt Brandy's night gown and it was drenched in sweat. More concerned, Jeanette tapped Brandy's shoulders with more force, trying to get her to wake up.

"Brandy!" Jeanette yelled. Frantic, she shook her furiously. "Brandy!" She patted her on the face a few times to try and revive her. Brandy suddenly let out a cough and moan. Brief relief came with the movement, until Brandy leaned over and vomited violently on the side of the bed and onto the floor.

Loud steps approached the door. "Is everything okay in there?" one of the guards asked.

"Brandy is sick. Go and get help!" Jeanette yelled. The footsteps hurried off.

Brandy vomited again. Jeanette lit a candle and grabbed a cloth off of the night stand, got it wet, and washed Brandy's mouth. Brandy's pulse was racing.

"What's wrong, Brandy?"

There was another knock at the door. "May I come in?" asked Emilia.

Jeanette replied and Emilia entered. "The guard said there was screaming and...oh my goodness!" Emilia exclaimed. Jeanette explained what happened.

"Maybe she just ate something. She probably feels better now," Emilia said. "I'll fetch somebody to clean up."

She started backing up when Brandy leaned forward again and heaved. Emilia covered her mouth in disgust. Jeanette looked at Emilia and said, "How about you get a doctor?"

***

An hour later, Jeanette paced in the hallway outside the bedroom. She watched the sun come up through the window across from her. The people of Pembrooke were starting their day, their special day. Smiles. Laughter. Cheer. It was the same uncertain excitement Addy and Brandy had during the festival in Emerleigh.

She turned from the window and caught the stare of the guards standing nearby, both of who quickly turned away. She was used to it now - the gawking.

Walking closer to the door, she listened but heard nothing. Cadmus had been in there the whole time with Emilia. The door finally opened.

"Come in, Jeanette," Emilia said softly, visibly shaken. Jeanette hurried in. Cadmus, packing a few things in his medical bag, rose to his feet. Maids had helped to clean and sanitize the room, but the stench of vomit still lingered.

Brandy lay on the bed, hair tied back and cheeks flush as she slept.

"Is she going to be okay?" There was a pause. Cadmus held Jeanette's glance. There was something different in the way he looked at her. Empathy? Concern?

"Cadmus?" she asked again.

"Brandy is seriously sick," he started. "There was blood in her vomit, which points to an infection in the throat or stomach." Cadmus reached down and placed the back of his hand on Brandy's forehead. "The infection is also causing the fever to get worse. I have given her some black walnut oil mixed with silphium juice to fight the infection and a sedative so she can rest."

"But she'll be okay, right?"

"With rest and medicine she should be okay, as long as the infection does not continue to spread. Have you noticed anything different about her lately? Any complaints about stomach issues or other ailments?"

"No. It just seemed to come out of nowhere."

He nodded. "I would imagine you two have had a lot going on these last few days."

"We need to let her sister know. She needs to be here," Jeanette said.

"I know the child is ill, but I don't think we need to interrupt the whole caravan, do you?" Emilia asked Cadmus.

"You are worried about interr..." Jeanette started.

"Guard!" Cadmus called. One of the guards in the hall stepped in. "Brandy's sister is somewhere nearby. Her name is Addy; she is one of the girls chosen as a cook from Emerleigh. Do you know the girl and where she is?"

"Yes, my lord. They are most likely in the middle of preparing breakfast for the caravan."

"Please find her at once and bring her here." The guard confirmed and left. "You can wait outside, please," he said to Emilia. She tightened her lips, crossed her arms, and walked out the room.

Jeanette sat down next to Brandy.

"Have you felt sick at all?" Cadmus asked.

"No. I think I am okay."

"Good. There is a lot at stake and I can't afford..."

"I don't mean to be rude, but I don't want to be here," she said still looking at Brandy. "I don't think I'm supposed to be here."

"I can only imagine how hard it is. I could try to tell you why I think you are truly special, but I have the sense that you won't believe me."

Jeanette looked at him. He seemed sincere. "It's nothing personal, but no, I wouldn't."

Addy suddenly appeared in the doorway. "What's wrong? Is she okay?"

"I am truly sorry for your sister's condition," Cadmus said. He explained his diagnosis to Addy. "We are doing everything we can. Right now, she is very weak and dehydrated."

Addy walked over and knelt beside her sister. "But, we're supposed to leave tomorrow. Will she be able to go to the castle?"

A sting of guilt coupled with a harsh realization ran through Jeanette. The first image of her visions. A lone figure...the castle on fire.

*If I go to the castle, someone I love will be in danger.*

*I can't go to the castle.*

"Do not think twice about it," Cadmus said calmly. "Assuming she is better in the morning, even if only a little, she should be okay to travel."

Relief fell over Addy. She looked at Jeanette as if searching for an answer.

*Addy, it's my fault Brandy is sick. I'm not supposed to go to the castle and she is suffering because I don't know what to do.*

How could Jeanette tell Addy or Cadmus? They would never believe her story about the visions. How could she leave Addy? Even if she felt she needed to, she was a Jewel of Amarin now, property of the kingdom.

Cadmus continued. "I hate to do this Jeanette, but I feel it necessary to supply you a new handmaiden, at least until Brandy gets on her feet again."

"But when she gets better, she'll be able to come back and serve with me, right?"

"Of course. But we need to make sure she is at full health. The requirements you will have, especially over the next few days, will be strenuous. You will need somebody with you."

Unable to think of one, Jeanette did not put up an argument. Cadmus called to Emilia and whispered something in her ear. She nodded and walked away. "I want you to know how sorry I am," Cadmus said. "I know it has not been easy, but we only have one hour before the festival. Please be ready."

As he turned to leave the room, Addy spoke up. "Master Cadmus, thank you for taking care of my sister."

"I'm just doing what needs to be done," he said, and left the room.

There was an awkward silence. Brandy lay silent while Addy stroked her hair. Jeanette sat down next to her. When she did, the fatigue set in.

"How could she get sick?" Addy asked. "She was so excited about coming to Pembrooke and seeing their festival."

Addy started to cry. Jeanette put her arm around her, but felt empty and powerless. Eventually, Addy wiped her eyes. "She never should have come." Jeanette knew it too, but it stung to hear Addy say it.

The door opened again and Emilia came in, escorting a young girl, average height, trim, with shoulder length brown hair hanging around her delicate face. Freckles dotted her cheeks and nose. "Jeanette, I would like you to meet your new hand maid, Auryn."

Auryn stepped forward and curtsied. "It is an honor to serve you, my lady."

Jeanette shook her head, "Please do not call me 'my lady'. My name is Jeanette." Auryn nodded.

"Auryn can help with whatever..." Emilia started.

"Right now she can wait outside," Jeanette said. "I will be out in a minute."

Auryn curtsied again and walked out of the room with Emilia.

"I'm sorry about that," Jeanette said. "None of this makes any sense."

"You need to start getting ready for the festival," Addy encouraged. "We can talk when you get back."

She had so much to say. The desire to reach out and give Addy a hug came, but she held it back. There was a distance building and it scared Jeanette, almost as much as going to the castle.

# CHAPTER 15

Jeanette walked past the guards to the end of the hall and opened the door to her room. She had spent the better part of the day being introduced to the people of Pembrooke. The final ceremony in the afternoon left Jeanette and Lorelei as the only two Jewels of Amarin.

*Is this what my life will be now; traipsing around with the prince, showing off my eyes? Do they really make that much difference?*

Auryn had stayed downstairs to talk to Cadmus. All Jeanette cared about was finally clearing the air with Addy. "We need to talk..." she started walking into her room. Silence surrounded her. Brandy's bed was empty and the linens changed. At the foot of the bed was a chest that Jeanette did not recognize. She looked over to her side of the room; all of her items were still in place.

Unease set in. She hurried out of the room and asked the guard, "What happened to Brandy?"

He quickly stood at attention. "Miss Brandy was moved, my lady."

"Is everything okay?"

"As far as I know. She was in the same state of health as

111

she was earlier."

"Why was she moved?"

"I do not know. I just came on a little while ago."

Jeanette left him standing and went down the hall, looking in and out of rooms. *What if she has been sent away? What if Addy went with her?*

At the end of the hall was a room with the door closed, but light flickered through the bottom slat. Jeanette inhaled and knocked.

"Come in," Addy said gently. Jeanette let out a sigh of relief and slowly opened the door. Addy was next to Brandy on the bed. Jeanette closed the door behind her.

"How is she doing?"

"The same," Addy said and then started across the room to dampen the washcloth. Brandy's breathing seemed calmer, but was still heavy. "Where's the new girl?" Addy asked.

"Auryn? She is downstairs."

"What's she like?"

"She seems nice enough. Kind of quiet. I'm sure she's surprised at how all of this has happened."

"Did the prince talk to you today at all?"

"No...not really. He was too busy being the prince. Why do you ask?"

"Don't take this the wrong way, but he seems to have more interest in you than he does in Lorelei."

Jeanette sighed. "I can't honestly believe that the Prince of Amarin likes me."

Addy smiled, "Why not? Can you imagine if you were the Princess of Amarin?" She laughed to herself.

*There is no way I will ever be a princess.*

"No, I can't imagine," Jeanette answered. "That's your dream, not mine."

"Eh, Braxton is not my type."

"And something tells me Rendall will never be a prince."

Laughter filled the space between them. It felt good, cleansing. The timing felt right. "Addy, we need to talk. There are so many things going on right now, so many things we need to talk about. Something has happened..."

"Of course somethings happened!" Addy responded, almost laughing to herself. "You have green eyes and my sister is on her death bed."

Jeanette stood in the silence. Addy sat back down and put the cloth on Brandy's forehead. A rush of guilt built in Jeanette. How could she tell Addy that she was responsible for Brandy getting sick?

"Addy, I need to apologize."

Addy stopped and eyed Jeanette. Jeanette worried whether her apology would be received. She was not good at apologies.

"For what?"

She moved a little closer, more guarded. "When my eyes changed I think there was something else that changed too. I think I am the reason Brandy is sick."

"Of course you're the reason she is sick!" Addy shot back, startling Jeanette. "If you hadn't picked her then she wouldn't be here in the first place."

Jeanette took a step back. A moment of silence passed and Addy started to cry. "Oh Jeanette, I'm so sorry. I don't mean to take it out on you," she said, wiping her eyes. Jeanette sat down next to Addy on the bed. Addy continued, "I'm just tired and hungry and worried."

"I know you are, and I'm so sorry that I picked Brandy. I didn't know any of this would happen."

"I know you didn't. I just...I was so excited when your eyes changed. Maybe I'm selfish, but it felt right that we would be at the castle together. Just us. I couldn't stand being there without you."

Jeanette reached out and gently touched Addy's hand, trying to reassure her before words were even spoken. "Addy, I can't go to the castle."

"What do you mean?"

"I mean, when my eye color changed I saw something, I felt something." Jeanette struggled for the words to have it make sense. "I feel if I go to the castle somebody I know and love will get hurt. I think that's why Brandy is sick."

"Jeanette, that doesn't make any sense," Addy said, moving the hair out of her face. She did look tired. The whites of her eyes were red, with dark circles lining the outer socket. Addy turned to go back to tending Brandy, but stopped and said reflectively, "We both just need some sleep. Some time to rest and think things through."

Jeanette agreed, feeling better that she had tried to share with Addy what she was feeling, even if Addy didn't understand. Jeanette touched her hand gently, "Get some sleep. Brandy is tough; she'll be fine."

"I hope so."

Jeanette left the room, closing the door behind her. She needed to move, to go and hide in her room, but her feet would not let her. The carriage rides, the guards, the people staring, the servants - everything had changed. Jeanette on one end and Addy on the other. Maybe it was a blessing that Brandy got sick to help bring it all to light.

Jeanette lowered her head, guilt stinging her for such a thought. That's when all the feelings started to flow. Running as quick as she could, she made it to her room. Auryn was still not back from talking to Cadmus, giving her the solitude she wanted.

Lying on her bed, it all came out - the hurt, the anger, the frustration, the uncertainty. Big sobbing tears and gasps. She had always been strong and willful, wanting to hide it all in, but this was beyond her. Her mind raced. She wanted someone to talk to. Not Addy. Not Auryn. Her dad came to mind, but her pride would not allow her to dwell on him.

Then she thought of Jaren. When he died, that is when everything changed. She started to cry again, but it wasn't uncontrollable. It was long, hard, and cleansing.

A knock at the door startled her. She quickly wiped her face and got herself together. "Who is it?"

"It's Cadmus," he said, opening the door. "Jeanette, is everything okay?"

"I'm fine."

"I was coming up the steps and saw you run past. It doesn't look like everything is fine," he said, opening the door. "Is there anything I need to know about, Jeanette? Is there something wrong that you have not told me of?"

"No."

"In light of your recent behavior, I am concerned."

Jeanette sighed.

"If you are nervous or unsure," Cadmus continued, "or having a hard time, we can talk about it. But one thing you cannot do is disrespect those who find hope and encouragement in the blessing that has been bestowed upon you."

*Blessing?*

"I didn't ask for any of this," she responded.

"We may not understand it all Jeanette, but you are special. It is simply a fact. Just a little patience...that is what I'm asking. Be patient with the people, and with Emilia, and me," he said. "And I know it's not easy, but even a little more patience with Lorelei," he said, with a slight grin.

Jeanette cocked her head to the side a little. She would not have expected him to be negative about Lorelei, in any way, but she respected him more for it.

"Everything has its purpose...you have a purpose. We just don't know what it is yet, but we'll figure it out." Cadmus waited for her to respond.

"I'm not supposed to be here," she finally said. She took

another deep breath and wiped her hands across her cheeks.

"Do you have a dream?" he asked.

The question took her by surprise. "I don't know. I thought I did, but this definitely isn't it."

"Life. It happens to all of us. Take Queen Devony. I assume you have heard about King Phillip and his...situation."

She nodded, remembering her dance with Prince Braxton. The dance that changed everything.

"You'll see that the king is good spirited, but definitely a handful. Yet I watch the queen care for him and the kingdom with grace and patience." Jeanette didn't understand, and the look on her face must have conveyed as much to Cadmus.

"All I'm saying is don't be surprised if your dream is still coming true, maybe just not in the way you had hoped. There is a purpose behind your eye color change, you will see."

Maybe she could tell Cadmus? Maybe more details about the visions might help bring understanding? Perhaps then she wouldn't be forced go to the castle against her will.

"I can only imagine how tired you must be. You just need some rest. Your nerves have been through the wringer. When is the last time you actually got some sleep?" He did not wait for an answer. "It's amazing what a good night's sleep will do."

Jeanette hadn't truly slept in days. Cadmus opened up his bag and started to rummage. He pulled out a small bottle. Jeanette went cold. She had seen the doctor in Emerleigh at her house far too often doing the same thing with her mother.

*I will not end up like my mother.*

She moved over on the bed and said, "I don't need whatever that is."

"Jeanette, look at me," Cadmus said, "this is nothing more than a light sedative. Its sole purpose is to tell your body that it is time to sleep. That's all."

She looked at the bottle again. A good night's rest sounded appealing.

"It will help you sleep, but if you do not wish to take it, I cannot force you. In my professional opinion though, just about everybody in the caravan could use some sleep."

"Okay," she conceded. She did not want to think about her eyes, the visions, Braxton...anything.

"Very good," he said, uncorking the bottle and pouring a small amount into a cup. She drank it quickly. It was bitter, familiar.

"I'll leave you now. I need go and see how Brandy is doing."

The door slowly opened. Auryn peeked her head in. "Is it okay to come in?"

"Please do," Cadmus said, grabbing his bag and standing. "Did you and Kellan talk to Emilia about the schedule tomorrow?"

"Yes, sir."

"Good. Jeanette needs a full night's rest. Please make sure she gets it."

"I will," Auryn said with a small curtsy.

He then turned to Jeanette. "I'll leave you be. You know where I am if you need anything." Jeanette nodded and Cadmus walked out of the room.

Auryn closed the door. "Are you all right, my lady?"

Jeanette's body tensed. All day long she had tried to get Auryn to stop calling her lady.

"I swear..." Jeanette pleaded, "if you call me 'my lady' one more time, the first thing I will do to you we get to the castle is have you tortured."

"I'm sorry, Jeanette," Auryn replied, hinting a smile. "I'm sorry you are feeling ill. Did you not enjoy the ceremony tonight?"

Out of all the festivities during the day, the one part Jeanette enjoyed - or at least was interested in - was the ceremony. Sitting away from the crowd with Emilia, Lorelei and the guards, she had watched Cadmus walk onstage with anticipation.

*What if another girl's eye's change? If the prince has more options, will it take the interest off of me? Please let another set of eye's change.*

"No change," Cadmus bellowed into the night. Over and over and over again.

"Not really," Jeanette finally answered.

"There were many more girls on stage tonight than there were in Emerleigh," Auryn noted.

"You were in Emerleigh?" Jeanette had not taken the time to find out anything about Auryn. If she had been with the caravan, then she would have been at the ceremony in Emerleigh.

"Yes."

"What was your assignment with the caravan before me?"

No response.

"What did they have you doing at..." Jeanette turned to see Auryn gazing at her.

Auryn turned away quickly. "I'm so sorry. I should not stare," she said quietly.

"It's okay," Jeanette reassured. Everyone since the ceremony had gazed at her eyes, trying to look through her. Looking for something. "What was it like when you saw our eyes change?"

Auryn's face lit up with excitement. "It was the most amazing thing I have ever seen! I was one of the assistants to Emilia and they let everyone come and watch. I was standing in the back. The whole crowd was silent. It was as if time stood still. And then you...," Auryn laughed a little, "you looked like you couldn't have cared less about being up there. I did not understand it, at least not then.

"As Cadmus went down the line, from girl to girl, the crowd...it was so tense. And then, when Lorelei changed and Cadmus raised her hand! I've never felt anything like that in my whole life." Auryn paused.

Jeanette didn't know how to feel. Hearing the events from Auryn's perspective gave her a different appreciation.

"Lorelei...I wanted to be her," Auryn said sincerely. Before Auryn could continue, Jeanette rolled her eyes. "But," she continued, "then your eyes turned and everyone was stunned. There was no way there could be two girls. And then I didn't care about being like Lorelei anymore...I wanted to be like you. You seemed...stronger. Real."

Jeanette felt sincerity in Auryn's words. "I'm sorry to have gotten you into this," Jeanette said. "I'm sure you were perfectly happy doing whatever you were doing before with the castle."

"You don't need to apologize. Being here with you, all of this...I would have never imagined it. Growing up I..."Auryn started, but stopped, as if restraining herself. "I'm sorry about Brandy." This time Jeanette knew she was being sincere. "I hope she gets better, I really do. But I'm happy to be here with you, for now."

Jeanette's attention was fading, the sedative setting in.

"Jeanette," Auryn whispered, lying on her bed, "the last few days have been the best of my life." She turned on her side to look at Jeanette. "Thank you."

Jeanette did not respond. The part of her that was still awake didn't know what to say. Her head became heavy. Closing her eyes, she waited for night.

Her body relaxed and her breathing slowed. And then she dreamed. She was aware, but still asleep. Vividly, the visions came again, but they were stronger, clearer. She could see the detail around them, as if she were there.

*A castle in flames. A lone figure hanging out of a window calling to Jeanette to stay away.*

*An old sign with a picture of an owl with green eyes hanging over a merchant shop.*

*A soldier with chains around his ankles standing across a large body of water.*

The feeling that surrounded her was strong and deep. It was more than anxiety; more than frustration or unsurety.

*I cannot go to the castle.*

She looked over to Auryn, who was fast asleep. Whatever or whoever it was, it finally sank in her heart and mind.

She repeated it softly herself. "I cannot go to the castle."

If she went, something would happen to someone. Something more detrimental than what Brandy was going through. There was something waiting for her at the shop with the old sign. Across a body of water, a soldier stood that she had to meet. She wanted to help, wanted to bring hope. But it wouldn't happen at the castle.

Her heart pounded and her chest swelled. She repeated it to herself again, a little louder, "I cannot go to the castle."

A sense of freedom swelled inside her. She quietly got out of bed and found a sack in her supply chest and started packing whatever she could find. Her mind filled with reality; she had no plan, no direction, no transportation. Only some images in her head and a feeling to follow.

"Jeanette? Is everything okay?" Auryn asked, sitting up in bed. Jeanette had not wanted to wake her.

"I'm leaving."

"What do you mean you're leaving?"

"I can't stay here. I can't go to the castle. I am not supposed to be here." Auryn watched Jeanette for a few seconds and then got out of bed. "What are you doing?" Jeanette asked.

"Well, if you're leaving, I'm coming with you."

"No, you're not."

"It is my job to stay by your side. And how are you going to get out of the house and where are you going to go?"

Jeanette thought for a second. "How *am* I supposed to get

out of the house?"

"You mean how are *we* supposed to get out of the house?"

"Auryn, I don't even know where I'm going. I just know that I can't stay here, or go to the castle."

"We'll figure it out, but you can't go alone," Auryn said, walking over to the window. It didn't feel right. She was supposed to go, but not with Auryn. But the fear of the unknown and the uncertainty of her quest begged her to take somebody with her.

"Thank you," Jeanette replied.

Auryn turned the lock on the window. "How good are you at climbing?"

Jeanette smiled, "Better than I should be."

# CHAPTER 16

The next morning, Addy sat next to Brandy, trying to keep her eyes open. The hum of night had caused her to drift.

"Addy," a soft, pained voice asked.

Addy woke suddenly. "Brandy! Don't move, just lay still," she pleaded as Brandy tried to sit up.

"Where are we?"

"We're in Pembrooke still, at the Mayor's house. You got sick...really sick."

Brandy closed her eyes and tried to swallow. Addy saw the hurt in her face. "I don't remember," Brandy said, her voice a little clearer.

"It's probably better you don't," Addy answered, swabbing Brandy's head with a damp towel. She felt her forehead. The fever had broke.

Brandy opened her eyes. "Where's Jeanette? I'm supposed to be..." she said, trying to rise out of bed.

"You are supposed to be resting, lay back down," Addy said, gently pushing Brandy back into bed. "Jeanette is just fine."

*Is Jeanette just fine?*

During the night, in and out of consciousness, Addy thought about going to Jeanette's room. Playing the conversation from earlier that evening over and over again, one thing stood out: Jeanette saying emphatically that she could not go to the castle. Why would going to the castle hurt somebody or cause pain? It didn't make sense.

Then again, a lot of things had happened that didn't make sense.

She wanted to apologize to Jeanette for not listening and placing blame, but she knew it best to wait. She would have a chance to talk to her today after some rest.

Addy wanted to serve the kingdom; it's what she always dreamed of. Go to the castle, improve her skills, come home, find a husband, and live a wonderful life with her beautiful family.

Simple and straightforward.

Yet Jeanette kept her life anything but simple or straightforward. Always a new adventure. Always a new drama. Never willing to settle and let well enough alone. Addy loved Jeanette like a sister, but she shook her head at the thought of how different they were.

Thoughts of their trip to training camp came to her memory and she smiled. They were good memories and she wanted to keep making those memories, even at the castle. But the reality of the last few days was setting in. Fear was growing inside and Addy did not know what to do.

*I need to stop worrying. Everything will be okay at the castle.*

Brandy motioned for a drink of water. She swallowed, and cleared her throat. "When are we leaving for the castle?"

"We're supposed to leave today, but I don't know if you are ready to go."

"I promise, I'm fine. I'm not missing going to the castle." Brandy coughed and grabbed the cloth from Addy to hold up to her mouth.

Shouting and commotion in the hallway rang in Addy's ears. "What is that?" Brandy asked.

Addy stood to investigate when Cadmus appeared at the door, startling her. "Do you know where she is?" he asked.

As she processed the question, Prince Braxton appeared behind Cadmus, out of breath.

"Do you know where she is?" the prince repeated.

"Where who is?"

"Jeanette. She is gone."

*I cannot go to the castle.*

The words echoed through Addy's ears. "What do you mean 'gone'. Gone where?"

"Emilia went to check on her this morning," Cadmus answered. Until now, Addy had not seen Cadmus absent his composure. "Their belongings were gone and they left the window wide open."

"What if they were...taken?" Addy asked, searching for any other explanation.

"That's a possibility," Cadmus admitted. "When was the last time you saw her?"

*Maybe I should have told someone she was talking of leaving? Did I ever really think she would want to come to the castle?*

"Last night, after she got home. She came straight up here and then...well," The debate in her mind ended quickly. "We were both tired and our emotions were high. We both probably said some things we didn't mean, but she...she said nothing about leaving." Addy was not used to lying, it was easier than she thought.

"Addy is telling the truth, my prince," Cadmus said. "I was coming upstairs to check on Jeanette when I saw her running to her room, emotional. We sat and talked for a while until she was calm. When I left, Auryn was in the room and promised to take care of her."

"So they both are gone?" Addy asked.

Emilia appeared. "The guards have searched the whole house and neither Jeanette nor Auryn are here."

"Find her, Cadmus!" Braxton demanded. His eyes had a look of power, like a man with something to lose. "Do whatever you have to do, but you find her," he said and left the room.

Cadmus turned to one of the guards in the hallway. "Assemble all the soldiers in the rear of the house in five minutes. We will send a search party after them, a messenger to the castle ahead of our arrival, and some men back to Emerleigh in case she went home." The guard nodded and left.

"If you hear anything from her – anything - let me know at once."

"Yes, sir."

"We will be leaving in one hour. However unfortunate the circumstances are, we still have a schedule to keep. Are you well enough to travel?" Cadmus asked Brandy.

Brandy tried to sit up and look healthy. She nodded.

Cadmus started out of the room when Addy spoke up. "Master Cadmus?" He stopped and turned. "Whatever is happening...whatever reason Jeanette has left, I can assure it is not with ill intent. I think she is just scared."

"I understand and I agree with you," he said, taking a deep breath. "But I am concerned for her safety. Word is just starting to spread. If she is noticed by others or caught by the armies of Tamir, it could be disastrous."

Addy had not thought about the situation in that light, and she didn't know what to believe. All she knew is if Jeanette had made her mind she was not supposed to go to the castle, she felt sorry for Cadmus and whatever army he was going to use to try and make her.

# CHAPTER 17

Later that afternoon, John's men relished in a rare victory.

"Did you see 'em turn tail and run?"

"They didn't stand a chance coming through us?"

"Little tree climbers...what did they expect...we would just let them walk right through?"

John walked through the camp as the men were enjoying dinner. Rations had been ignored and there was a feeling in the air that had been missing for some time.

Victory.

He could hear it. He could feel it.

John had reluctantly followed the orders to sit and defend the outskirts of Samdon. There was to be no scouting missions or offensive attacks. They were to wait for the Brown Eyes to come on their own. And they had.

John's men held them off with a decisive battle. But listening to his men celebrate, he did not share their joy. It did not feel like a true victory.

"Hey, Eugene..." one of the soldiers called out. "Play something upbeat. Play it loud!" All the men nearby laughed and shouted their approval.

"I got just the one," Eugene replied and started in on a tune. John cracked a grin as a few of the men stood and started dancing. He shook his head at their sorry attempt. Regardless of his own reservations, he enjoyed seeing his men happy for a change.

Another soldier came up beside him, "It's good to see them with such high spirits, eh?"

"No question, Wesley."

Wesley was one of three lieutenants who served under John. They made their way to the command tent and found Zachary and Gabriel, the other two lieutenants, waiting. As always, Burleigh was close by.

"Everyone report. We'll start with you, Wesley."

"My crew is doing okay. Morale is high after the victory..."

"I would hardly call it a victory," Zachary interrupted, in his usual serious tone. "If anything it was more of a hold than an outright victory."

"But compared to the other options of a slaughter or retreat," Wesley continued, "I believe the men have reason to celebrate."

There was a short pause. John looked to Gabriel for his input. "I agree. It's been too long without a fight. The men need to remember our purpose. To defend Amarin and fight to protect her."

John focused on the men's eyes, trying to read their true feelings. The only soldier he had ever opened up to about his personal misgivings was Burleigh. Though he trusted his lieutenants, weighing them down with his own concerns was not the way he wanted to lead. But if they had reservations, he needed to know.

"Yes, we did win and I think it's okay for the men to let off some steam, as long as the celebration does not go on too long," Zachary added.

All eyes were on John.

"I think what happened over the last few days is a good thing," John said. "We were called not only defend, but to also protect the freedoms of the people of Amarin. When we have the opportunity to fight for those freedoms, we do. As you said, Wesley, that's what the men signed up for. But, as was also said, this was not a victory. The men cannot get complacent. We temporarily drove the Brown Eyes back, nothing more. Today, we can celebrate the opportunity to protect our kingdom, and that's what we must help our men to remember," he said with conviction, ensuring each lieutenant understood.

"And the celebration?" Wesley asked.

"The men are allowed this time to celebrate, but it will end tonight. I will speak to them before the next watch begins," John said flatly. "Is there anything else?"

All three shook their heads.

"Thank you for your efforts. Dismissed."

They all saluted and left the tent, leaving John and Burleigh alone. John was leaning over the table staring at the map, troubled.

Burleigh came closer. "What's eating at you? I thought the conversation went pretty good."

"What's eating at me? In no time, the kingdom will return with our next orders and it will be the same as it has always been. Sit and wait."

"Come on, John," Burleigh said, aggravated, "The men fought! You led! We won! Seriously, for the love of pud, can't you just enjoy yourself for one day?"

John focused on the map, trying to decide where the Brown Eyes were. Pointing, he said, "We should have followed them back into the tree line and advanced to finish the job. It just makes more sense. Instead, we are sitting here, waiting for the same enemies to strike again. We have to take the fight to them if we want to win."

"Well, why didn't you then?" Burleigh said gruffly. "I'm sick of listening to you prance around it like a sick gelding. Your horse, Cheswin, is more of a man than you sometimes!"

"What can I do?" John said, voice raised.

There was a glint of hope in Burleigh's eyes as he kept prodding. "Do you want to fight?"

John walked closer, right up to Burleigh. Next to each other, Burleigh was a good four inches taller than John and forty pounds heavier. Burleigh raised his voice and asked, "Do you want to fight the Brown Eyes?"

"Of course I do."

"Well, I'll ask you again...why don't you?"

"Because...because I can't," John stammered.

Burleigh grabbed John by the collar and maneuvered him over to the tent door. He opened it and turned John around, saying, "Look. There is a whole camp of men that *you* command. Why can't you go fight?"

John pulled the flap closed. Burleigh got toe to toe with John and stuck his finger in his chest. "Answer me!" Burleigh insisted. "Why won't you just take your men and go fight?"

John backed away, avoiding the taunt. Burleigh was his closest friend, but John's anger built. His face turning red, he warned, "Burleigh, stop it! I'm warning you."

"No," Burleigh said, taking another step, pushing his finger into John's chest again. Burleigh looked John straight in the eye. "Why won't you just take the men..."

Poke.

"...into the forest..."

Push.

"...and fight them like a real soldier?"

Shove.

John yelled, grabbed Burleigh's wrist with his left hand and swung his right fist directly into Burleigh's jaw. Burleigh didn't back away in time and found himself on the floor with a bloody grin.

He wiped the side of his lip with his hand and winced, "I didn't think you'd get me."

John's blood was pumping. He stood stunned. He finally let out a small laugh of disbelief.

"Hardy har," Burleigh said, pulling himself to a sitting position.

"Was all that really necessary?" John asked.

"Well, the way I see it, you needed an attitude adjustment, and I figure that's why you keep me around."

John turned around and walked back over to the table and leaned over it again, sweaty and tired. Burleigh stood, wiping his mouth with his sleeve.

"It's in our nature as soldiers to follow orders. It's what we do. But what do you do when you disagree with an order?" John asked.

"That's the problem," Burleigh continued. "You keep fighting with yourself. Unless you are going to stand up to the kingdom and disobey orders, then lead the troops, celebrate the victories, and quit complaining."

"But what if this grand scheme of the kingdom doesn't work? All of this," he said, waving out over the maps, "all the running, all the waiting, all festivals...all of it will have been in vain. I owe more than that to..."

"Stop, stop, stop!" Burleigh was shaking his head. "Listen. When was the last time you asked yourself, honestly, if maybe the war council know what they are doing after all? Maybe, just maybe, you're not right?"

"Are you saying you would rather not fight and just run around the country haphazardly waiting for..."

"No, I'm not!" Burleigh said flatly, desperation for understanding in his eyes. "What I am saying is that our one little unit by itself is responsible for certain things and we are not going to change this war by ourselves. The council has a better vantage point to make broad strategic decisions. If they say we fight, we fight. If they say we defend, we defend. You don't have to create strategy, that's not your job. Your job is to lead these men and when you are frustrated, despairing, and unfocused, that is hard to do. We will follow you, as long as you *lead*!"

Like a punch in the gut, it hit John. Everything Burleigh said was right. He sat down, weary. For the first time in his career, John thought about quitting and it scared him.

John looked up, "So what do we do now?"

"Well," Burleigh said, "what are the orders?"

"The messenger hasn't arrived back from Captain Barrett's camp with them."

"Sounds like we enjoy the moment until he does," Burleigh said extending his hand. John was still not so sure it was as easy as Burleigh was making it, but he took his hand anyway. "There you go, lad. Put on a face and let the men see you enjoying yourself; that's what we do for now," Burleigh said, slapping John on both shoulders.

As they were about to leave the tent, loud cheers and cries came from outside. John motioned for Burleigh to go out and investigate. A moment later, he stuck his head back in. "It's the messenger, he's returned."

"I don't remember the men being that enthusiastic about a messenger coming into camp?" John said. The messenger made his way up to the front of John's tent with a crowd of soldiers around him.

"What news do you bring?" John said, exiting the tent.

"I come with good news. It's about the girls, sir."

"Girls? What girls? What are you talking about?"

"It's finally happened. It's worked! There are finally green eyed girls in Amarin, sir," the messenger said with a smile. He then looked at the crowd and shouted, "Prince Braxton will have a green eyed bride. Long live Amarin!"

A chorus of cheers returned from the crowd.

None of the messenger's words registered with John. All he knew is that the celebrating in his camp was now bubbling over. He grabbed the messenger by the coat and led him through the crowd into his tent. Once inside, he threw him into the chair.

"You seem upset sir. I thought you would welcome the news."

"Concrete, solid news is your duty as a messenger. What you bring sounds like rumor. Can you verify it for certain?" John was staring him down. Burleigh entered the tent.

"Uh, well, yes, I mean..." he stuttered. "It's traveling swiftly all over the kingdom."

"Get out!" John said forcefully. The messenger quickly exited.

"Well, John, I told you...you don't have to save the kingdom by yourself," Burleigh said with a smirk, wiping blood from his lip again. "The kingdom has found some girls to help you."

John listened to the celebration outside and tried to understand the optimism around him, but the last thing he wanted was false hope. The leaders of the kingdom had given him little too hope for lately.

# CHAPTER 18

Addy rode in a large carriage with five other girls, all squished together; two from Lynnhaven, one from Crespin, and two from Pembrooke. They would all be working in the kitchen. It had been a long, silent, unsure ride to the castle from Pembrooke.

Over and over in her mind, she had played the last conversation with Jeanette, trying to put the pieces together.

*I can't go to the castle.*

Jeanette never said why. Maybe she didn't know. Was she running away from something or toward something? Prince Braxton had feelings for her, of that much Addy was certain. Maybe that was the great motivator. Jeanette could not stand the remote possibility that she could be the prince's bride, even if it meant saving the kingdom.

The more Addy considered, she too couldn't stand the remote possibility. It wasn't Jeanette.

"There it is, look!"

All of the girls squirmed to get a better view. Addy saw it rising over the hill. The castle of Amarin. Soldiers walked along the security wall between the four towers, one on each corner.

Hard stone with thick, earthy vines snaked halfway up the side. There were no visible windows and the only entrance appeared to be the vast metal gate that rose as the carriage pulled into the courtyard. Large, green banners with the kingdom's crest hung off the walls on each side of the entrance.

It was everything she had imagined. All of her royal fantasies about stealing away at court and finding true love all took place in a structure like the one in view. A guard opened the door, motioning for them to exit. Addy noticed two large carriages holding back: the one carrying the prince and the one with Lorelei.

A couple of guards opened the medical carriage with Brandy inside. They hoisted her onto a transport and started for a side entrance. Brandy waived. Addy's heart sank. How could she ever have not wanted her sister with her?

A stocky, bald man came over. "All you servants, leave your trunks here and get over to the front steps and form a reception line, now!" Addy stood surrounded by a dozen young people, all her age. Each wearing the same timid, unsure look on their face. "Quickly now!"

The girls were shewed into two lines, one on each side of the small stone path from the carriage drop off to the door. Addy was positioned closest on the right side of the steps. Her glance moved up the castle walls and to the tops of the majestic towers above.

*I am here.*

The entrance to the castle opened and out walked two men wearing black berets with dark green cloth shields, bearing the sign of Amarin, long trumpets at their hips. A crowd of castle royalty had gathered. The two men raised their trumpets high into the air and blew forth a fanfare. The two remaining carriages pulled up as the king and queen appeared on the steps.

The queen's posture was perfect, high cheek bones on skin

that was once without blemish. The gold crown on her head fit perfectly in the braided nest of light brown hair that was precisely in place. The king looked older. His salt and pepper hair was wild and went in every direction. Hunched over slightly, the gray eyes that sat above his large nose looked aloof from the proceedings.

The trumpets died and the queen motioned to the carriages. Cadmus stepped out of the first carriage, followed by the prince. A smile formed on the queen's lips. Addy could not help but feel the queen was anxious.

The first carriage rode on and the second carriage pulled up. Cadmus and the prince walked up to the steps and knelt before the queen. The prince stood less than three feet from Addy.

"I hear you bring good news," the queen asked. Cadmus and Braxton stood.

"We do, your highness," Cadmus replied. "The serum has worked. We have brought a potential bride for the prince." Queen Devony's smile widened. The king stood, swaying slightly in the wind with no response.

"There is another one, mother," Prince Braxton pointed out. "We need to find her."

"Hold your tongue," the queen said between her teeth. "You have brought with you everything we need. Forget about the other girl."

*Why would the queen not be worried about Jeanette?*

Cadmus turned to the carriage, signifying for the occupants to come forth. Everyone around stood in awe. Addy noticed the prince did not share in the revelry. He looked much like his father, the king, standing on the steps - defeated.

Lorelei wore a yellow dress with a green sash. The beaming sun radiated her eyes. She looked regal. Emilia exited the carriage after Lorelei, followed by Kellan. Lorelei made her way forward and stood between Cadmus and Braxton.

Cadmus took Lorelei's hand and walked her forward, closer to the steps. "My queen, my king, may I introduce Lady Lorelei of Emerleigh," he said with a bow, extending Lorelei's hand out, closer to the queen. Lorelei gave a perfect curtsy as the queen took her hand.

Suddenly, King Phillip stepped forward, pushing his wife's hand out of the way. "You must be my new nurse! 'Bout damn time you made it here! How good are you at giving baths?" Lorelei stood, frozen.

The queen pulled her husband's hand back and spoke something into his ear. Disappointment flashed across the king's face as he crossed his arms, pouting. The queen reached out for Lorelei, again, and pulled her up onto the steps next to her. "What King Phillip meant to say is that we have waited decades for someone to help instill a new hope into our kingdom, into the people. Today, she stands before us."

At these word Lorelei's demeanor brightened and the prince stiffened. With no mention of Jeanette, Addy sensed the queen had already made her choice.

"Long live Lady Lorelei," the queen called out, "and long live Amarin!" The trumpeters gave another blast while the king and queen walked back into the castle amid the celebrating in the crowd, Lorelei on the queen's arm. Cadmus and Braxton followed with Emilia and Kellan close behind.

Addy stood still until the door to the castle closed behind them. A loud voice interrupted the spectacle. "Time to show you where you newbies will be staying," the gruff man said.

*** 

A few moments later Addy shuffled along the small hallway, scrunched close to the other girls around her. They had entered the servant's quarters through a separate entrance near the back of the castle.

"Hurry up everyone, there is a big day ahead," said the loud woman moving the group of young ladies forward. The girls' trunks were being delivered to their rooms as they were led down the tiny hallway.

Girls were siphoned off one at a time. The line stopped, a girl was taken into a room and given instructions, and then the group would continue on. Addy was next in line.

"Come in. What's your name?"

"My name is Addy," she responded, peering into the room. It was small. There were two beds, one on each side wall, with a storage chest at the foot and a small table and chair for each occupant.

"This will be your room. Your roommate's name is Marah. She will be your mentor in the kitchen. Get your things stowed away and report to the servant's lobby at the end of the hall in ten minutes."

Addy nodded. The group continued on down the hall.

*Marah.*

Other than the blankets on the bed, which Addy still had to make, her only belongings were those in her trunk. She curiously looked over to Marah's side of the room. The bed was made, trunk closed, and on her table were a few papers, a quill and a bottle of ink. A small hand mirror hung on the wall.

Addy's side of the room seemed barren and cold. The only light coming in was from the torch in the hallway. No windows.

She started to unpack her things and she thought what Marah might be like. Where was she from? Would she be fun? Would she have wonderful stories about life in the castle? Would they stay up all night talking about it? Would she be...

*Jeanette.*

Addy unpacked her things and then sat on her bed, tired.

*How am I supposed to handle Lorelei on my own?*

She fought back the tears that wanted to come out and

finished unpacking as someone bellowed down the hall, "Time's up."

Addy stood, catching a glimpse of herself in Marah's mirror on the wall. She rearranged her hair and ran her hands down the front of her dress to try and straighten the seams.

*I can do this.*

She wanted to believe it, but for the first time in her life, she truly felt alone.

"Where are you Jeanette?" she whispered before heading out into the hall.

# CHAPTER 19

"Jeanette?" came a still whisper. Jeanette opened her eyes slowly and listened. It was dark, damp, and bumpy. "We're getting close to the city, I think. We need to go," Auryn said.

Jeanette felt the surroundings around her, trying to remember where they were.

Dirty.

Wet.

Walking.

And walking.

It was two days since escaping from Villard's house. With no energy left, they hid in the back of a vegetable wagon on the way to Enzion.

*Enzion.*

The visions were a puzzle, clues to what Jeanette needed to do. The only conclusion was to listen to them. After the festival it felt like a weight was on her shoulders. The closer she got to the castle, the heavier it got.

*I cannot go to the castle.*

As soon as she listened and acted, the weight lifted. There was still confusion and uncertainty about where she was headed, but she knew it was right. Her green eyes were not for the castle, or the prince, but they did have a purpose. And the only option she felt left was to follow the visions to help her better understand that purpose.

*An old sign of an owl with green eyes hanging over a merchant shop.*

Her promptings heeded her to Enzion. Whatever she found at the merchant shop, assuming there was one, would help her. She had to believe it.

Jeanette started to get up and Auryn placed her hand on her shoulder. "Quietly."

Together, they lifted up the cloth covering they were hiding under. At the head of the wagon was a large, middle-aged man whistling a tune, oblivious to their presence. The sun was rising.

They quietly crept to the back of the cart and looked out. All clear. Jeanette held up her fingers to count. One. Two. Auryn's eyes got big and she held up her hand to wait. She leaned back and started grabbing food and stuffing it into her bag. Jeanette had a mixed look of worry and necessity. They had been on the road for two days without any food or means to pay.

Jeanette grabbed two apples and slung herself over the rail. Auryn following behind. They rolled to the side of the road as quickly as they could.

Crouching down in the knee-high grass, they looked around. "I don't think anybody saw us," Auryn said.

Jeanette looked down at the apples in her hand and then felt the pain in her stomach. It was a pain that she had never felt before, but over the last two days, she was starting to understand it better. She took a soft bite. She closed her eyes as the flavor burst in her mouth. Her stomach quieted as if it had received the message that food was coming.

"Get down!" Auryn said sharply, tossing her food to the side and practically jumping on Jeanette to cover her. There was another wagon coming.

"Traffic is going to pick up over the next hour. We better get moving," Auryn said. She looked up at Jeanette's eyes, "You need to keep your hood on, and down."

*These stupid eyes.*

She had spent the last few days with her hood on and head down, not able to take all the parts of the kingdom she had never seen before. Word of the 'Jewels of Amarin' had already spread throughout the kingdom and any notice of Jeanette would have been a hindrance.

Walking head down had gotten tiresome, but it had worked thus far to keep Jeanette's eyes hidden. It also helped her come to know Auryn more, and trust her.

At first, it seemed odd that Auryn wanted to come with Jeanette. But as they traveled, Auryn opened up some about her circumstances and her willingness to leave. Young, orphaned, feeling like a slave to the castle. "I fully understand that I have been blessed to have the comforts the castle offers," Auryn had said, "but at the same time I feel so trapped. I don't have any freedom to live my life as I choose."

Jeanette understood exactly how she felt. Although the relationship had grown in the few days they had spent together, Jeanette still was reluctant to share her own thoughts. More than anything, the visions inside her longed to come out, to express themselves. Jeanette ached for the ability to share them, to seek guidance and advice. But she couldn't.

Not with Auryn. Not yet.

As they walked, Jeanette watched the shadows beneath her feet appear and disappear as the sun tried to break free. Every few yards she would pass a puddle and catch her reflection...wavy, but enough. Finally, at a large puddle, she stopped.

Kneeling down, she saw her face. She was filthy and her hair messy and tangled, but her eyes were still as bright and glorious as they had been back at her room a few nights ago.

Auryn tapped her on the shoulder. "We must keep moving. We don't want to draw attention." Jeanette turned back to see more wagons on their way. She stood up and resumed her pace.

"Have you ever been to Enzion?" Auryn asked.

"No."

"You have never been to a place quite like it. There are people everywhere. People barking at you, trying to sell you things. There are entertainers, musicians, oh and the food...there is all kinds of food. And there will be people who we want to stay away from."

"You seem to know all about this place," Jeanette said.

"Working at the castle has taken me lots of different places," Auryn responded. "But none more colorful than Enzion."

\*\*\*

"Get the best wares from Bandar...must sell today!"

"Tools! Tools! No one makes better tools than Morton's of Vulsini!"

At the center of town there were people everywhere. Men, women, children, old and young, all varying degrees of status and profession were scurrying from vendor to vendor. It was hard for Jeanette to stay focused on staring at the ground. All Jeanette wanted to do was look up and gawk at the scenes around her.

There were people from Bandar, the blue eyed kingdom to the north, known for their fishing lifestyle and knowledge of medicines. Dressed in simple coverings, their sunned skin and white hair testified to their simple life by the water.

There were people from Vulsini, the purple eyed kingdom in the mountains to the east. They were gifted in stone and metalwork. They also had a talent for keeping to themselves. The men of Vulsini were strong and determined, their bodies stout and solid. Jeanette passed a cart with a purple eyed woman wearing a thick, silver bracelet on her wrist and a necklace wrapped tight around her neck shone with various stones.

Of course, there were no Brown Eyes.

She glanced up quickly to see a street three times as wide as any street in Emerleigh. On each side was door after door of buildings housing permanent shops. Running down the middle of the street were two rows of tables filled with peddlers, merchants and others selling their wares. The lanes were jammed with foot traffic.

As Auryn led her through the crowd, Jeanette's senses reeled in every direction. To her left sizzling flesh was being spit and shaved. It was a large, bird like creature she had never seen before.

To her right were baskets of brightly colored fruits and vegetables. One in particular was small, oval, and had a velvet skin that was fuzzy dark lavender. "Those are mountain rounds, from Vulsini," Auryn said. "They are not much to look at, but when you cut them open they have a dark red center that is juicy and..." she closed her eyes, as if tasting something sweet.

"Tell me again how you know so much about Enzion."

"I have done a lot of traveling," Auryn answered.

The deeper they got into the crowd, the harder it became for Jeanette to keep her eyes down. Auryn tried to steer her, but they kept bumping into other shoppers and sometimes carts or tables, people giving them unkind stares.

"How much further until we are through the main market?"

"Just hold on," Auryn said, tightening her grip around Jeanette's arm. Halfway through, Jeanette tripped on a passing foot and stumbled into a small table with jewelry. Some of it spilling and breaking on the ground.

"Oh come on, look what you did!" said the lady behind the table. Jeanette caught a glimpse of the woman as she walked in front to see the damage. Her eyes were solid violet. "Father, come quick, they broke some of our goods."

Auryn grabbed Jeanette and pulled her up. A small crowd started to gather. A large man, stout, with a bushy beard came out from behind a curtain. Jeanette lowered her head, causing her hood to drop and shield her eyes. She could only see him from the waist down, but he was massive.

Jeanette's instinct was to run, but Auryn held her arm tight, encouraging her to stay still. Auryn inched closer as the man moved in front of the table to survey the damage.

"Look here, you broke my goods. You gots to pay up for them," the man said moving closer. The crowd continued to grow.

The man took another step. "I said, my goods need to be paid for!"

Auryn stepped in front of Jeanette. "We are sorry for the trouble sir, I hope this is enough?" she said handing him two silver pieces. He looked at the money in his hands and then at his goods on the ground. He snorted and retreated behind the curtain again. The crowd dispersed.

Auryn led Jeanette away from the table. Jeanette tried her best to keep her hood on. "What happened? Where did you get that money?" Jeanette called out from behind her.

"Just keep walking." Auryn didn't answer until they got further down the street, away from the heavy traffic. "In the commotion I swiped it off the table next to us. Nobody was paying attention."

"How much did you get?"

"I don't know exactly, a few coins. Enough to save our back sides...and to get something to eat."

They stopped in front of a food cart and Auryn placed an order. Jeanette could feel her stomach drop with anticipation. Auryn retrieved more silver out of her dress and handed it over to the vendor. The cooked meat and bread filled her with warmth.

"We need to keep moving," Auryn encouraged.

Outside of the main town square the road branched off into various directions. Back alleys and side streets were still humming with activity, but not with the vibrancy that had been on display in the heart of the city. There were no more carts or peddlers, just shops. Some were active with buyers while others were vacant.

Stomach satisfied and away from the crowds, Jeanette felt at liberty to peek out of her hood and get a better look. "Where are we going?"

"We are leaving the main district. Next, we'll be in the residential area. I don't know exactly where you want me to go."

Neither did Jeanette, but she felt they needed to keep moving. At a cross section, Auryn looked left and Jeanette looked right, down the less crowded streets. As Jeanette strained to see, something pulled her attention away from Auryn. She started walking, leaving Auryn standing in the middle of the road.

As she got further down the lane, she saw it distinctly and stopped. Auryn finally caught up. "What's wrong?" Auryn asked.

"Do you see it?"

"Do I see what?"

Jeanette brought Auryn to her eye line and pointed down the road. "Look down on the right. Do you see that sign...the one with the owl?"

"Yeah, I see it."

*An old sign hanging with a picture of an owl with green eyes hanging over a merchant shop.*

It was the sign. Though the owl on the sign had black eyes, instead of green, she felt it pulling her closer. Any doubt she had about the visions left her. She was not supposed to go to the castle. She was not going crazy. She would have more answers.

"That's why we came here, whatever is in that shop." Auryn looked confused, but kept following. The closer they got to the sign, the faster Jeanette's heart pounded. She could feel the blood pumping in her ears.

"What do we do now?" Auryn asked when they got to the sign.

The storefront showed no indication of what to expect inside. Large display windows flanked the front door. They were dusty and dirty, both inside and out. Items in the display lay strewn about: old pots, statues, candle holders, and various other trinkets all piled together as if they had sat there for ages. Everything about the place said go away, including the sign in the window which read 'closed'.

"How can they be closed; it's the middle of the day?"

Auryn knocked. Jeanette grabbed her hand as quick as she could. "What are you doing?"

"What do you mean what am I doing? You said this is the place, right?"

Jeanette sighed. She did not know what to expect, but whatever it was, a hesitance remained. Who or what is going to be in here? Will they know that I'm coming? Will they be happy to see me?

After a few seconds, there was no answer. Jeanette reached out for the handle and gave it a turn.

Locked.

She turned harder and pushed.

Nothing.

She looked around to see if anyone on the street was

paying attention. She put her shoulder into the door and it creaked as the wood shifted. Some of the items in the display window rattled. Jeanette gave the door another shove with her shoulder, but it did not budge. She finally took her hand off the door and stepped to the side to look through the windows. "It's sealed up tight."

Auryn stepped forward, pulling a pin out of her hair. She stuck it in the keyhole and moved it around carefully. After a few seconds, there was a *click*.

"Well, I didn't know you could do that," Jeanette said.

"Are you sure we should go inside?" Auryn asked, ignoring the comment.

Jeanette nodded and turned the knob. The door was still stuck. Auryn and Jeanette shared a curious glance. Auryn shrugged.

"Stand back," Jeanette said, looking up and down the street. "Let me see if this works now." She gave a grunt and lunged at the door with her shoulder.

*Crack.*

The door flew open with wood splintering all over the room. Auryn stepped in behind Jeanette. "It was barricaded," Auryn said, picking up a piece of wood off the floor.

"Let's just hope the person who barricaded it is happy to see us," Jeanette said, removing her hood and running her fingers through her hair.

The place was abandoned. There was a makeshift counter on the right that was starting to lean. On the left was a storage shelf that ran the length of the wall. Dust was everywhere.

Jeanette took a step forward and the whole floor creaked, the warped boards bent and hissed off of each other. She retracted a little and lowered the other foot more carefully, but it still produced the same sound.

"What is this place?" Auryn asked.

"I don't know," Jeanette said, still gazing around. She

walked over to the shelves and looked through them for any clues. Nothing but old junk. She turned around and walked to the other side of the room. Auryn made her way over to another bookshelf on the far wall where a handful of old books sat arranged haphazardly.

"I'm not sure we are going to find anything here, Jeanette."

Jeanette walked behind the counter. Still nothing. She sat down on a chair, a puff of dust rising behind her. "I fear I may have brought you on a pointless adventure," Jeanette said defeated. "Look at all this junk. Nobody has been here for years. What am I doing here?"

Auryn was still looking at the books on the shelf. She reached for one of the books and it didn't move. She pulled harder. The book didn't budge.

Jeanette titled her head slightly. "What are you doing?"

Auryn had both hands on the book, twisting and turning. "It won't come out."

Jeanette stood up to walk over. "What do you mean it...?"

Auryn gave one last tug and the book came unattached from the shelf with a splintering crack. Eyes wide, Jeanette walked over.

The wood was mangled and ripped out where the books had been. On the wall, they found a hole large enough to fit a fist through. Auryn got closer, about to peer in, when the tip of an arrow came protruding out of the hole. She slowly backed up and looked at Jeanette, fear in her eyes.

"Don't move! Stay right there!" came a voice from behind the arrow on the other side of the wall. Auryn froze. Jeanette glued herself to the wall, thinking frantically of what she should do.

"Who are you? What are you doing here?" It was an older male voice.

Auryn looked to Jeanette, still stiff with fright. Jeanette nodded permission for Auryn to speak. "Uh, I...uh...just saw the shop and wanted to look around," Auryn said unconvincingly.

"It was locked for a reason. You shouldn't be snooping around. You need to leave and don't come back." The voice was shaky and nervous.

"Who are you?" Jeanette asked. The arrow moved over toward Jeanette as far as it could go. Auryn took the moment to crouch and flee to the opposite corner.

"Leave and don't come back, both of you!" the voice insisted again.

"I'm sorry sir, but I can't do that," Jeanette continued, her heart pulsing.

"Who are you? What do you want? You didn't just come to look around did you?" he asked, the tension growing in his voice. His arrow moving around looking for a target.

Jeanette took a breath and her confidence increased. She moved closer to the shelf. "No we didn't. We have been traveling for a few days from Emerleigh. Were you expecting us?" Jeanette asked.

"Of course I wasn't expecting you. That's why the door was locked! You are not supposed to be here...go away!"

She had come this far and was not turning back. Every instinct within her told her to keep moving forward and not to be afraid. She stepped in front of the bookshelf facing the arrow. She put her nose right up to the hole so that he could see her eyes.

"I am supposed to be here and you are supposed to help me."

There was a gasp. The arrow disappeared behind the hole and there was a thud as if the man behind the wall fell to the ground.

"Hello? Hello?" Jeanette called through the hole. There was silence. "I think he passed out." She looked through the hole and could see a small dwelling, but could not see the man.

She turned around and looked at Auryn. "I think we should go and wake him and introduce ourselves properly."

# CHAPTER 20

"Are you insane?" Auryn whispered harshly as Jeanette tried to push the bookshelf out of the way. "He wanted to shoot an arrow into my brain!"

"Be quiet and help me push." They both pushed as hard as they could against the bookshelf, but it didn't budge. Auryn fell to the floor, tired. "Come on, get up," Jeanette encouraged, inspecting the shelf. "There has to be some way to get into the back room."

She walked over behind the counter, moving things around, looking for any sign of a door or a hole. A pot lying on the counter fell, echoing across the room.

Auryn quickly backed up against the wall away from the hole. "Be quiet. We don't want to wake him up." As Auryn was moving back, Jeanette noticed a rug at the base of the bookshelf. Jeanette walked over to it and knelt down. Reaching out, she grabbed it and tried to lift.

It didn't move.

Auryn's eyes got big. They crouched around it, took hold, and pulled.

Nothing.

They felt around the rug and still could not find a way to get it to move. Jeanette lay down on the floor to see if there was a gap underneath it, but it was flush. She laid her cheek on the floor and, looking sideways, focused past the rug toward the bookshelf. On the bottom of the shelf, there was a lone book. It looked out of place by itself.

Jeanette, her face still firmly pressed against floor, reached over to the book, grabbed ahold and pulled.

*Pop.*

Underneath the rug, a latch come undone. She smiled at Auryn.

Pulling herself up to her knees, she reached down and pulled. This time the rug lifted with ease. It swung open to reveal a small ladder descending into a passageway. "Whoever this guy is, he certainly doesn't want anybody coming to visit."

Auryn bent over to look down the ladder and then back to Jeanette. "I happen to agree with him." Jeanette could see in Auryn's eyes that she was uncertain about their prospects. Jeanette wasn't sure either, but it was one step closer. She jumped down the ladder.

On the other side of the small, makeshift tunnel, Jeanette slowly lifted the door at the top. She opened it just enough so she could see.

"Well don't go slow now! Hurry up before he wakes up," Auryn whispered from below.

Jeanette raised the door all the way and could see the man's body lying nearby. She climbed out and Auryn followed.

They were in the middle of a crude dwelling. To the right was a makeshift bed and living space. To the left was a kitchen area. In the middle of the room was a workbench, full of glass bottles, pots, burners, and kettles. Below the workbench was row after row of labeled bottles of herbs and plants, vegetables, fruits and an assortment of other items.

"Well, what now?" Auryn asked.

"If I told you I had no idea, would that make you upset?"

"I think I'm past the point where I'm supposed to be upset."

The man on the floor started moaning.

"Quick, we need to tie him up," Jeanette whispered. "He's probably not going to be happy when he comes round."

"Tie him up with what?" Auryn asked, looking around.

"There," Jeanette said, pointing to some rope on the back wall. They tied him up as quickly as they could and when they stepped away, Jeanette got her first good look at him. He was old, with long gray hair that covered most of this face. His clothes were simple and dirty, just like his lodging. He was of medium build, not fat, but not in good shape.

"Uhhh..." he moaned again, moving his head to the side. When he did so, his hair fell away from his face and Jeanette and Auryn took another step back.

Jeanette studied his face. "It looks like burn marks."

The burn that covered the left side of his face carried over his nose, making it seem larger than it was. His left ear was shriveled and the same side of his lip curled slightly downward, almost to a frown. But it was his eye that made the deepest mark. When he opened his eye, the slightly rigid flesh that was still there serving as lids revealed a black, round orb that showed no sign of life. It was a stark contrast to his other eye that was normal and gray.

"Well with all of...this," Auryn said, indicating the workshop materials, "he probably blew himself up. Who knows what he's cooking back here?"

His breathing became heavier. He appeared shocked and tried to move his hands. He did not pay any attention to Auryn, but had his gazed fixed directly on Jeanette. He struggled to a sitting a position. "Whatever it is that you are looking for, it is not here. I promise you. Please just go," he said, solemnly, almost begging.

Puzzled, Jeanette stepped closer and knelt down in front of him. "Do you know who I am? Do you know why I am here?"

"The news is all over town about the girls from Emerleigh. But I don't know why you are here. You can take whatever you need and then leave. I promise not to tell anyone."

"Maybe we should go, Jeanette," Auryn prodded.

"What is your name?" Jeanette asked.

He stopped struggling and continued to peer at Jeanette. "Hermes."

She repeated the name to herself and then waited. Maybe there would be some clarity.

Nothing.

As he continued to hold her gaze, Jeanette sensed there was more to him; something inside of him that he was not sharing. She didn't know how to get it.

"What is your shop for? Do you live here alone?"

He sighed and repositioned himself again, and said, "Yes, I live here alone. Now would you please untie me? I promise I won't hurt you."

She slowly walked behind him, catching another glimpse of the side of his raw and rigid face. It made her insides squirm.

"Jeanette," Auryn said with a look of uncertainty.

"It's alright Auryn," she said, cutting the rope. "We are the ones that were uninvited. It will be okay," Jeanette answered, not completely sure of their safety, but confident in the feeling that told her she could trust him.

He brought his arms around in front of him and massaged his hands. "The whole kingdom is probably looking for you," Hermes said. "How long have you been traveling?"

"Two days."

"Why did you come here? I don't have anything that you could possibly need." He stopped, his look turning suspicious.

"Did somebody send you here?"

"I told you, I don't know what brought us here. I was hoping you might have some insight. I just saw this place – the sign out front - and knew I had to stop."

He tried to stand up, wobbled a bit, and caught himself on a desk. "There is nothing here but an old shop, this little room, and me. It's time for you to go," he said, pointing to the hole in the floor they came through.

Jeanette stood motionless. She wanted to argue, but he was right. The problem was, if they left, she didn't know where else to go. He started moving towards them, hands outstretched, as if to slowly prod them along. "I'm happy to give you some food and some money if that will help."

Jeanette looked at Auryn for some guidance. The situation was at a crossroads. Auryn spoke up. "That's kind of you, sir. Come on Jeanette. Having some food and money sounds good."

He kept moving forward. Jeanette took a step back and looked at him, focused on his face. "Have you ever seen someone with green eyes before me?" Jeanette asked.

"I told you, it's time to leave," he said, a shift in his voice from aggravation to anger.

Auryn knelt down next to the opening in the floor. "Come on Jeanette," she encouraged again.

"I'm not leaving," Jeanette said flatly. "There's something you have, something you know, or something you can do that can help me."

"I don't want to help you. I cannot afford to help you. You don't even sound like you know what you want help with. You need to go. Go home or to the castle...I don't care."

"We have nowhere to go. It's just you." Jeanette knew she was pushing Hermes' limits. He looked like he would force them leave if he needed too. Why was she here? She tried to remember what brought her here in the first place.

The feeling.

The vision of the shop with the sign.

What else? What was she missing? Hermes and Auryn were both staring at her as if waiting for her to make the next move. Jeanette closed her eyes and focused on her feelings.

*You are in the right place.*

*He can help you.*

*Rebekah.*

The name came as a tingle on her lips. What did it mean?

*Rebekah.*

"Rebekah". It came out low, almost as a question.

Hermes stopped, visibly shaken.

"Rebekah," she said again.

His one good eye squinted with uncertainty. "What did you say?"

Finally. She could see the recognition in his face. "I said, Rebekah."

"How do you know that name?" There was a pause and Jeanette did not know how to answer.

Jeanette shook her head solemnly. "I don't even know who she is."

Hermes placed his hands on his head and turned away in desperation.

"Hermes, who is Rebekah?"

His whole aura had changed. He was calm again. "I don't know why you are here, and I don't know who sent you. And I don't know how you know that name. But..."

She had pricked something. He was considering her plea for help.

"I will let you stay here tonight...out back. But you will need to leave tomorrow. Do you understand?"

Jeanette wanted more. She wanted to keep digging.

"That is kind of you sir, thank you," Auryn said, looking at Jeanette to take the offer.

"Okay," Jeanette finally answered.

Hermes looked intently at Jeanette and said, "But you have to leave, in the morning. No more questions."

Hermes led them to a makeshift shed behind the shop. "There's room on the floor and you'll find some blankets on the shelf. I'll grab some supplies and leave them by the door, but I want you gone in the morning." He turned and walked back inside before Jeanette could say anything.

Auryn found the blankets and laid them on the floor. Tired, Jeanette sat down, her body grateful for the rest. "I wish I knew how to get him to open up more," Jeanette pondered out loud.

"I am just grateful we get to rest. I know you say that he knows something or can help, but I think he might be a little crazy. I don't know if we can trust him."

"Well, he probably doesn't trust us either, at least not completely. But I got through to him. I just wish I knew what else to say."

"How did you know to say that name?"

"It just came to me," Jeanette answered. "I can't explain it."

"Maybe if you just get some rest, your mind will be more at ease. And who knows, maybe Hermes will change his mind."

"It's him...I know it's him, Auryn."

"You keep saying that," Auryn said. "But what do you mean?"

There was a lump in Jeanette's throat. She didn't know what to say or how Auryn would take it. She didn't want her to think she was crazy. Right now, Auryn was the only person she could depend on.

"Did I tell you everything that happened when my eyes changed?"

Auryn shook her head.

Jeanette's muscles tensed. If she did tell her, Auryn would

not understand. But she needed to tell somebody. She had been holding it in for too long.

"It's not just a feeling I get. I have these pictures...in my head, I can see it. Like the sign. I saw it the night of the festival."

"You mean like, you can see the future?" Auryn asked, eerily. "Did you know I was going to come along? Did you know we were going to leave the camp? Did you know..." she started firing off questions.

Jeanette held up her hand. "It's not like that. So far it's just the same scenes with the same feelings."

"So, is this man," she said pointing back to the house, "somebody you saw in one of your visions?"

"I don't know," Jeanette said, softly. She was unsure and exhausted. "Getting this far doesn't do much good if we don't know what we're doing here, does it? I'm so sorry I got you into this, Auryn. You have no business being here. I don't know what I'm doing," Jeanette said, tears of worry and self-doubt building behind her eyes. She wiped her eyes and moved her hair out of her face. "Ouch," Jeanette called out. She reached up and patted her head. When she lowered her fingers, there was blood.

"You must have cut yourself or scrapped something going through the tunnel," Auryn said, taking a cloth out of her pocket and wiping it. "It doesn't look serious. I think we both just need to get some rest and we'll figure everything out in the morning."

Jeanette laid down and tried to relax. At this moment, she welcomed rest. "Thank you for your help, Addy. I wouldn't have gotten this far without you."

Auryn smiled, "My name is Auryn."

"Of course it is. I'm so sorry, Auryn. Thank you for everything." Jeanette's breathing slowed and for the first time in days, she drifted off to sleep on solid soil.

# CHAPTER 21

Addy had only been in the royal kitchen for a few hours, but she already knew it was not going to be what she expected. It was the largest kitchen she had ever seen. Four cooking pits, row after row and shelf after shelf of utensils. Three wash bins. Tables for this, spices for that. Fresh fruit, vegetables and meat. It was captivating.

She had always dreamed of cooking for a royal feast, but that would have to wait. Tonight, her responsibility in preparing for the royal dinner was to only clean and prep.

Addy walked back through the kitchen door after cleaning off some tables in the dining hall, almost running Marah over.

"Sorry, I didn't see you," Addy said. Marah had short, brown hair, skinny fingers and an air of confidence. Even though they were roughly the same age, Marah seemed taller and older than she really was. They had only known each other for a few hours, but Addy felt comfortable with her.

"Is anybody out there yet?" Marah asked, walking back to her station to butter the bread.

"A few people have started to arrive. Is every dinner like

this?" Addy asked, looking around at the hustle and bustle.

"Get those rolls done, Mar! I can't wait all day," came a booming voice from around the corner. Tilly, the head chef, was in charge of the kitchen. Big and loud, she was a commanding presence.

"I am getting them!" Marah screamed back, shaking her head. It was going to take time to get used to the atmosphere. "No, we don't usually have feasts like this," Marah said. "Only when blonde tramps come to the castle."

Addy stopped, confused. "You mean, Lorelei?"

"Whatever her name is," Marah said, " I don't like her."

How did Marah not like Lorelei? She hadn't even met her yet. Either way, Addy couldn't argue with her. "She is...interesting," Addy said.

"You know her?"

"Yes, she's from my village. Emerleigh."

"I heard there were two girls from your town. The other didn't make it to the castle. Ran away or something." Addy didn't respond. She didn't know how.

A hint of music came through the kitchen door. Tilly came around the corner. "Alright, my darlings, look alive; it is about to begin. Does everyone know their place? Marah, why don't you and the new girl take up in the hall during dinner. I don't care about the other mucky mucks, but if the head table needs anything at all, you come and get it. Understood?" Tilly asked, her bulging cheeks read and sweaty from hours of screaming.

Marah nodded and took Addy's arm. "Where are we going?" Addy asked.

"You heard her. Me and the new girl - that's you - are going be stationed by the head table."

"Who sits at the head table?"

"Who do you think? The king, the queen, the prince..."

"And Lorelei!?" Addy said with a fearful understanding.

"The yellow haired hussy? Yes, her too!"

Addy reluctantly followed.

***

Fifteen minutes later, Addy and Marah were against the wall behind the head table. Other tables ran down the walls on opposite sides of the room. Royal dignitaries of the court sat waiting to see the new prize of the kingdom – Lorelei. Music from the quartet echoed joyfully off the walls.

*I am at the castle. The king, queen and prince of Amarin are sitting in front of me.*

Outside the hall, three loud knocks came echoing through the chamber. Queen Devony waived to the musicians and the music quickly changed to a processional. The door opened and Cadmus entered far enough to see everyone. "My king and queen, Prince Braxton, and the royal court of Amarin, it is my pleasure to present to you, Lady Lorelei of Emerleigh."

Heads craned and chairs squeaked to get the first look. Lorelei walked past Cadmus to the center of the room. The dark green, silk dress fit her slim body perfectly. Her golden hair was pinned up, showing her neck in full glory. Though her eyes were radiant and her bosom protruding, it was her smile that captured attention. It was warm, beautiful, and confident.

The queen leaned over and whispered to Braxton, "Is she not magnificent?"

The prince did not respond.

Queen Devony rose and welcomed Lorelei, who curtsied. Then Cadmus led her to the table. As Lorelei sat, Braxton stood, and bowed.

"My Prince, it's an honor," she said. Lorelei sat to Devony's right. To the left of Devony were the king, Braxton and Cadmus.

"Let the feast begin," Devony announced. The doors to the kitchen opened and servant after servant placed food on the tables.

As the dishes arrived, the king took his utensils in hand with excitement. The queen put her hand on her husband's shoulder and turned back, getting the attention of a woman standing not too far from Addy. She was wearing a nurse's bonnet. "Fetima," the queen called, "if he gets out of line, I will need you to take him away."

Fetima nodded.

"What do you think of the castle so far?" the queen asked Lorelei

"Honestly?" Lorelei answered.

Devony laughed and turned to Cadmus. "Cadmus, how did you find her? I like her already! Yes, of course honestly."

"I still can't believe I'm here," Lorelei started. "I have some sense of the magnitude of my..." she searched for the right word, "my position. But I know I do not fully appreciate it yet.

"I hope that the prince and I can get to know each other and build a relationship of mutual respect and admiration," Lorelei said in her best sing-song voice, smiling at Braxton. He did not smile back.

Devony leaned in closer to Lorelei, out of Braxton's ear shot. Addy titled forward to hear. "You do understand that there is only you now. The other girl...the one who ran away..."

"Jeanette," Lorelei interjected.

"Yes, Jeanette. She has already shown herself unworthy of this opportunity. I have nothing against the girl personally, but fate has put you where you are."

Addy saw the satisfaction in Lorelei's face. Anger was not an emotion to which Addy was prone. She found it stressful. But in the moment, it was building.

"You might have to be a bit persuasive," Devony continued. "Braxton is somewhat hesitant, but I think he is coming around. He is a good man with a decent heart. He needs, and has always needed, the right woman to help him realize his true potential."

"I am the woman for the job and will not let you down, my queen," Lorelei said, shooting another smile to Braxton who was not looking.

Devony and Lorelei resumed their meal. Out of nowhere, the king started throwing chicken legs out onto the dance floor, screaming, "Fly away! You can be free!"

The queen looked at Fetima, who quickly came over and escorted the king out of the dining hall. Addy smiled and glanced at the prince, who sat picking at his food.

Did he really have a choice? If Jeanette were here, would it make a difference? Addy continued to listen as Cadmus leaned over to the prince.

"So, my dear prince, what are your impressions of Lorelei?"

"She seems like a...nice girl."

"That's all, just nice?"

"I can't say I know her that well."

"I am so glad you said that," Cadmus said with a smirk, arising from his chair.

"Oh, please Cadmus, no," Braxton begged, looking to his mother. She called Braxton over and whispered something into his ear. He nodded reluctantly and Cadmus motioned to the musicians and the tempo slowed to a waltz.

Cadmus looked to the crowd, "Who here tonight wants to see the prince dance with Lady Lorelei?" Cheers of agreement fill the air.

After some reluctance, Braxton made his way over to Lorelei. "Would you like to dance?" he asked, leading her out onto the floor. Addy could not see the queen's face, but imagined the look of pleasure on it.

Addy noticed Marah with a look of spite on her face. "Are you okay?"

"I'm fine, just...just keep still and look forward."

The prince and Lorelei twirled about the floor while the whole room watched. The queen turned to Cadmus. "What of the other girl? Is there any update on her whereabouts?"

"We do not know, my queen. I take full responsibility for her escape. Security should have been tighter."

Devony waved off his apology.

Cadmus continued, quieter. "I sent a scouting party out from Pembrooke as soon as we knew she was missing. Unfortunately, we have no idea where she could have gone. I have not had any updates as of yet. I don't think she left because she was scared. I think she left for a reason. I just don't know what it is yet. If I may say," Cadmus continued, in a more personal tone, "you do not seem overly upset with the development."

"Upset. Not hardly. One girl; that is all we needed. And there she is," the queen said, pointing to Lorelei. "It's hard enough for Braxton to accept his fate as future ruler of the kingdom, can you imagine if there were more than one option for a wife? How difficult that would be for him?"

"But what happens when we find her?" Cadmus asked.

The queen thought about the question. "Maybe we don't find her?" she said, more as a statement than a question, eyebrows raised knowingly at Cadmus.

Cadmus nodded.

Addy watched the prince and Lorelei continue to dance and for the first time thought maybe Jeanette was right to run away.

# CHAPTER 22

Jeanette heard the world around her slowly coming into consciousness as she awoke. Her body did not want to get up, but she was being forced.

"Stop it," she cried. Her eyes opened slowly. It was still dark outside, but a light shined down on her.

"Wake up," the man said, poking her in the shoulder.

Her eyes finally opened and adjusted to the man standing over top of her. It was Hermes. She could not tell if the look in his face was urgent or angry. A patch now covered his scarred eye.

She sat up, putting her arm in front of her eyes to shield the light. "What's wrong?" As soon as she asked, she saw another man standing off to the side. He was holding Auryn, who was tied up.

Her instincts kicked in and she tried to jump to her feet to help Auryn, but Hermes intervened. "Calm down, just calm down," he said. "Nobody's going to get hurt."

"What are you doing with her? Untie her right now!"

"Would you be quiet? You'll wake up the whole street." He turned to the man holding Auryn and said, "Deacon, let her go for a second." The man holding Auryn did not move. "I said let her go!" Deacon finally let go.

"Listen girl," Hermes said to Auryn, "come over here and sit down next to....next to..."

"My name is Jeanette."

"I know your name. I was going to tell her to sit down next to her friend. But I don't think that applies anymore."

Jeanette's heart raced, eyes glued to Auryn. Auryn looked haggard, tired. As she got closer, Jeanette could see that she had been crying.

"Auryn, what's going on? Did they hurt you?" Jeanette reached out to console her. Auryn flinched and moved back, avoiding her touch. Finally, their eyes met and Jeanette saw in Auryn something that sent chills down her spine - guilt.

"I'm so sorry, Jeanette," was all Auryn could get out as she began to cry. "I never meant to hurt you."

"It seems she wasn't along just for support," Hermes said.

"I don't understand? What are you talking about?"

Hermes pointed to the window on the second floor of his shop. "That second story is not there for show. My good friend here is up there to make sure people leave me alone. If he would have been home yesterday when you barged in I wouldn't be in this situation.

"I was honest when I said you could stay the night and I was honest when I said you had to leave in the morning. Your story I believe," he said, looking at Jeanette. "But you," he said, turning to Auryn, "there was something about you that didn't sit right. So I made sure Deacon kept an eye on you last night."

"Nothing happened last night. We both fell asleep," Jeanette said, looking to Auryn for reassurance.

Hermes shook his head. "No, you were not both asleep. Your friend snuck out in the middle of the night."

Jeanette looked at Auryn, who was looking down at the ground. Jeanette knew it was true from Auryn's posture. Her heart sank with betrayal.

"Deacon followed her through the streets and to one of the inns in town. According to Deacon, she met with a fellow, gave him something. The man she talked to then left in a hurry and Auryn came back here. Now here we are in a messy situation. I knew I should have stuck to my gut and sent you both packing while I had the chance," he said, disgusted.

Jeanette looked at Auryn. "Who did you meet with? What did you give them?" Every inch of her was crawling with uncertainty.

Auryn still did not respond. Angry, she crawled over to Auryn and lifted up her chin. "Look at me!"

"I'm so sorry, Jeanette. I didn't have a choice."

"So nothing over the last few days was the truth? It was all a lie? Everything I told you, all the things I said...I trusted you."

Through her tears, Auryn pleaded, "It's not like that. I promise, I meant everything I said."

"Well then who did you meet? What did you give them?"

"He's a messenger. They are spread throughout each city of the kingdom."

"A messenger for who?" Jeanette and Hermes asked at the same time.

Auryn looked at both of them and then focused on Jeanette. "A messenger for Cadmus."

The words did not process with Jeanette. She looked at Hermes, who turned pale.

"I don't work for him, not really..." Auryn stumbled for the words. "After Brandy got sick he thought it was a good idea to keep an eye on you, to have somebody with you. In case..."

"In case what?"

"In case you ran away."

*How did Cadmus know what I was thinking?*

"He made me follow you. I didn't have a choice. Cadmus wanted to make sure you were safe, that's all."

"But you led him straight to me," Hermes interrupted. Hermes seemed overly concerned with himself and his own safety. He turned to Deacon, "Tie her down so she can't escape. Whoever is coming; she can be here to greet them. I need to go." He turned and walked into the house.

Jeanette didn't have any fear of Cadmus, but she knew she could not go to the castle. Hermes was the one who was supposed to help her. She needed to keep going, to figure out the visions.

Auryn turned to Jeanette. "Jeanette, please, I am so sorry. You have to forgive me. I did not mean to betray your trust. I don't want to go back to the castle. You can't leave me here, please take me with you!"

"Then help me understand. How can I trust you?" She waited. Auryn turned away. Jeanette's heart sank at the realization she could not trust anybody.

Jeanette ran into the house after Hermes, "Why are you running from the castle? What are you not telling me?"

"What you have started you cannot stop," Hermes said, walking methodically from spot to spot, as if going through a checklist.

"What have I started? That's why I need your help; I know you know things that you aren't telling me."

"I have no time to talk. I have to leave."

"Take me with you," Jeanette begged.

"That is out of the question."

"Hermes, you know I don't have anywhere to go. You know there is a reason I am here. If you don't want to tell me what you know, fine, but at least get me out of the city, away from the castles grasp."

He stopped and bent his head over. "That's it, do you hear

me. Out of the city and that's it. No more."

"And you promise nothing will happen to Auryn," she added.

"Whoever comes from the castle will find her unharmed. I promise you, they are already on their way."

"Thank you."

Hermes walked past her and grumbled, "Don't thank me yet."

# CHAPTER 23

Cadmus felt uneasy.

Looking around the table as lunch was served he saw all the pieces - the pawns - he had in play. The overall goal was still in sight, but the current game was slipping out of his grasp. Every time he lined up his next move, new events would cause him to rethink his strategy.

Auryn and Jeanette had been gone for days with no word. Maybe Auryn wasn't as trustworthy as he thought. He needed Jeanette back, soon.

No matter; he would find a way. His current focus was Braxton. He knew the prince better than anyone. Braxton could not have true feelings for Jeanette in such a short amount of time, but the idea of going against his mother's wishes would be too much for him to see reason. He was transfixed on Jeanette and would be stubborn about his forced feelings. Cadmus needed to help Braxton accept his reality...to accept Lorelei. She was his future bride, whether he liked it or not.

*One step at a time.*

"I would like to make a toast," Cadmus said standing, lifting his glass. Around the table sat the queen, king, Braxton, Lorelei and Emilia. Everyone, except the king held their glass up.

"To Amarin and a peaceful future." He pointed his glass subtly to Braxton and then to Lorelei.

"Here, here!" the queen added.

As soon as Lorelei lowered her glass, the king gave her a wink. "Phillip, that is quite enough," Devony reprimanded. He lowered his head like a punished child.

A servant came through the kitchen doors. "Dessert will be served shortly."

"Woo-hoo!" King Phillip cheered, his frown quickly turning to a grin. He picked up his spoon and held it at the ready. Devony shook her head and waved the servants to come in and clear lunch. Marah was one of them.

Cadmus noticed the coldness that came from Marah. Her pleasant manner around the prince had shifted. He knew about her close friendship with the prince. Braxton seemed clueless about or uninterested in Marah's affection, which is exactly how it needed to be. If the prince had shown a desire for any type of relationship with the girl, Cadmus would have to intervene. Thankfully, it had not reached that point.

"Have you enjoyed the first few days?" Cadmus asked Lorelei.

"Yes, everyone has been so pleasant and patient as I learn."

Devony smiled, "There is a lot to learn, that is for sure. But it will come. You seem like you are a quick learner."

"Yes, your grace," Lorelei responded, giving Braxton a smile, "I certainly am."

"And what of you, Prince Braxton?" Cadmus continued. "Have you and Lorelei had some time yet to become better acquainted?"

"Um, no. We unfortunately haven't."

"But I am most looking forward to it," Lorelei chimed in. "How do you like to spend your free time, my prince?"

"I find ways to try and stay busy," was all he could manage.

"Our good prince," said Cadmus, "is an accomplished horseman."

"Really?" Lorelei asked, eyes wide with excitement. "I love riding!"

Lorelei was going to need some coaxing to tone it down a bit. Cadmus was already fighting an uphill battle. Two servants came out carrying the dessert trays.

Before the bowl could be put in front of King Phillip, he already had a spoonful in his mouth. "Yummy!" he exclaimed, filling dripping from his face as he shoveled another bite in.

"I agree," Devony said, "this is delicious."

"This is wonderful," Lorelei added. "I could get used to eating like this."

"I hope you do," replied the queen. "We have some of the best chefs and bakers in the kingdom."

"I would hope we have *the* best," Cadmus added.

"And I hear that they are especially good at making *cakes*," Devony added.

"Yes mother, I'm sure they are," Braxton said, squirming. For a fleeting moment, Cadmus felt sorry for Braxton. But it was time for the prince to grow up and take more responsibility. The wedding had to go as planned. Cadmus depended on it.

"Is there any news on the location of Jeanette?" Braxton asked, changing the subject.

"I hope there will be soon. She is not safe out on her own"

Devony chimed in, "Yes, of course we want her safe, but I personally have lost respect for the young lady. Running away from the caravan...who would do that?"

"Enough with the pansy talk, more pie!" the king shouted.

"A messenger for you, Master Cadmus," a servant called from the door. Finally, some news.

"Excuse me," Cadmus said, wiping the corners of his mouth. As he walked to the door, his pulse quickened. He was normally calm, calculating, and in control of his emotions, but this news would change everything.

He pulled the messenger aside. "Did you talk to Auryn?"

"Yes, sir. They are at an old shop in Enzion. The shopkeeper let them stay the night. She is hoping she can convince them to stay longer."

A peace went over him. It was all going to work out. He instructed the messenger to send a scouting party to retrieve both of the girls quickly and to tell no one. As soon as the messenger left, Cadmus felt a small pang of guilt for not trusting Auryn, but she had come through, as she had before. He knew she would. She depended on him; she had no other choice. He needed Jeanette. Only once had he let someone as special slip away, and he couldn't – wouldn't – let it happen again.

"I'm sorry to interrupt, my lord," another servant said, interrupting his thoughts. "There is a visitor who is demanding to speak with you."

"Who is it?"

"The girl who ran away; it's her father, Jacob. And he has a boy with him as well."

Cadmus sighed. He had hoped her family would be content with the promise that Jeanette was their highest priority. Apparently, it was going to take more effort that he did not want to give, but he was used to being flexible. It was the price he paid to stay in control.

# CHAPTER 24

Later that evening, Corwin stood in Cadmus' office, his adrenaline still high from the ride. What was he doing at the castle? Did it have anything to do with Jeanette?

It had been a week since arriving at the Royal Academy. Word had spread quickly throughout the kingdom that Jeanette did not stay with the caravan. His fellow soldiers prodded and poked to try and get information out of him.

"You're from Emerleigh, what do you know?"

"Did you know her? What was she like?"

*Is she safe?*

The last question startled him, realizing the gravity of the situation. Ever since he and Jeanette shared the dance at the festival in Emerleigh, everything had changed. Not his feelings – he had always had feelings for her – but his outlook on reality. She had never given him any reason to believe she liked him, and that drew him in even more. He had hopped the dance would build a foundation and help her understand his true feelings. He would go away and fight, come home a hero, and she would have matured in her acceptance of him.

Then her eyes changed.

Corwin had watched as she bent over, obviously in pain. He wanted to help, to protect her. He knew her well enough to know she had no desire to be a part of the caravan, or to go to the castle, or to have green eyes. Maybe the pressure was too much?

The door opened and in walked Cadmus and the prince. Corwin started to attention and then stopped, noticing others behind them.

"Jacob? Tristyn? What are you doing here?"

"They came seeking information about Jeanette," Cadmus said. "You must be wondering why you are here."

"Yes, sir."

"Well, we need your help."

"Is Jeanette okay? I heard that she ran away."

"Unfortunately, that is correct," Cadmus replied. "We have word that she is in Enzion. This morning we dispatched a scouting party to find her and bring her back to safety."

"If there are others already going to find her, how can I help?"

"Her father has asked that he and Tristyn be allowed to go rendezvous with the scouting party," Cadmus replied. "As any father would, he wants to make sure Jeanette is safe and makes the right decision to return to the castle. He feels having you there would also be of great benefit."

"I will serve however I can," Corwin said, "but how do we know where she is?"

"Master Cadmus felt something was not right with Jeanette's behavior from the beginning," Prince Braxton chimed in. "After her handmaiden became ill in Pembrooke, Cadmus had a trusted servant fill in for her. The new servant was given express instructions to stay close to Jeanette and if something like this happened to report their location at the first opportunity."

"We received a message from the handmaiden, Auryn," Cadmus said. "We know they are staying at a shop in the city run by a man named Hermes. We have the directions to them."

"Why me?" Corwin asked Jacob.

Tristyn answered, "Because we know you care about her." Jacob smiled and nodded, confirming Tristyn's response. In his eyes, Corwin saw understanding. There was no question Jacob knew how he felt about Jeanette.

"I don't mean to bring you into this, Corwin," Jacob said, "but your help means a lot."

"Assuming we do find her, we need someone she trusts," Cadmus continued. "I believe, sergeant, that this young lady is scared of what the future holds and I want to have the opportunity to bring her back and put her mind at ease before she gets herself, or others, hurt."

"What if she does not want to come back?" Corwin asked.

"Just to be clear," Cadmus said, "she unfortunately does not have an option. She is far too valuable to the kingdom."

"She belongs here at the castle, with me," Braxton added.

Corwin bristled at the prince's words. He looked to Jacob for reassurance.

"I agree, Corwin," Jacob said. "She is a danger to herself and to others. The safest place for her is here at the castle."

It was not what Corwin wanted to hear, but he nodded. "What if we meet up with the search party and she is not with them? What if she has already fled from Enzion?"

"I certainly hope that is not the case, but if it is, then your mission is to track her and to report back as soon as you have a verified location," the prince answered. "Under no circumstances should you try to apprehend her yourself."

*Apprehend her?*

"What if Jeanette has run from Enzion? Then what of Tristyn and me?" Jacob asked.

"In all honesty, it is best for you to go home and support your wife and your village," Cadmus said. "If she is not on her way here now, then there is nothing realistic that you could do to help. We cannot afford more civilians falling into the wrong hands. There may be force required to bring her in, that is the reality of the situation, but we would not expect that force to come from you or her family." Cadmus looked to Jacob for approval of his words. Jacob eyed Corwin.

"I give you my word," Cadmus said, "our only concern is her safety. And the safest place for her is here, with us, guarded in the castle until we can figure all this out."

"We will leave as soon as possible," Jacob spoke up, "if that is okay with you."

Braxton and Corwin both nodded.

"I do have one more favor," Corwin said. "One of the girls from our town, Addy, came with the caravan. I would like to speak with her."

"I am happy to let you, but we have already talked to her about the situation and she doesn't seem to know anything. From what I understand, she and Jeanette were close."

"They have been best friends forever," Jacob said. Corwin could not remember a time that he did not see them together.

"Understood," Cadmus said, walking over to a desk against the wall. He pulled out some parchment and began writing. "Guard, please escort them to the servant quarters so they can speak with Addy; and then Corwin, take this to the quartermaster. He will supply you with funds, a fitted horse, and the official seal of the kingdom that will allow you to travel freely. I hope you understand the importance of this mission."

"I will do everything I can to help bring her in and keep her safe," Corwin replied, saluting again.

"I have no doubt that you will."

# CHAPTER 25

Addy finished brushing her stubborn hair and shivered. It was beautiful and warm outside, yet the basement stone in the castle was cold on her feet. She quickly jumped into bed.

She couldn't remember working so hard and was excited for the prospect of sleep. It had been three days since arriving and she was still adjusting to castle life. Thankfully, Marah made the adjustment easier.

Having Marah as a roommate was a blessing. Not that she held anything against the other girls, but she found she could talk to Marah. There was something familiar about her. Marah was comfortable in her own skin and not afraid. That's exactly what Addy needed.

"How long have you been at the castle?" Addy asked.

"About a year I guess. I arrived from festival last spring." Addy already knew she was from Lynnhaven on the eastern side of the kingdom. Addy had never been, but from listening to Marah, it was very similar to Emerleigh, except it was closer to the mountains of Vulsini.

"So you only have one year left?"

"That's what they tell me," Marah replied, placing her hand mirror back on the wall. Marah fiddled with it constantly. Addy did not have the nerve to ask her about it. Not yet.

"Do you like it better at the castle than in Lynnhaven?"

Marah smiled, "Yes."

Addy nodded, wanting to agree. A knock turned both girls towards the door.

"Who would come down here this time of night?" Marah said, pulling her nightshirt on tighter and walking to the door. She opened it slowly.

"Corwin!?" Addy exclaimed, getting up from her bed. "What are you doing here?"

Marah opened the door fully, revealing Jacob and Tristyn. Warmth ran through Addy. She would not admit that she missed home, but seeing them made her homesick.

"The prince is asking me to help bring Jeanette back," Corwin said. He gave a polite nod to Marah. "Sorry to interrupt, but do you mind if we talk in the hall quickly."

"Sure," Addy said. "I'll be right back."

Marah looked giddy. "I can't wait to hear the update."

Once in the hall, Addy asked, "So they found Jeanette?"

"Sort of," answered Corwin. "They know where she is and have sent some soldiers to bring her back. They asked me to go with Jacob and Tristyn to try and help."

"Soldiers? But she didn't do anything wrong."

"We know that, Addy," Jacob said, "but she is not safe since her eyes have changed and the best place for her would be here at the castle."

*Would Jeanette be safer at the castle?*

"Did she give you any reason of why she left?" Corwin asked. "Was there any hint of her motive?"

Addy hesitated. "She said she was afraid...afraid to come to the castle. She kept saying she felt something bad would happen if she came. I think, in her mind, going towards the castle had something to do with Brandy getting sick."

"How is Brandy?" Tristyn asked.

"Much better, Tristyn. Thank you," she said and then turned back to Corwin. "I have been playing our last conversation over and over again in my head. She did not leave any clue as to where she thought she needed to go." Addy scanned the faces before her. Did Jeanette know the trouble she was causing everyone? Was she really that selfish, or was it something more? "Are you leaving tonight?"

"As soon as we're done talking," Corwin said. She could sense the anxiety and nerves in his voice.

"If you do find her, tell her...tell her...," Addy started. "Tell her I miss her and I hope she's okay."

"We will. Thank you," Corwin said and they left down the hall. After they were gone, Addy went back into the room.

"So, what did they say?" Marah sat on the bed, wide eyed. "I still can't believe you were best friends with the green eyed girl who ran away. What's she like?"

Addy had avoided the conversation until now. "She is..."

*Inconsiderate.*

*Impatient.*

*Insecure.*

*Crazy.*

*The closest friend I have ever had.*

"She is the exact opposite of Lorelei," Addy finally answered.

"Then I like her! I like her very much," Marah said. "Where do think she is?"

"I don't know; but wherever it is, I imagine it's not very safe."

# CHAPTER 26

"Thank you, Bertha," Hermes said to the buxom lady who dropped two dinner plates in front of them. Jeanette glared at the food in front her. She was starving; she had not eaten since morning.

"I'm sorry to pop in on you like this, but it was kind of an emergency," Hermes said.

"Hermes, it's been forever. You are always welcome," Bertha said, with an eye glancing in Jeanette's direction. "You don't usually bring guests." Jeanette lowered her head, letting her hood dip down lower.

"Have you seen any fighting up here in Samdon lately?" Hermes asked, redirecting her attention from Jeanette.

"A few days back on the outskirts of town there was a tussle. I think we held them off." Hermes thanked her for the food and Bertha walked into the back.

Jeanette lifted her hood slightly and grabbed the meat off the plate and started chewing. She had never been this far outside of Emerleigh. Samdon was a border town, northwest of Enzion, closer to the Bandar border.

"How do you know Bertha?" Jeanette asked, taking

another bite.

"I used to travel through this way a lot. She keeps a few rooms and offers meals. She's handy to know."

"Back at your place it didn't look like you did much traveling," Jeanette said, remembering all of the odd materials back at his house. "What is it that you actually do?"

"It's none of your business," he said without looking up, wiping his fingers off on his shirt.

The night had settled in and she couldn't help but think about Auryn. Is this what her life was going to be? Lack of trust and constant running?

"Thank you for bringing me with you, Hermes. I know you didn't have to." She took a sip of her drink before adding, "Where are we going tomorrow?"

He stopped mid-chew and spat out his bite. "*We* are not going anywhere! I kept my end of the deal. You can stay here for a day or two. It will be safe. Then you can go home, or to the castle, or wherever. I honestly don't care."

"Well you need to care," she snapped back. "All this sneaking around, secret rooms above abandoned stores, fleeing in the dark of the night. There are people who would be in interested in what I could tell about you? I don't care about this town and I don't care about these stupid green eyes. Don't you get it?" Jeanette asked. "I am supposed to be doing something. Why won't you help me?"

"Jeanette, it will lead to no good. Trust me. Go home, kiss your family, and get as far away from the castle as you can."

Bertha came out of the back. Jeanette quickly turned away and pulled her hood down again. "I heard some fussing. Everything okay?"

"Oh, everything is fine, Bertha. My friend is just tired and a little out of sorts. I'm sorry for the disturbance. It won't happen again." Bertha smiled and walked away.

Jeanette moved her hood back to see his face better. "I am

not going back. I must keep..."

A sound from outside interrupted her. She stopped to listen. A long cry. "Does Bertha have a child?" Jeanette asked.

"I don't think so," Hermes said, looking around confused. Apparently, he heard it too. The sound was not infant and innocent.

Then another cry. It came from outside. It was more distinct.

"What was that?" Jeanette asked, walking closer to the window.

Then a blood curdling scream echoed through the town, followed by another and then a relentless barrage of horrific sounds. Fright filled the space in Jeanette's veins.

*Rogues.*

She saw them coming from all directions, as if appearing out of thin air. Instinctively, Hermes dropped to the floor. Jeanette was mesmerized; she had never seen one before...alive. She could not count all of them. They looked like people – human – but they were savagely dressed, unshaven, and unclean.

It was their face...the look in their face. It was expressionless. But the red in their eyes pierced the night.

"Get out of the window," he whispered, pulling her down. "Go over there and blow out the light."

Jeanette paused and looked, trying to think.

"Don't think child, just do it," he said forcefully. She got up and went over and blew out the candle. He went to the other side of the room and blew out another candle.

Bertha came out of the back. "What on earth are you..."

"A Red Eye attack. Get in the back and hide," he said. Bertha didn't hesitate.

"Come here," he called over to Jeanette. "Take these," he said, handing her food from off the dinner plates and stuffed them into the cloth she was holding. The warm juices and syrups ran down her hand. He took all the utensils and the plates and laid them on the floor. Turning the table on its side, he placed the plates and utensils as if they had fallen on the floor. He took what remained in the mugs and also poured it out.

"What are you doing?" Jeanette asked, stupefied. He didn't answer. There was continued screaming and cries from outside. Jeanette started to shake.

"Go in the pantry and find a box, a bag, anything to carry items. Put that in there," he said pointing to the leftovers in her hand, "and then start taking stuff from the pantry and start filling it up. I am right behind you."

Jeanette looked at him, her face asking why.

"Go!"

She found a crate in the corner and collected everything she could find. As she filled, Hermes was knocking down items and spreading his own chaos.

"What are you doing?"

"I need to make it look like one of them already came in here and cleaned it out." Jeanette found a table to hide behind and in the dark, waiting, as Hermes ran to the back.

Footsteps on the porch made her skin crawl. The noise that had been so terrifying outside suddenly disappeared. She could hear everything perfectly: her breathing, the dripping of the spilt liquid from the table, Hermes whispering to Bertha. The footsteps got closer to the door and she ducked her head further under the table.

The door slowly opened. The Red Eye walked in and kicked the plate on the floor, sniffed the air, and then waited.

Jeanette tensed. Maybe Hermes' plan had worked. Jeanette looked over towards the back room and saw Hermes standing, back against the wall. He held his finger up to his mouth.

The Red Eye slowly turned back toward the door. Jeanette closed her eyes, thankful. As it reached the door, Jeanette gently leaned against the table she was hiding behind. It moved across the floor, the sound echoing. The rogue turned quickly and ran toward the table.

"Run!" Hermes yelled.

Jeanette leapt up and tried to make it to the back room. The Rogue caught her from the side by the hair and slung her across the room. Her body slammed against the wall near Hermes.

As she hit the wall, she felt a tear in her elbow. Shrieking, she tried to slide to safety. Before Hermes could do anything, the rogue was on her.

Jeanette held up her hands and pleaded, "Please! Don't!"

She saw his face for the first time. The anger and savageness quickly changed to shock and surprise. They were staring at each other. He looked at her – at her eyes – pondering. The next minute he dropped her to the floor and ran out of the house.

Panting on the floor, Jeanette turned to see Hermes, looking at her, shocked.

"What did you do?" he asked.

"I...I didn't do anything. I just looked at him."

"I don't know what you did, but get over here before another one comes back."

She slid across the floor into the back room, her elbow throbbing in pain. As she tried to stand, her legs became weak. The last thing she thought as her mind faded and her body dropped was she hoped Corwin would catch her.

# CHAPTER 27

"What about you, Tristyn?" Corwin asked. They had rode through most of the night, stopped for a few hours rest, and were back on the trail toward Enzion. "How has this adventure been so far?"

Tristyn thought for a moment and replied, "Adventurous."

Corwin smiled. He did not know much about Tristyn, other than what others said.

*Spliteye*

That's the name he had heard other boys call Tristyn on a couple of occasions. Cruel.

"You are what, Tristyn, fourteen...fifteen?"

"I'm fourteen."

"I was your age when I started on rotations," Corwin said. All he ever wanted to do was grow up, get trained, and go fight. Obedience was in his nature. He built bonds easy with the other men and felt a call for leadership. He was currently a bit out of his comfort zone.

"How has training at the academy been?" Tristyn asked. But before Corwin could answer, he added, "I hope they let me go to the academy when I am old enough,"

"Tell us again about finding that Red Eye," Jacob interrupted. Corwin could sense Jacob changed the subject because the chances of Tristyn being able to attend the academy were nonexistent. He had never heard of someone with two eye colors being allowed to serve.

"Do you hear that?" Corwin asked before Tristyn could speak. There was pounding of hooves up ahead.

"It's a royal squad," Tristyn said, pointing to the banners the lead man were carrying.

A squad of six men, all on horseback, rode up. Corwin waved them down.

"We are on official business, soldier. We do not have time to stop," the lead guard said. Riding with one of the soldiers was a girl, tied up.

""I am on an errand for the kingdom, under Master Cadmus' orders. Is that Auryn?" Corwin asked, searching for any sign of Jeanette.

"How do you know her name?"

"Where is the other girl? The girl that was with her," Jacob asked.

"Yes, her name is Auryn. She was with the green eyed girl who ran away. Unfortunately, by the time we got there, the other girl was already gone."

Auryn looked distraught and weary. "You were with Jeanette?" Corwin asked.

Auryn did not answer.

"Where is she now? When was the last time you saw her?"

Nothing.

The guard spoke up. "She hasn't said a word. We searched the home where we found her and discovered nothing."

"Where are you taking her now?"

"Back to Cadmus."

Auryn bristled at the name.

"We need to be going, if that is all," the guard said.

"Where did you other men go?"

"They stayed in Enzion hoping to pick up a trail. Now if you will please move out of the way." The soldiers resumed their pace down the road.

"What do we do now?" Tristyn asked. "Go back?"

Corwin didn't know, but going back wasn't an option. He needed to know Jeanette was safe. "We need to keep moving forward and try to find her."

"I think the only thing we can do is follow behind the guard and see if they missed something at the shop where Jeanette was," Jacob added.

"You're right," Corwin said. "Maybe we will get lucky." It wasn't much, but it was all they had. They kicked the horses and picked up their pace toward Enzion.

# CHAPTER 28

John could not believe the scene before him. It's not that there were bodies - he was a soldier and death was inevitable - but he had never seen anything like this.

The whole reason his camp had come to the outskirts of Samdon was to insure the supply line was intact and that the kingdom's goods got through the northern pass unharmed. His men had heard the cries for help on the outskirts of the village, but by the time they got into town, it was too late.

He turned to Burleigh. "Have we found the mayor yet?"

"Dead."

"Where's Zachary?"

"He went over to get a final count of the wounded and to make sure the survivors were okay."

"And we won't have word from the kingdom until later today, assuming the messengers are swift," John said. He was tired and upset. "This shouldn't have happened, Burleigh."

Burleigh did not respond.

"How did we not see anything last night? Not even a warning."

"We all heard it at the same time. By the time we got here they were gone."

"What's the damage?"

"All of the houses were pretty much cleaned out of food and supplies. All except one."

John's ears perked up. That didn't seem right. Why would they hit every house except for one? "Which one?" John asked. Burleigh pointed towards the house and they walked over.

"Who lives here?" John asked.

"A woman named Bertha. Runs it kind of like a small inn."

"What about the man of the house?"

"She claims there isn't one."

Inside, it was a mess: a dinner table knocked over; chairs, plates and food strewn on the floor. John walked to the pantry and discovered some of the food had been taken, but not all of it. Out of the back door, he found two sets of tracks. Something wasn't right. It did not look like the work of a Rogue.

He then walked out of the house, toward the line of people waiting for a meal. They all looked tired, hungry, and still shaken from the experience.

"Which one is she?" he asked. Zachary pointed her out.

"Excuse me ma'am," John said. She took a step, along with the rest of the line, toward the rations cart. She said nothing.

"I said excuse me, ma'am." Finally, she turned to face him. "I know it has been a trying night for you, but would you mind stepping over here so that I can ask you a few questions?"

Her eyes were scared, worried. "Um, of course."

He escorted her back to the house and walked through the door. She was hesitant to enter. "The kingdom will be sending representatives down and I have to be able to give a detailed report. The Rogues are something we take very seriously. Your insight may help keep these types of attacks from happening in the future. One of them was here in your house last night, is that correct?"

She nodded.

"Did you see it?"

"Him."

"Excuse me?" John asked, confused.

"It was a man...I mean; it was a man with red eyes. Yes, I saw him. I've never seen anything like that in my life."

"Did it...did he see you?"

"I don't think so. He seemed pretty intent on just beating up the place and was looking for food."

"Then do you know why he did not take any?"

She shrugged, "I don't know, maybe one of his friends called him or it was just time for him to go?"

"Thank you, Bertha. I just wanted to see why your house was the only one in the village that wasn't foraged. I appreciate your time," John finished.

Bertha was quiet as she left to retake her place in the rations line. John looked at Burleigh and asked, "Why would she lie?"

"What do you mean?" asked Burleigh.

"There were two places set at the table for dinner last night. Somebody was dragged out of the back door; if you look on the floor, you can see spots of blood. The same person, I assume, was dragged out into the woods. You can see the indentation in the ground leading out from the doorway. I just haven't figured out why she would lie about it, or why that would stop something like a Red Eye from foraging from food"

"I can't think of any reason why it would matter," Burleigh said. "John, right now our concern needs to be these people and helping them get settled. We have graves to dig and homes to repair. Not to mention, it is still our duty to keep the supply line protected."

"Go have Zach and Wes' men start burying the dead. Then

have Gabriel and his men assist repairing homes." Burleigh saluted and walked away.

John started down the main street of the village, taking in the site before him. Destruction and despair is all he saw.

Hopelessness.

Defeat.

The same feelings he had been struggling with lined each and every face he passed. It wasn't just the soldiers who were discouraged; it was the kingdom at large, the people. All of Amarin is living in a bad dream.

John's thoughts turned to the trail out the back door of Bertha's home. Where did the blood come from? Who had left?

Whoever they are, they are lucky they got out alive.

# CHAPTER 29

Jeanette opened her eyes to a splintering pain in her elbow. The earth moved beneath her. She tried to get up.

"Ow!"

"Don't move," Hermes said.

She put her head back down on top of the makeshift pillow. It took a moment to adjust her eyes. It was daytime, but inside the back of the wagon only the slightest hint of light spilled in through the canvas.

"What are we doing?"

"We're trying to stay alive, which is why I need you to keep it down." He moved closer to the front, opened the flap slightly, and exchanged words with the driver.

"Who is driving the wagon?" Jeanette asked, trying again to sit up. She finally did with considerable effort. She touched the wound on her arm. It was wrapped.

"It doesn't matter. For now, we should be safe."

"What happened? How did we..." she was trying to recall everything.

*Dinner.*

*Screams.*

*Hiding.*

*Rogue.*

"He was right there in front of me. How did we get out?"

"I honestly don't know, Jeanette. All I know is he threw you against the wall, stared at you for a few seconds, and then ran out the door. You were out cold. They didn't come back and after they left I made sure Bertha was safe and dragged you out of the house. I was able to find a wheelbarrow. It wasn't easy getting you into it. At the next village, I got us a wagon."

"Where are we going now?"

Hermes exhaled. He looked pained and tired. "Tell me Jeanette, why did you have to come? Why did you have to find me? Why all of..." he looked around searching, "this?"

"You knew I was coming, didn't you?" she asked softly, without accusation.

"No, I didn't," he answered. "I figured maybe someday somebody would. But I didn't know it would be two days ago and I didn't know it would be you."

A surge of confidence rushed through her. "But...but...I don't understand. Why were you so reluctant to help me? What are you so afraid of?"

"How did you know where to find me?"

"I just knew. I saw it. I could feel it. But I wasn't completely sure it was you because..."

"Because I didn't have green eyes?"

*The owl with green eyes.*

She stared. "How did you...?"

"Jeanette, I have lived many years. I have not always been the disfigured, old man that you see before you. Unfortunately, something drove me to that."

"Was it Cadmus?" she asked, forgetting about her pain for a moment.

"No. Not really. Mostly it was myself dealing precisely with what you are dealing with now."

"How do you know Cadmus?"

Hermes ignored the question. "Jeanette, if you would have left and turned away we wouldn't be dealing with any of this. But you are not going to do that are you?"

"I can't Hermes. I don't know how many ways I can make you believe that. I don't know what happened that day, but whatever it is moving me forward won't let me turn back. I can't see the full picture yet, but this is not the end."

"Well you are better than me. Because it tried to push me forward and I fought it. I fought it long and I fought it hard, and it ruined my life. That's why you found me...working... *alone.*"

Jeanette was quickly trying to connect the dots. "So your eyes used to be..."

"Green, yes," he said. The wagon moved along slowly. Jeanette was lost in the moment.

"But...but..." she stumbled, searching for more questions, more answers.

"One day, out of the blue, my eyes just changed. That's all I know. It was right around the time Braxton was born. The whole kingdom was so excited. I didn't know what to do.

"I did not see it as a gift; I saw it as a curse. I saw things, felt things as you say, but I fought them. I had other pursuits I was trying to accomplish with my life. At the time, I thought the promptings wanted me to go the wrong way. Over time, the more I fought, the more intense the visions came. The kingdom was falling further and further into decline. My spirit was saying help, but my head and my heart were yelling no. Eventually, broken and ashamed, the promptings left and the color left. For me it was a release. I shunned it out and was finally able to get on with my life."

He paused. Jeanette hung on every word. For the first time she felt like she understood, at least a little. "So you know what

I'm going through. You understand what's been happening to me."

He started shaking his head emphatically, "Jeanette, I don't understand it. Not in the slightest. I have no idea what it is about. But the only reason you are still with me and I have not left you on the side of the road is because I cannot bring myself to do it. I can't let what happen to me happen to you.

"As a scientist, I don't believe in fate. It is no coincidence that you found me. The odds are incalculable. As much as I would like to push you away - as I have done with the rest of my life - I can't."

"Does this mean you'll help me?"

"Well, you are still in the back of this wagon, aren't you? But I do have one request."

"What is it?"

"You cannot tell *anyone* what we just discussed. About my green eyes or anything. You have to promise me."

"I promise," she said sincerely. She needed his help and would keep his secret. "Thank you. I don't have anybody else I can trust."

"You keep thanking me. You need to stop that."

There was an awkward moment of silence. A connection was formed. If not a friendship, at least a working partnership. "Is it okay if I ask where we are going?"

"Well, I guess I should be asking you if you have any idea of where we *should* be going next."

All she knew was she needed to follow the remaining visions.

*A soldier standing across a large body of water.*

"I don't know for sure, but I know there is a soldier and he is standing across a body of water."

Hermes smiled. "It sounds like we're heading in the right direction then."

"Where?"

"As far away from the castle as we can get," Hermes said. "They will have people looking for us."

"You still haven't told me what connection you have to the castle."

"We don't need to worry about that now."

"And Rebekah?"

"We don't need to worry about her either. Lie down and get some more rest. We still have some travel ahead of us before we cross over into Bandar."

# CHAPTER 30

Cadmus moved quickly through the halls of the castle. He was furious. "Is the girl here?" he asked the guard standing in front of the door to his laboratory. Part of the lower level of the castle, his workshop was tucked out of the way of normal foot traffic.

"She is safe in the room, sir,"

"What happened? Where is Jeanette?"

"They must have known we were coming, my lord. When we got there, we found the girl tied up; like somebody left her as a present. She hasn't given us any information. We searched the workshop and found nothing. I sent the other half of the guard to try and find a trail."

Cadmus wanted to scream at the incompetency. "You are relieved of your post." The guard left without hesitation.

Cadmus opened the door to find Auryn sitting, her hands tied in front of her. She was staring at the floor. "Where is she, Auryn?" he said between his teeth.

Putting her hands up to her face, she started sobbing.

"Tell me where she is?"

Auryn muffled something into her palms. Suddenly, in a rage, he grabbed her by the hair and picked her up. She screamed out as he slammed her up against the wall.

"Please be quiet," he said, trying to compose himself. "Perhaps you don't understand the situation we are in. I gave you one simple task and you have failed. Where is she?"

"I'm so sorry," she stammered.

He wanted to slap her, but he did not. She moved away from him and retreated back to the chair. Taking a deep breath, he pulled his robe back down, and straightened his sleeves. He didn't like feeling desperate. Maybe he needed to change tactics.

"When was the last time you took your medicine?" he asked, more somber.

"About two days ago."

"Auryn, do you remember the talk we had before you left? It's the same talk we've had a number of times."

"Yes, of course."

"The only reason you are here – alive – is because of me. If you did not have my medicine, you would have died long ago. I keep you alive because it benefits me. Do you want to stay alive?"

"Yes."

"Then tell me something. Anything."

Auryn paused, "When I snuck out of the house the old man had a spy follow me. He saw me hand off the message. They didn't know anything other than they couldn't trust me. That's why they fled."

"Old man, what old man?"

"In Enzion, the one...the one Jeanette wanted to find. The one..." she stopped.

"The one?" Cadmus asked.

Auryn looked backed to the floor and answered, "The one who let us stay the night."

He eyed her suspiciously. Cadmus wondered how much Auryn actually knew. Did she know just how special Jeanette was? Did she know how important it was to have Jeanette at the castle?

"What about the other task I gave you? Did you get it?"

Auryn nodded and reached inside her pocket and pulled out a cloth. It was stained with a tiny smear of blood. She handed it to Cadmus.

"Well, that's a start."

"I'm sorry I wasn't able to bring her back."

"Tell me again about this old man. Are they together now?"

"I don't know. They tied me up and left me. They could be anywhere."

He walked over to his workbench, lined with bottles and vials; some empty and some containing various liquids and powders. "What was his name again?"

"His name is Hermes."

It didn't sound familiar. He picked up a bottle with blue liquid and poured a small amount into a bowl. "It's not your fault that she ran away," he continued. "You were doing what you were asked." He picked up another glass and poured a white powder into liquid. Mixing it, he walked over to Auryn. He held out the bowl, inviting her to drink.

Auryn was apprehensive, but reached up and took the bowl. She drank the concoction quickly and wiped her mouth. "What's going to happen next?" she asked, voice shaking.

Cadmus debated with himself. There were a few options available, but which one was best? He had finally found the time to study the burned rogue body found during the festival at Emerleigh, but it was burned beyond hope. He could not produce a specimen worth studying.

Would he still need Corwin? How was he going to get Braxton to come to terms with Lorelei? Who was Hermes?

*I have Jeanette's blood. Do I even need her anymore?*

He didn't know. But there was one thing he did know, and it was that he needed to cover his tracks.

"Don't you worry about what will happen next," he said, placing a gentle hand on Auryn's shoulder. "You have done your part and everything will work out in the end."

# CHAPTER 31

Later that night, Tristyn stood on Jacob's shoulders outside of Hermes shop. "Be careful," Jacob whispered. Tristyn was trying to open one of the windows around the back of the building.

Corwin knew the other soldiers had already been here and found nothing, but there was no information to which way Jeanette went. It was worth a second look.

They had already looked inside the shop on the ground floor.

Nothing.

But upon further inspection of the back yard, Corwin noticed a window that seemed out of place. There were no steps or ladder on the first floor that led to the second, so the only way to the second story was to climb.

"Got it," Tristyn said, popping the window open and climbing through. "I found a staircase."

Corwin and Jacob quickly entered the first floor again and listened. Corwin followed the creaking of Tristyn's footsteps to a door in the wall. Opening it, he found nothing but a simple cupboard.

The next moment the wall at the back of the cupboard opened to reveal Tristyn.

"What kind of person has a secret staircase in their house?" Corwin asked.

"I don't know, but apparently the guards didn't find it," Jacob said, leading them up the steps.

At the top was a small dwelling, barely furnished. Corwin walked over to one of the two windows in the room. It overlooked the main street.

"Whoever this man is," Tristyn said, "he doesn't want to be found."

"Well there has to be some clues here somewhere," Corwin said. "We don't know where to go next unless we find something."

"Something like this," Jacob said. He held up a piece of parchment from the trash bin.

*Farthing Tavern. Debt owed....*

"Is there a name on it?" Corwin asked.

Jacob smiled and answered, "Deacon."

\*\*\*

Thirty minutes later, they stood in front of Farthing Tavern on the outskirts of town

"If only we knew what he looked like," Corwin said, anxiety building. "He might not even be here."

"It's the best lead we have. Do you have another idea I don't know about?" Jacob asked.

Corwin exhaled. "Do we just go in and start asking around if people know him? I mean, what if we ask someone who happens to be chummy with him? That's a dead giveaway right there."

"For goodness sake, Corwin, are you a soldier or a sea

urchin? Try to relax. Let me handle it and you just follow along. Does that sound okay?"

Tristyn stood next to Corwin and snickered.

"You lead the way," Corwin replied.

Jacob turned to Tristyn. "Normally I wouldn't have a problem with you coming in, but we don't want to..."

"I know. I'll wait out here."

"Corwin, we are just two men on our way to Enzion stopping for a drink. That is all you need to worry about. I'll take care of the rest."

The pub was twice the size of any Corwin had been in. It was twice as loud too. Corwin had seen men in their element before, but this was a different breed of men than he was used too. They looked meaner, scrappier and drunker.

Jacob leaned over and whispered, "I hope you wore your big boy breeches."

"Get out of my way, little pisser!" an older gentlemen demanded, pushing by Corwin, almost knocking him over. Eyes wide, Corwin watched as he stumbled by. Jacob grinned.

Tables and stools filled the pub. In a backroom, there were more tables set up with men playing games of chance and where most of the noise and bickering was coming from. A few ladies waited tables.

Jacob raised his hand, summoning the bartender. A big, bald, unattractive man walked over. "Two pints," Jacob said simply. Corwin focused on the faces in the room. How were they ever going to find Deacon in a place like this? What if he wasn't even here?

"That'll be one piece," the bartender said.

Jacob paid him and then asked, "We're in town for some business and I need to get a message to Deacon. Do you know if he is around tonight?" Jacob's words were simple and had no hint of untruth.

The bartender shook his head, uninterested, "Can't say. I've never heard of him."

"Really?" Jacob asked surprised. "Hmm, I was told this is where I might be able to find him. Odd."

"Yes, it is odd," the bartender said, wiping off the counter and walking away again.

Jacob took a sip.

"Now what?" Corwin asked and also took a sip. Corwin's face stretched with disgust after the first sip. "Ugh."

Jacob laughed. "Don't worry, it will put some hair on your chest. And the bartender knows Deacon, it was all over his face. So now, one of two things should happen. Either nothing happens. Or, if he is here, the bartender will motion to him and let him know we were asking questions. If that's the case, he'll grab us down the road once we leave to find out what we wanted."

"Well that doesn't sound good. So what's the backup plan?"

"Well, other than the bartender, who else is likely to know all the people in a tavern?"

Corwin thought about it for a second. One of the girls walked by, her busy body bouncing along the way. "Need something my dear?" she asked Corwin with a smile.

He looked at Jacob. Jacob urged him on with a nod. "Uh, yes ma'am, actually I do," Corwin said.

She stood, waiting. He looked at his glass and then, holding his breath as best he could, chugged down the foul tasting substance. Jacob watched in delight.

He sighed long and hard. "I need," he said slowly, the ale sitting firm in his stomach, "another one of these."

"You too?" she asked to Jacob.

"Yes ma'am."

She came back with the drinks. "I've never seen you two in here. What are you here for?"

"Business," Jacob replied.

"Ha! Aint everybody."

"Do you know where I can find Deacon?" Jacob asked bluntly, sliding an extra coin across the table. She picked it up and slipped it into her shirt.

"I'm sure I have no idea what you are talking about," she said, gesturing her eyes toward the backroom to a table with a man eating alone.

Jacob smiled and said, "Thank you." Jacob downed the rest of his drink and wiped his chin. "You ready?"

Corwin hiccupped. His head spun and his stomach turned sour. Yet, he felt lighter. "I think so," he said, trying to bring Jacob into focus.

"Look, just follow my lead, and if you can't help, just stay out of the way."

"I can carry," Corwin started, and hiccupped again, "my weight."

"Sure you can," Jacob said, patting him on the shoulders. They made their way back to the table. Deacon took another bite of stew and ignored both of them. Corwin watched over Jacob's shoulder.

"I don't want any trouble," Jacob reassured. "I just need to find my daughter. I heard you might know where she went."

Deacon finished chewing and looked up. He thought for a minute. "Nope. Don't know nothing about a girl. Sorry I can't help."

Jacob pulled the other chair at the table out and sat down. Corwin looked around, nervous. Deacon smirked.

"Well this particular girl is special," Jacob said. "She has green eyes."

Deacon eyes shifted from Corwin, to Jacob.

"I don't want any trouble," Jacob said again, "I just want to know where she went."

"Like I said," Deacon said, slowly pushing his chair back,

"sorry I can't help." Then with a groan, Deacon heaved the whole table forward at Jacob and Corwin. It landed on Jacob and Corwin fell backwards. Deacon ran for the front door, trying to jump over the table, but Jacob reached up and grabbed his leg. Deacon's body slammed to the floor. Corwin watched as the bar patrons whooped and hollered with excitement at the duel.

Jacob pushed the table off of him and grabbed Deacon by the coat and turned him over. Jacob landed a couple of punches to the face before Deacon kicked him against the bar. Corwin moved out of the way just in time. He looked down to see Jacob grabbing his head in obvious pain.

"A little help," Jacob said.

"Of course," Corwin said.

Deacon was already up again and coming toward Corwin. Corwin swung and Deacon dodged and landed a punch to the stomach. Corwin doubled over as the ale in his stomach felt like it wanted to come back up his throat.

Deacon made for the front door, but not before Corwin came up from behind and jumped on top of him. They both went crashing through the entrance, toppling to the ground. The crowd continued to cheer and followed them out.

Outside, the lanterns hanging on both sides of the splintered entryway shined down on Corwin and Deacon as they exchanged blows. Corwin felt his adrenaline rising with each punch he landed and with each crack to his face. Almost as if he couldn't feel it; like he was enjoying it.

The crowd formed a circle around them. Corwin was getting weary, and could tell Deacon was too. Corwin swung a long, hard right and when Deacon moved out of the way, it sent Corwin spilling over, onto the ground. Before he knew it, Deacon was on top of him.

Deacon raised his fist, but before it fell, Jacob came up from behind and placed his blade under Deacon's chin.

Corwin rolled out of Deacon's grasp and breathed deep. Tristyn ran over to him. Deacon's eyes showed defeat.

"This isn't personal you understand," Jacob explained, "but I need to know where my daughter went."

Out of breath, Deacon finally answered between breaths. "They went to Bandar."

Jacob threw him back on the ground and walked over to Corwin.

"You could have stepped in a little sooner," Corwin said, putting his hand to his mouth, wincing at his first collection of battle wounds.

Jacob grinned and then looked at Tristyn. "Remember how I said one day I would take you to visit your people up north."

Tristyn nodded.

"You can thank your cousin for helping me keep my word."

# CHAPTER 32

Bandar.

It didn't feel any different than being in Amarin. The Tamblin river ran east and west across the northern border separating the two kingdoms. Halfway along the border it cut south and ran directly opposite of Pembrooke and then snaked out into the great sea.

*A soldier with chains around his ankles standing across a large body of water.*

Having crossed the river, Jeanette felt hopeful that they would find whatever soldier she was looking for. He was the next piece to the puzzle.

"We need to get going, out of the open," Hermes said.

She lay on the sandy edge of the river, drenched and cold. The afternoon sun hinted it's warmth through the branches. Her body told her to stay still, close her eyes and sleep.

The last twenty-four hours were spent in the back of a wagon. Hermes slept most of the way, though Jeanette was not sure how. Between the rattling of the wagon and the bumps in the road, sleep had come sporadic for her. But there had been a connection and more information.

Hermes once had green eyes. How? What kind of visions did he see? Why was he hiding? How did he know Cadmus?

Every time she looked at him, hoping to gain more answers. She tried to imagine his eyes, wide open and shining with the true color, but all she saw was an old man and burnt flesh.

"We need to go Jeanette," Hermes said again, making his way into the tree line.

Jeanette stood, twisted the water out of her shirt one more time, and followed behind him. The forest was not as dense as the Amarin side, but still wooded.

As she walked, Jeanette held out her hand, a tingle in her fingertips. Like the trees and the brush were somehow tempting her, calling her. Her body warmed and there was a surge of feeling that ran through her, a swelling. She stopped and put her hand firmly. The cold left and she felt a spark on the inside. It's as if the tree were providing sustenance, life.

"Would you come on!" he scolded. She let go of the tree feeling safe, protected.

*What does it mean to have the true gift?*

Did Cadmus have the gift? Or Braxton? What about Lorelei? Though Jeanette did not want to admit yet that she was grateful for the color change, she was gaining understanding. She knew she had a purpose.

"And you have to promise to do whatever I say," Hermes continued. "It has been a while since I have been here. And," he said sternly, "you cannot repeat anything I told you about my history and my eye color. That is strictly information between you and me, is that clear?'

"I understand," she said, even though she didn't. "How do you know all of these places? The inn at Samdon, the shortcut through the river, where we're going now?"

"I've been around," is all he said. "Now, if we can keep moving, I think..."

A large net fell from above, trapping the two underneath.

Jeanette tried to stand. The net was thick and heavy. Trying to reposition herself on the ground, her elbow moved slightly and pain shot through her arm. The wound opened again.

Six men came out of the trees, each holding spears. Their eyes were blue against the brown of nature. Each wore a skirt and a loose shirt. Their heads flowed with white hair.

They communicated to each other in hushed tones as they approached.

"Everything will be okay, Jeanette. Just let me do the talking," Hermes said.

"What brings you into our land?" one of the men asked.

"I am a friend of Larrick," Hermes said. The men looked at each other, surprised. "It has been a while since I have called on him. But I can assure you he will be willing to accept my arrival. My name is Hermes."

The lead scout whispered something to one of the soldiers. The other man nodded and ran off.

"What now?" Jeanette whispered.

"Well, if Larrick is still alive, then we will be welcomed into the village. In a little while we'll be dry and fed and all will be well."

"*If* he's still alive?"

"Like I said, it's been a while."

Jeanette rested her cheek on the ground, the net hanging heavy on her head. She closed her eyes and tried to remain calm. Addy came to mind. Was she happy? Had she made friends? Was Lorelei making her life miserable? It had only been a week since they were together, but a week was six days longer than they had ever been apart.

Finally, the scout returned. "Let them free," he yelled from a distance. Without hesitation, the other men removed the net. Jeanette rose while a couple of them helped Hermes up. "I am sorry for the net; it was only a precaution."

"That is okay. Better to be safe," Hermes said brushing off.

"So it is true," one of the other men muttered, gazing at Jeanette as she brushed her hair back out of her face.

The lead guard quickly moved to chasten him, but Jeanette reached out her hand and said, "No, no, it's okay. He's okay to ask. Yes, I am one of the girls from Emerleigh." She glanced at Hermes, wondering if she was saying the right things.

He smiled. "We should head to the village now." Three of the Bandar men led the way, walking in front of Jeanette and Hermes, while three followed in back.

A gathering of people met them as they entered the village. A change came over Hermes as they did so; a peace appeared that hadn't been there before. His pace quickened and there was a smile on his face. He turned to Jeanette. "You are going to like it here."

Down the center of the village was a path with crude, tented dwellings on the left. Further down on the right sat Tamblin's shore.

"You have gotten old my friend," an elderly gentlemen in the middle of the group called out to Hermes. He was average height, lean, dressed as the scouts had been, but his hair was longer. A simple braid also donned the patch of hair on his chin.

He opened his arms as Hermes got closer. "Larrick," Hermes said, kissing his friend on both cheeks. "It has been far too long."

Larrick grinned from ear to ear. "It is so good to see you." Larrick caught a glimpse of Jeanette over Hermes shoulder, and respectfully bowed his head. "And you have an important companion with you."

"Larrick, may I introduce, Jeanette."

Larrick stepped forward and extended a hand of welcome to Jeanette. "My dear, you have come a long way. And we are so happy to accept you. Welcome to Norbrook."

Jeanette was transfixed. As he reached out and took both of her hands in welcome she felt calmness radiate through her.

"Oh Larrick, let the dear child go," came a voice from behind. A woman stepped beside Larrick. She was the most beautiful woman Jeanette had ever seen. She had white hair that let off a golden hue. It hung down to her waist, flowing freely. She was the same height as Jeanette. Her skin was smooth and the tunic she wore was as white as the hottest sun, it complemented her clear, blue eyes perfectly. Behind the woman stood a young girl, not much younger than Jeanette.

The woman put her arms around Jeanette. "Am I the only one that can see this child is hurt?" she asked. "What happened?"

"We were attacked by a pack of Rogues in Samdon," Hermes answered.

The woman shook her head. "They are getting closer and closer to our border every year it seems. It won't be long before they are ravaging all the kingdoms."

"No need to worry now. You are safe with us," Larrick said, putting his arm around his wife. "This is my wife, Vanora."

"We need to get this one looked at," she said, pointing to Jeanette's elbow.

"Everyone back up and make room," one of the scouts said, walking in front of Larrick. The crowd moved obediently, but still gathered in as close as they could to watch Jeanette pass. They were curious, but not like the people of Pembrooke. Pembrooke was fever pitched with cheering, loud calls and pageantry. This was different; it was reverent. It stayed quiet, even after Jeanette was inside.

Inside the tent was a small cot and the wall was lined with bags, vials, and instruments.

"Jeanette, don't worry," Hermes said as she got on the

table. "Larrick is one of the best physicians in Bandar."

"Well, that may be pushing it a bit, my friend," Larrick responded, taking hold of Jeanette's arm. She winced.

"I am sure it needs stitches, but I was not able to do it myself as we traveled," Hermes said to Larrick. "I got the wound to stop bleeding, but it reopened today."

Larrick took the makeshift sling off and removed the bandage. The wound was bigger than Jeanette had thought; dark blood caked along the crevices as fresh blood seeped through.

"It will certainly need to be closed," Larrick said, walking over to the wall and pulling off a vial. Tension built at the thought of a needle going in and out of her flesh.

Larrick took the vial, full of small seeds, and poured some of them into a bowl. He ground them into powder and added a small amount of water. "This will help sterilize the area."

Putting some of the mixture on his finger, he ran it over the wound. Jeanette winced, waiting for pain.

None came.

Hermes chuckled. "It's easy to forget that the people of Bandar have the gift of healing. A wonderfully blessed gift indeed."

Jeanette focused on Larrick. When he reached out his hand to welcome her, the feeling of calm. Was that also a gift?

"Can you give her some waning leaf mixture?" Larrick asked Hermes, pointing to another bottle.

Hermes took the bottle and poured some of it into a separate bowl. "This will help you relax," Hermes said, handing it to her. Jeanette took the cup in her hand and put it to her lips. It was distinct and smelt familiar. She was sure it was similar to the sedative Cadmus gave her in Pembrooke. She swallowed it. Hermes watched close and Larrick took the cup back.

"How do you feel?" Hermes asked, standing right in front

of her.

Jeanette sighed. "I'm hungry, tired, aching...I've had better days."

"Go ahead and lie down. When the medicine starts working, you will feel a little light headed." She did not hesitate. She lay back on the table and closed her eyes. The animal skin on the table was soft and welcoming. This was a peaceful place.

For a moment.

Then behind her lids, she saw flashes. The same images, but they were different. They were clearer than before. She wanted to reach for them; wanted to grab them, but this time she waited. She waited for them to come to her.

*A castle in flames. A long figure hanging out of a window calling to Jeanette to stay away.*

*An old sign hanging with a picture of an owl with green eyes hanging over a merchant shop. A young couple is underneath the sign.*

*A soldier with chains around his ankles standing across a large body of water. Around him lay dead bodies.*

Jeanette woke up, her body dripping with sweat. Her mouth was open to scream, but she didn't. She sat up on the cot, not noticing the fresh bandage on her arm.

"Everything's okay, Jeanette," Larrick said calmly. "The medicine is wearing off. Your will be fine," he said.

"I saw more."

"More of the visions?" Hermes asked. Confusion filled Larrick's face.

"Yes."

"How many times have you had these visions?"

She wiped her brow and thought. "At the festival with Cadmus, that's when I first saw them. Then the night that Auryn and I left Pembrooke. And then now."

"And they just happened, just random, for no reason?" Hermes asked.

The first time she saw the visions was at the festival. Cadmus gave her the vial, she drank it and waited. The change wasn't instant, but after the color came, that's when the visions came. The second time was also with Cadmus. She was upset and frustrated; he gave her something to calm her. She lay down and...

"I don't know about the first time, but the second time, Cadmus gave me some medicine to calm me down. I cannot remember the name. It was a sedative. The visions came after I took it," she said. "What did you give me tonight?"

"Something similar, it sounds like," Larrick answered.

"What does a sedative do?" Hermes asked. "It helps to calm you down, to relax. Maybe you just need to try and relax, Jeanette. To get your body and mind into a state where it can focus."

*Focus.*

Everything over the last few days had made it almost impossible to focus. All the questions and concerns. Running from the kingdom that was supposed to protect her. Feeling a sense of mission to obey the visions. So far, they had not led her astray, but she wanted it to be clearer.

"There is only one way to find out if the medicine triggers my visions," she said, lying back down. "Larrick, give me some more."

"I don't think that's such a good idea, Jeanette. When I said you needed to focus more, I didn't mean to go and pour more medicine down your throat."

"But it has to be that. I am tired of the visions coming a little at a time. I need to know what to do next, where to go. I can feel it wanting to come out."

"And it will, as you control it," Hermes added.

She looked at both of them in disbelief. "But we are so close, Hermes. This last time I saw more."

"I'm not sure what visions you are talking about, Jeanette,"

Larrick said, "but forcing medicine for an unintended purpose is not wise."

"We can talk about it more as soon as you lie down and get some more rest," Hermes said. "We are safe here. We can take it one step at a time."

"I'm perfectly fine," Jeanette said, trying to stand. As soon as she did, the blood rushed from her head and she fell to the side. Larrick caught her and maneuvered her back onto the table. Her stomach felt ill. She didn't say anything, just closed her eyes, and drifted.

The last thing that crossed her mind before falling asleep was Addy.

*Addy will keep me in control.*

# CHAPTER 33

Addy stood with a serving tray, waiting for Marah to place the freshly cooked sausages on it. Addy was tired.

After meeting with Jacob, Corwin and Tristyn a few nights before, her and Marah talked late into the night. The same thing happened last night. Addy was hesitant to tell her too many specifics about Jeanette; she did not want to feel like she was boasting – 'my best friend, you know, the jewel of Amarin that ran away.' Marah was pleasant and seemed to welcome the tales.

"Were you able to see Brandy this morning? Do you know if she's doing better?" Marah asked.

"Not yet, I'm hoping to go after breakfast." Brandy had been steadily getting better, but was bored out of her mind. Addy made trips as she could to keep her spirits up.

Marah finished putting the sausages on the platter when Tilly walked in. "Alright ladies, let's get a move on. Lady Lorelei is waiting in the garden."

Addy and Marah exchanged looks. They had talked about Lorelei, too.

"Make sure to put on your best face for ol' bright eyes," Marah said, fluttering her lashes. Addy laughed, took off her apron, and grabbed one of the serving trays.

"Does it really take five of us to serve breakfast?" Addy asked as they lined up to leave the kitchen.

"Welcome to the castle!" Marah said as they went out the door.

A few moments later, they lined the courtyard, ready to enter. As soon as Addy saw Lorelei, her stomach turned.

"It's about time," Lorelei blasted, "I certainly hope it's not cold."

Addy felt her stare. The kitchen staff placed all of the items on the table. Marah asked, "Is there anything you need, my lady?"

Lorelei looked over at Emilia, who joined her for breakfast, to see if they needed anything. "I think we are fine." Marah gave a nod and the kitchen staff started walking away.

"However," Lorelei said, after biting into one of the sausages, "is there any way, if the food is not to my liking, to get it prepared again? Or perhaps ask for something different the next time altogether? Too much meat does not sit well with me," she said putting her hand over her stomach, comfortingly.

"Of course my lady, anything you wish," Marah said, without hesitating.

Lorelei smiled approvingly and then pointed to Addy in the line, "You...step forward." Addy went rigid and turned blush red. She paused for a moment and then obeyed. "What is your name?" Lorelei asked. Heat built on the back of Addy's neck. She had known Lorelei since they were little girls.

"I asked you what your name is, girl," Lorelei asked curtly. Addy tried to stop her face from contorting into what she was feeling. She remembered all the times she saw Jeanette's face after mentioning Lorelei.

Before Addy could open her mouth, Marah stepped up, "Her name is Addy; she is new, my lady."

Lorelei's eyes pierced through Marah and then turned back to Addy. "Addy, you will stay here, standing, while we eat our breakfast, just in case anything is out of sorts. Is that clear?"

Addy shot a glimpse to Marah and then looked back at Lorelei. For the first time in her life, she hated Lorelei. "Yes, my lady."

Lorelei nodded and took a sip of tea. Emilia excused the rest of the girls and Addy stood, watching Lorelei nibble and banter with Emilia. Addy felt cold and alone.

Steady breaths contained her anger. She didn't like feeling angry, but the freedom that came with it was refreshing.

# CHAPTER 34

Everything around Jeanette was foreign: the tents, the lack of tension, and the sense of family and togetherness. Everyone seemed at peace.

In front of Larrick's hut the fire crackled. Earlier, she had tried to fight rest, wanting the visions to come, but her body gave in to the need for sleep. Now the sun had set and dinner was ending. She had never seen the orange species of fish that she had eaten. It was tart, but filling.

A large group of onlookers had gathered when Jeanette first came out of Larrick's infirmary. "That is enough for one night," Vanora said in her stern, matriarchal way. "Everyone has had a good look, now back to your homes." The crowd obeyed, slowly turning and heading back the way they had come, some periodically turning back to get one last peek. Jeanette could see their bright blue eyes through the fire light of the night.

"I'm sure you're sick of being ogled over, my dear," Vanora said.

"I've gotten used to it," Jeanette said. "No more than me

catching a glimpse of any one of your eyes. It's different; it's beautiful."

"Another wonderful meal, mother" Larrick said. Around the fire sat Hermes, Jeanette, Larrick, Vanora and their niece, Salinda. She had been standing behind Vanora when Jeanette first arrived.

"Do you always eat dinner outside?" Jeanette asked Larrick.

"As long as the weather is nice, why wouldn't we?"

"It is beautiful up here in the north country," Hermes added, lying back with his eyes half closed. The gentle, cool breeze from the nearby river ran across Jeanette's skin, accentuating his point.

"What about the war? How has it affected you?"

"Thankfully, we have avoided it," Larrick said, with a sense of relief in his voice. "We get reports, but nothing more. Our goal all along has been to avoid it." Larrick turned to Hermes, "Is there any end in sight?"

"Seems to be getting worse every year. The armies of Tamir are literally walking right over us," Hermes said. "This is sorry for me to say, but I don't know how they haven't just rammed us through yet. It doesn't seem like we put up much of a fight."

Larrick shook his head. "Thankfully, we have been spared. Not since we were driven from our homes," Larrick looking around the village. "We're safe here. We've learned to call it home and manage."

"This isn't your home?" Jeanette asked.

"Well, it is now," Larrick said, reaching out for Vanora's hand. "Has been for some time. Back where we are originally from - more north, closer to the coast – the situation became complicated. Bandar avoided the conflict between your people and Tamir for a long time, but eventually, the Brown Eyes needed somewhere to find more resources. It started out slow, at first. Our people wanted to avoid a conflict with them; military is not our strength. We would give them what they wanted just to leave us alone. After a while, they realized they could take it: food, materials, medicines, and even labor. They came one day and took and unfortunately," he said, with a sorrowful glance to Vanora, "we weren't ready."

"Are all people of Bandar in hiding?" Jeanette asked.

"No, we are not a kingdom like you are used to. There is no king and queen, nor any ruler to govern the people. Each clan has their own say. Some chose to stand their ground and fight; while others like us chose to try and find a safe place to wait it out, out of the reach of Tamir."

There was a moment of tense silence. Jeanette knew the general story of the people of Bandar: quiet and reserved people who lived off the sea. But she had never heard this story before.

"My cousin, Tristyn, he is part Bandar," Jeanette said. "His mother was killed." Salinda, who had seemed disinterested in the conversation, perked up. "I know it has been hard on him."

"Do you really know how hard it's been?" Salinda asked.

"Salinda, not now," Larrick said.

"I just want to make sure I understand," Salinda continued, agitated, "that the girl with green eyes who gets to go live in the castle knows what it's like to have your land and your parents taken from you?"

"I said that's enough, Salinda," Larrick demanded. Salinda kept her eyes on Jeanette, waiting for an answer. When none came, she got up and walked into her tent.

"I apologize, Jeanette," Vanora said. "She is a spirited young girl trying to find her way."

"It's okay," Jeanette said, but Salinda's words sat with her, weighing her down. She didn't know what it was like. Did she really know Tristyn? Would she have really run away with him to Bandar?

"Well that's enough action for me for one day, I'm ready for slumber," Hermes said, getting up. Larrick followed suit, said his good nights and went to bed. Jeanette could not bring herself to leave the comfort of the fire or the presence of Vanora.

"After all you've been through today, I thought you would be ready to pass out," Vanora said.

"I just have a lot on my mind," Jeanette responded. "Sitting here, feeling the fire and listening to the river...it's nice."

"Well," Vanora started, "I'd much rather be back up north. If you think this is peaceful, you haven't seen anything. When you are next to the shore with sand as far as you can see; that is peaceful. The water birds talking over your head. The boats creaking by the dock. You can see the moon. It looks like it's this big," Vanora said, stretching out her hand to make a huge circle.

Jeanette laughed.

"But, that is no more," Vanora continued. "Tamir came without warning. Took what they wanted and burned the rest." She paused and there was sadness in her eyes as she looked toward the hut. "Salinda's parents didn't make it. There were quite a few that didn't. She is angry and bitter...and has every right to be. She's had trouble finding her own peace."

Thoughts of Jaren came to Jeanette's mind. She hadn't made peace with his death, not yet. And she knew Tristyn hadn't made peace with losing her mother. In a small way, she understood Salinda's emotions. "Why didn't you fight?"

"We had no army to speak of, at least not covering the whole kingdom. It was every clan for themselves. Some fought, but it was of no use. We could not stand against the Brown Eyes."

"Why didn't Amarin come to your aid?"

"I don't know for sure," Vanora shrugged, "but I'm sure Amarin's focus is, and will continue to be, on Amarin."

*Amarin.*

A recent history of doubt, fear, and disgrace. Jeanette was now part of that history.

"How do you know Hermes?" Jeanette asked.

"Hermes is a physician by training. When we first met, the war with Tamir was still young; it wasn't near as bad as it is now. Travel was not as restricted and it was easier to move around the land. He was retired and seeking ways to enhance his work, gain a greater understanding of his field of practice, to..."

"So he came to learn from Larrick about the traditions in medicine," Jeanette said.

"Exactly," Vanora said. "That was when we still lived back home. We used to enjoy his visits. He had great insight, particularly with childbirth. He wanted to understand more about our ways, but he also taught us. He is very gifted. Larrick has always been leery of outsiders, regardless of who they are, but there was something about Hermes that he trusted. I did to. He was - is - a good soul that wants to do well. Larrick could see that. They became very fond of each other."

"What about the scar on his face?" Jeanette prodded.

"He had the scars when we first met him. We never felt the need to ask and he never felt the need to share."

*Jeanette, you can't tell anyone about my green eyes or anything.*

She wanted to ask about the castle and about Rebekah, but she didn't. Why all the secrets? If Larrick and Vanora did not know, how would she ever find out?

"What about you? What are you doing here? What's your history," Vanora asked.

"I feel like I'm floating and don't have any way to direct the way I'm going."

"My mother used to tell me that the waves can fight

against the moon all they want, but it's still going to drag them to shore." Jeanette thought for a moment, trying to give the words meaning.

"Stop fighting it," Vanora said. "Those beautiful green eyes you have are not coincidence. They are taking you where you need to go. Something tells me it's going to do all of us a lot of good in the end."

Vanora's voice was calming and Jeanette felt her sincerity, her faith. "Thank you, Vanora."

Jeanette stood up and started to walk toward the tent, but she found herself wandering toward the river shore. The sky was clear and the night was quiet; everyone else had gone to bed.

On the shore, the sand cool to the touch, she thought of Vanora's words.

*Don't fight it.*

She hadn't been fighting it, had she? She was trying to do everything the visions and the feelings had been telling her to do. At least that's what it felt like. But she wanted answers. She needed to be in control.

As the river flowed, she felt the cool breeze off the waves run across her cheek. She picked up a stick sitting next to her and tossed it in. It landed on top of the water and washed downstream.

*I'm not in control.*

The thought came loud and clear. She wasn't in control, and for the first time she felt it and her mind didn't argue.

*What am I supposed to do next?*

She thought of the visions.

The lone figure at the castle, in peril. She wasn't supposed to go to the castle, and she didn't. Was the person safe?

A sign with an owl had led her to Hermes, who once had green eyes. She was supposed to find him and he led her to Bandar. Across the shore, but there was no soldier.

The warrior standing, chained, in anguish. Dead bodies all around him. She needed to find an answer, to know where to go. The soldier was her next step.

Jeanette looked across the river. Trees. Darkness.

No soldier.

She situated herself more comfortably and breathed slowly. Closing her eyes, she cleared her mind and tried to remember what she could.

A river. Across the river, on the shore, a soldier. He was too far away though, she couldn't see.

*Don't fight it.*

Her body slumped a little.

*I won't fight it.*

Instantly a flash of light came before her eyes and she was hurdling across the shore, over the water, and to the other side toward the soldier.

*A soldier with chains around his ankles standing across a large body of water. Around him lay dead bodies and dead trees. Enemies approached from behind, hidden behind the branches.*

She still could not see his face, but he was guarded, unsure, and held his sword ready to attack. He stood, surrounded by death, around him bodies and old, famished trees. She had never seen trees like them. The enemy was upon him.

He needed her help. She needed to unchain him.

She opened her eyes, peering out across the river. Blinking, she could not erase the image from view, as if the soldier was there, standing across the shore from her.

Excited, she jumped up and ran back to the village and into Hermes tent.

"The soldier in my vision...the one across the river. I saw more this time."

"What do you mean you saw more?" Hermes asked, sitting up, rubbing the sleep from his eyes.

"He's across the river, near a field of trees. I can't describe them, but they were once beautiful. Does that mean anything to you?"

Hermes eyes woke instantly. "Yes," Hermes said. "There is only one place like that. It's the sakura tree that you describe. They used to grow in Brighton. It is north of Samdon. We passed it on the way here in the carriage."

Jeanette did not remember anything from the wagon ride other than being groggy from lack of sleep and the pain in her arm.

"Are you sure we need to go *back* across the river?" Hermes asked, a tired look in his eye. Doubt hit Jeanette. The vision had told her to come across the river to find the soldier. She had crossed the river and now knew where he was.

"Yes," she said firmly. "He is in Brighton. He has to be."

# CHAPTER 35

"Well," Jacob said, wiping the water from his face, "we are now officially trespassing." They were cold and wet and walking in the Bandar forest. They left the horses tied up near the bank, hidden from plain view. Stepping quietly, carefully, they walked in a single file; Corwin in front with Tristyn in back. Corwin wondered how ready Tristyn was for whatever may happen.

At the sound of rustling, they all three suddenly turned together. Corwin put his hand on the hilt of his sword.

"We need to find cover," Jacob whispered. Corwin held his finger up to his lips and began to draw his sword. In an instant, two tiny objects shot past his ear, one right after the other. One flew into the brush behind them, the other one hit Tristyn in the upper left arm. Tristyn cried out in pain.

Darts.

Corwin peered into the forest, trying to find the assailant.

Nothing.

Another dart flew by and Corwin saw its origination point. Men were running towards them. Tristyn's eyes started to wander and he wobbled. Jacob caught him before he fell.

Corwin turned to yell at Jacob as a dart pinged off his sword. Another dart came from the left and missed Jacob, hitting Tristyn in the leg. The boy did not flinch; he was out cold.

"Take Tristyn and start back over the river," Corwin yelled.

"It's too late," Jacob exclaimed, "we are surrounded!"

They huddled, covering Tristyn. But it did not matter, when the net hit them they fell to the ground.

Corwin looked around at the Blue Eyes hovering over them. "You are not supposed to be over the river. Why are you in our land?" the soldier demanded.

"I am sent on official..." Corwin started.

"We are looking for my daughter," Jacob interrupted. "We think she may have come through here and she might be in danger."

The guards exchanged a look of uncertainty. "You will come with us," the soldier said.

Later, they appeared in the village, their hands bound and sacks over their head. Corwin could not see anything through the darkness. Finally, they were stopped and commanded to get on their knees. Corwin obeyed.

"Larrick, we found them just off the river shore. One of them is an Amarin soldier," the lead scout said throwing Corwin's sword on the ground.

"Why are you here?" Larrick asked, the sacks pulled from their heads. Corwin looked around to find that Jacob and Tristyn were near him, though Tristyn still lay on the ground, unconscious. Their horses had also been brought.

"We are looking for my daughter, Jeanette," Jacob replied. "My name is Jacob, I am her father. Have you seen her?"

"I have no reason to believe you are who you say you are," Larrick said, not answering the question. Larrick's eyes shifted to the lead soldier. Corwin could tell Larrick knew something.

"My daughter would have been traveling with a man, an older gentleman...she's seventeen...she has black hair that goes down past her shoulders..."

"And green eyes," Corwin blurted out. Jacob closed his eyes as if remembering that yes, his daughter did have green eyes.

A crowd of villagers began to form as the drama unfolded. "If you are Jacob, the girl's father, then who are you?" Larrick asked Corwin.

"My name is Corwin. I have been sent from the castle to help find her." Behind him, Corwin heard Tristyn roll over and start to get up. Larrick looked at Jacob and pointed at the boy, questioning.

"This is my nephew..."

"His name is Tristyn," Salinda blurted out. Corwin felt the adrenaline from knowing Jeanette had been here. Tristyn tried to stay on one knee, but was wobbly.

Jacob looked past Larrick, at Salinda. "So Jeanette has been here?"

"They were here yesterday, but left this morning."

"Where did they go?" Corwin asked.

The murmuring in the crowd built. Larrick looked at Salinda with restraint. He turned to his people. "We have, for the second night, guests to our village. I know there is a lot of excitement and I thank you for your concern, but all is safe. Please return to your tents."

Everyone started to disperse. Larrick told his soldiers to untie Jacob, Corwin and Tristyn.

Tristyn reached his hands up, rubbing his eyes. "Where are we?" he asked, hazy.

"Shhh..." Jacob responded. "Everything is going to be okay."

Larrick walked over to Tristyn. "The affects should wear off after a while. We will give you something to drink to help."

Salinda put one of Tristyn's arms around her neck to steady him. Tristyn looked up briefly and said, still groggy, "Uh...you have blue eyes." Salinda smiled and did not respond as they headed into one of the tents.

"Where did they go?" Corwin asked. "What do you know about this man she's with?"

"What I am about to tell you may be hard to believe, but it is all true," Larrick started. He then told about Jeanette's travels, Hermes, and the visions.

"What do you mean visions?" Corwin asked, trying to make sense of the news.

"She believes she has a purpose," Vanora said.

"To do what?" Jacob asked.

"I don't know, but she is searching for a soldier who she says is across the river. She thinks he will help her know what to do," Larrick said.

Jacob and Corwin exchanged glances. Was she looking for Corwin? Did she know that he was trying to find her?

"I am going after her," Jacob said. "This has gone too far."

"The boy is in no condition to travel," Larrick said, referring to Tristyn. "It would be better if you wait here, to see if she returns."

"What if he stays here with us?" Salinda said.

"I don't think that is a good idea," Jacob said. "We sincerely appreciate your hospitality, but he should be with me."

"I would like to stay," Tristyn whispered from the tent door. He looked groggy and unsteady, but there was a hint of excitement in his eyes.

Jacob looked at Tristyn and then at Larrick. "He is welcome here among our people and I promise you, he will be cared for," Larrick said.

Vanora walked next to Larrick and took his hand in hers. "Yes, it is alright for him to stay with us. He will need rest to fully recover."

"Very well. It is a kind offer. Corwin and I will track Jeanette."

A knot stuck in Corwin's throat.

*Under no circumstances should you try to apprehend her yourself.*

"I have to report back to the castle," Corwin said, unsure of the pronouncement.

"Are you sure that's the right thing to do?" Jacob asked.

"She seemed very determined to avoid the castle," Larrick suggested.

Corwin struggled. Everything Cadmus said had made sense. She needed protecting. She needed to avoid running around the kingdom, unguarded. She would be safe at the castle.

"I think the castle cares very much about her and wants nothing but her safety. If she continues to run around the kingdom, looking for...whatever...how safe can she be?"

"You have honorable intentions, young soldier," Larrick started, "but I wish no danger to come to me or my people. We have avoided the conflict long enough."

"The end goal for all of us - me, Jacob, and the castle - is to find her and keep her safe. Maybe they can help. If we don't find her, it could end up causing more trouble for your people."

Corwin's heart said Jeanette knew exactly what she was doing, but his understanding of Jeanette knew that his heart wasn't one hundred percent trustworthy.

"As long as Amarin knows we have not provoked anything," Larrick said. "All we want is peace."

"That is what we all want," Corwin said, mounting his horse. He reached his hand out to Jacob. "Good luck. If you find her, I hope you can talk some sense into her."

"I've been trying for years, no reason to stop now."

At Corwin's kick, the horse bolted back toward Amarin.

# CHAPTER 36

"Every bit of intelligence that we have says that the Brown Eyes should be making their way to us in two or three days," Wesley said, running his finger along the map.

Since the cleanup of the rogue attack in Samdon, John's men had moved a little farther north following the main road. John had never been to Brighton, though he had heard of it's beauty. Sakura blossoms far and wide that stretched forth like small, pink balls of cotton. But now there was row after row of lifeless bark and branches with no color. Time and war had changed everyone, everything.

"They should be coming this way and our orders are to hold them off," Wesley added.

The other lieutenants in the room agreed. Burleigh, as usual, was standing unassumingly in the background. Usually this would be the point where John felt flustered. His heart urging him to do more than just defend. To fight.

The feeling did not come.

"If we hold here, here, and here, that should cover all the possible routes. It's a straight fight, man for man, we just have to be ready and fight harder."

All of the men looked up from the map at the same time. There was a commotion coming from camp. Men were cheering and getting louder by the second. John motioned for Burleigh to go and see what was going on.

"Have there been any more rogue sightings?" John asked.

"None, thankfully," Gabriel answered.

Burleigh ran back into the tent. His mouth opened, but no words came out.

"Well?" John asked. He could not wait any longer and finally pushed Burleigh aside to go out and look for himself. Burleigh put his hand on John's chest to stop him.

"Just wait," he nodded. "She's coming to you."

"She? What are you talking about?"

"John, it's her, it's really her. Everything they said is true. A green eyed girl. And she's here!"

John heard what Burleigh said, but it did not translate logically. He motioned for the other men to leave the tent. "What do you mean a girl with green eyes?"

"Just like it sounds, " Burleigh said, shouting over the noise. "She's here and she wants to talk to you." Burleigh opened the tent flap again to look outside.

"Why does she want to talk to me?"

"How do I know? Crunch, she really has green eyes!"

If there was a green eyed girl, why was she coming to him? What was he supposed to do with her?

"She is right outside the tent," Burleigh said softly, waving John over to the door. Burleigh leaned over and ran his palm along John's hair. John batted him away quickly.

"Well, let her in. Let's see what she wants."

Burleigh grinned. "I'm so excited." Burleigh opened up the flap and stepped outside. John wiped his brow and exhaled.

Burleigh came back in. "Captain, may I introduce..."

"Jeanette!?" John exclaimed.

"John!?" Jeanette answered.

"Well that spoiled all my fun," Burleigh said. "I take it you two know each other."

"We grew up together," Jeanette said. Hermes also walked in, standing behind Jeanette.

"We're from the same town," John corrected. "So it was you," he chuckled. "Amazing!" After the initial shock of seeing someone he knew, he had finally focused on her eyes. Bright, clear and green. The thought registered that he found her taller, older, and more beautiful than he remembered.

Being a few years older than Jeanette, he did not know her very well. Over the years he had built respect for her father, Jacob, and was friends with her brother, Jaren. All John ever wanted was to leave home, to go and fight. To get away from the girls in town eying him and his father trying to push him and his sister up the social ladder.

"Look, I don't know if this is some kind of farce or a prank to get back at my sister for always tormenting you, but I have nothing to do with it and I don't need you here."

Hermes and Burleigh exchanged looks.

"How is dear sweet Lorelei anyway?" John continued.

"You haven't changed at all," Jeanette said, crossing her arms and shaking her head. He felt the sting in her words. The look on Jeanette's face changed quickly. "What do you mean how is Lorelei doing? You haven't heard?"

"Heard what?" John said, frustration continuing to build.

"John, what have you heard about the green eyed girls? You did hear that there were two, right?"

Two girls.

Emerleigh.

The realization came to him suddenly.

Jeanette continued, "Lorelei is the other girl. She is at the castle. More than likely she will be Prince Braxton's wife."

There was a moment of silence, then a loud, piercing

laugh. Full of animation, it took everything John had to stay upright. Finally, he finished with a loud cough.

Jeanette looked at Burleigh, who just shrugged.

"What is so funny?"

"Right," he said sarcastically. "There is absolutely nothing funny about it." John's brain was trying to keep up with the situation. He could not take it. A part of him felt like he was having a breakdown, living in some alternate reality. "If Lorelei is at the castle, then what on earth are you doing here...and who in creations name are you?" he said, pointing to Hermes.

"My name is Hermes. I am Miss Jeanette's...escort. I am here to help."

"Of course you are," John said. "Everyone's here to help. So why has the kingdom sent you here? On a grand tour, to boost morale, give us a hip hip hooray speech as we watch ourselves go down in a ball of glory? I'm surprised my sister didn't come herself to rub her newfound position in my face."

"No," Jeanette said boldly, "the castle has no idea I am here. I broke from the caravan before it ever even reached the castle. Chances are they are looking for me now. I've been on the run."

"On the run?" John said puzzled. "On the run from what?"

"On the run, looking for you. I've come to help."

"You? Come to help?"

"Young man, do you know what this young lady has been through to get here?" Hermes said.

"Do you have any idea what we're doing out here?" John shot back. "This isn't a game of chance or eye color. It's war!"

"I know its war," Jeanette stated, stepping forward, her eyes firmly locking into his.

John had had enough. He moved closer, visibly angry. He was toe to toe with Jeanette, so upset he was spitting. "Have you seen a man have his arm cut off in the middle of battle?"

Jeanette did not answer.

"Have you seen a man have an arrow go through his eye and come out the other side with part of his brain attached to it?"

Jeanette looked away.

"Have you heard a man begging for mercy while his leg was being sawed...?"

"Enough!" Hermes yelled. "That's quite enough."

"Yes, I would say it's quite enough. I am sorry your trip has been in vain, my lady. You can offer no help here," John said, signaling Burleigh to see them out.

Jeanette did not move. Hermes placed his hand on her shoulder, "Let's go, Jeanette."

As Burleigh opened the door to the tent, John felt the excitement spilling in from the rest of the camp. As Jeanette walked out, the whole camp cheered.

John's words came back to him.

*You? Come to help?*

John saw confidence in his men's faces. He groaned. What was he supposed to do? His hands were already tied and if she wasn't here on official business from the castle, wouldn't that only make things worse? Did he even care anymore?

Jeanette did not walk out into the crowd. She turned around and came closer to John. "You don't have to give up. I know you have lost hope. I don't know what I can do to help, but I want to help."

His head told him to listen, but his emotions were in control. "I told you to leave," he said, trying to walk past her. She reached out and grabbed his arm. John stopped and looked at Jeanette. "You can't just show up and change everything. It doesn't work like that." He looked at her hand on his arm. She finally moved it.

"I know that, John. That's not the point. You need to take the men and empty the camp, tonight. The townspeople, too.

Tamir is lying in wait to attack."

John stopped and turned around, attentive.

"You are waiting here for the Brown Eyes, so you can stop their march. You think they are coming tomorrow. But they are not. They are coming tonight."

"How do you...?" he stepped forward a bit. His eyes searching.

"It doesn't matter how I know, I do. The same way that I made it here to find you. Haven't you wanted to fight? Haven't you wanted a change?"

The words stung. Deep.

She stepped a little closer and talked softer. "John, all I know is that I was supposed to come find you..." she said, pausing to make sure he was listening, "and tell you that you can make a difference. Whatever you have wanted to do, it's possible. That is all I know. You can change the tide of the war. Tonight!"

John looked up and let out a groan of frustration. He could still hear the clamoring outside in the campground. Jeanette took another step back.

It did not make sense. How could she know so much? Why did she come, prodding him to follow his heart? He had told himself multiple times he was not the answer. One man cannot change the tide of war, right? One girl with green eyes couldn't either, could she?

"No, I don't...I don't need this right now. I don't need you here with your silly stories of being chosen, and I don't need you here giving my men false hope. I told you to leave." As he said the words, he couldn't look at her. "Please, just leave," he wasn't angry anymore, he was distraught.

She left him in the tent more confused, unsure, and depressed than when she arrived.

# CHAPTER 37

The trip back to Norbrook was quiet. Jeanette was thankful Hermes had stayed silent. She fumed from the encounter with John.

"I am sure you left an impression," Hermes finally said. "Hopefully it will set in." She was riding along beside him, sullen. She did not respond.

What could she have said differently? Didn't John understand that she was led to him? He was the soldier in her vision and if he didn't trust her – if *he* didn't know – then there was nothing else to do. The journey and the mission would be over...whatever it was in the first place.

Without warning, Jeanette stopped her horse, jumped down and walked off the road to lean against a nearby tree. Hermes also dismounted, taking the reins of both animals. He walked to the edge of the road, but did not encroach.

Jeanette opened her pouch, took a drink of water and then let it fall, the strap bouncing off her shoulder. She closed her eyes, the shade cooling her neck. Uncertainty and anger built. She looked up and down the road and saw no one.

"It's okay, Jeanette," Hermes said from behind, giving her

permission to express how she truly felt.

She started to tremble, as if she would slide down the trunk of the tree. But she didn't. She let out a scream. Deep from inside, primal. She wanted to swing and punch the tree. It was right in front of her. The immovable force that she wanted to battle. But her fists told her not to. Instead, she grabbed the strap on her shoulder. She flung off the water bottle and started to swing it.

She let out another cry as the water pouch slammed against the tree. It made a thud. She swung it again over her head and slammed it a second time.

Another scream.

Finally, with all of her strength and energy and sweat pouring down her face, she hurled it against the tree and the pouch burst open against the bark, water spraying everywhere. The loose strap hung loose in her hand. Her cry still echoed through the trees. The water which splashed on her face mixed with the tears on her cheeks. She fell to the ground, spent.

Hermes walked over, knelt next to her, and placed his hand on her shoulder. She did not move, but stayed, sobbing on her knees with her hands over her face.

When she was finished, she wiped her face off in her hands, sniffed, and drew in a breath. Exhaling slowly, her shoulders dropped.

She looked up at him. "I can't do it. I'm done."

Hermes looked away, down the barren street and then back to her. He patted her on the shoulder. "Today, you don't have to do anymore. You have done enough," he said quietly. "For now, we just need to make it back to Larrick's."

She wanted to lay down in the shade of the tree and sleep. In the breeze of the afternoon, it was calm and cool; she wanted to drift off.

Hermes extended his hand to help her up. She took it and stood. She dusted herself off and they started back down the road to Norbrook.

# CHAPTER 38

John's gait was slower. He walked with Wesley and Gabriel through the parade ground making sure everything was ready for the next day. The men stood in formation.

"The men are in fine form sir," Wesley said with an air of confidence. "I must say, having the lady show up to the camp, they saw it as a wonderful sign. They are encouraged about the direction..."

"Enough about the girl," John said, cutting him off coldly. "Are the scouts back with intel?"

"They arrived not long ago. Everything seems to be just as we had expected. The Brown Eye army to the northeast will arrive here sometime mid-day tomorrow. We will be ready sir."

"How many did they say?"

"Around two hundred, sir."

The number did not sound accurate. It should be more.

John walked past row after row, man after man. He could see the renewed courage in their eyes. Something had changed; something as simple as a fresh, colorful pair of green eyes. They were ready for battle, more ready than he had ever seen them.

He turned quickly to one of the soldiers. "Soldier!"

"Yes, sir!" he replied, stiffening

"What are your thoughts about this girl with green eyes coming into camp?"

The soldier did not pause in his response, "I think it is wonderful sir. She was a glorious sight."

"Do you believe we can beat the Brown Eyes?"

The soldier, up until now, had been looking forward, not making eye contact, as trained. Turning his head slightly to meet John's eyes, he answered, "Only if we actually fight sir."

He could not look the soldier back in the eye. He wanted to, but he couldn't.

*They are coming tonight.*

*What if Jeanette was right?*

He stepped back so he could see his men before him. All of them had followed orders on faith, out of a sheer desire to serve the kingdom. What if there was a better way to serve the kingdom?

He called to Burleigh and spoke with him out of earshot of the others. "The girl did have an impact on them, didn't she?"

"John, the men are more determined than I have ever seen them."

"And all because of Jeanette?" John said, still not able to grasp it.

Burleigh paused for a moment, and then nodded. "You have to admit, it is pretty awe inspiring. You saw her."

John paused, "Yes I did." He turned once more and looked at his army. They were patiently waiting for their orders. His heart started pounding. Putting both hands on Burleigh's shoulders, he asked, "Are you willing to follow me no matter what?"

"No matter what," Burleigh replied.

"Well, it's time for a little change."

With more courage in his step he walked back to face his soldiers. "Men, there was going to be a battle. As you probably know, we have received word that the Brown Eyes would be upon us, coming from the northeast, by tomorrow night. Our orders were to secure this area and Brighton from any attack. We are to defend at all costs."

There was a collective deflation in the crowd. On some faces, anger. John's last words completely ripped from the men their newfound courage from Jeanette. Many were shaking their heads, some were cursing under their breath. Like John, they were sick of only defending.

John held up his hand. One of the lieutenants gave a call for order.

"But men, hold steady," John started again, his entire body on fire with a passion he had not felt in ages. He was pacing up and down the line, searching the men. "The Brown Eyes will not make it to our hold, because today, this night, we are going to take the fight to them. It is time to stop waiting." He stopped in his place. From within came a voice that he had never used before, but was crying to emerge. It echoed over the valley where he stood with his men, "It is time to start fighting!"

A shout went up. It rang hard, loud and long, bouncing off the ears of all present. Afterward, silence filled the air as everyone waited. The whole plan had changed.

"All men report back to your posts for further orders." All the men broke off with excited chatter. The lieutenants raced to John.

"Do you really think the girl was right?" Wesley asked. "I don't know," John answered honestly, adrenaline rushing through his still body, "but either way, we are going to fight. Whether the castle wants us to or not."

# CHAPTER 39

Light from the torches bounced off the stone walls and played with the shadows. With every unfamiliar turn the guard took, Corwin felt like they were going deeper into the castle.

*Why is she running away? Who is the soldier she is searching for? Maybe she is following fate. Maybe she really knows what she is doing.*

Reaching a dead end and an unmarked door, the guard knocked. It echoed along the corridor. They waited. The guard knocked again.

"I told you to please not disturb me...," Cadmus said, finally opening the door. "Oh, Corwin, it's you. Wonderful! Guard, if you can please wait out here in the hall," he said, inviting Corwin inside and closing the door. Cadmus took his apron off and balling it in his hand said, "Did you find her?"

Corwin explained to him everything that had happened. Cadmus listened attentively as the night lamps flickered.

"Did you ever actually *see* her yourself?"

"No sir, I didn't. But there was enough proof that she had been in Norbrook, and was going to be back. The leader of the village, Larrick, assured us they would be back."

"Who is they?"

"She is with a man named Hermes. Larrick said that he was helping her with whatever she was doing," Corwin answered.

"And what of her father and the boy, the one with the blue eye."

"Tristyn stayed with the villagers and the father was intent to continue to look for her."

"This is great news, Corwin. I am glad Jacob recommended getting you involved. I just wish I knew why she felt the need to run."

"Would you like me to lead a group of men back to Bandar for when she returns?" Corwin asked. If Jeanette was going to be brought in, he wanted to be there. He wanted to hear from her own mouth why she was causing so much trouble.

"You have invested a lot of time and energy and I can understand why you would want to return, but you are needed back at the Royal Academy."

"But if you wanted me to originally go, why would you not want me to go now?"

"You have feelings for Jeanette, don't you, Corwin?" Cadmus asked.

"I care about her very much, sir, and just want to help."

"I appreciate that and I tell you what I will do. As soon as she is safe and sound back with us I will make sure you receive word. On my honor, I promise," Cadmus said.

Corwin felt his sincerity and respected his position, but he wanted an answer. "Did you send me just to appease Jacob?"

Cadmus took a deep breath. "Yes. How could I not fulfill his request? But we need all available young men training at the academy, learning how to better fight so we can win this war. It is nothing against you personally, but we have trained soldiers who can help bring her back."

*Trained soldiers who can't even check a house completely for clues.*

"I wanted to appease Jacob, I can only imagine what he's going through," Cadmus continued, "but now it's time for you to return back to your original post."

It wasn't what Corwin wanted to hear, but it made sense. "Thank you, sir. You should also know that if soldiers are sent to Bandar that the people in Norwood do not wish to be involved in any type of conflict. Jeanette went to them uninvited; they are not complicit in her avoiding the castle."

"I will certainly keep that in mind. Thank you again for your work Cadmus; the prince will be very pleased to hear this update," Cadmus said, walking him to the door. "And please know what your service means to the prince. I know great things are in store for you."

With everything going on, the last person Corwin was worried about was himself. "Sir, what about the girl?"

"Which girl?"

"The one that returned. The handmaid, I believe Auryn is her name."

"Ah, yes. What an ordeal for her; but she is doing well and has been put back to good use with us here."

Cadmus opened his door to allow Corwin out into the hallway. "Guard, allow Corwin to go to the kitchen and get a good meal in him before heading back to the academy."

"Thank you, sir," Corwin said with a salute. Cadmus smiled, bid him farewell, and closed the door behind him. Corwin followed the guard, hoping he had made the right decision.

# CHAPTER 40

"Corwin!" Addy said, face lighting up. The other servants in the kitchen watched in earnest as she ran over to him. She grabbed his arm and led him around a corner, out of the view of the rest of the staff. She had promised Marah she would introduce him next time they met, but Marah had disappeared as dinner cleanup was winding down.

"Did you find her? Is Jeanette back?"

"Not exactly."

"Then why are you here?"

"I needed to report to Cadmus." He shared with Addy the current situation and all that had happened.

"Do you think Jacob will find her?"

"It doesn't seem like she wants to be found."

"I know that feeling," Addy said.

"What is it about her?" Corwin asked. "Why am I so drawn to her when she keeps running away?"

Addy smiled. She had not heard Corwin speak so honestly. "What are you saying?"

"I'm saying that I wish she was a normal girl. Regular,

every day, stay put, normal girl. No adventure. No trouble."

"No you don't. That's why you like her so much."

Corwin shook his head. "Well, it doesn't make it any easier. Cadmus wants me to go back to the academy."

"And you think you need to keep looking for her?"

Corwin didn't say anything. His silence answered the question.

"Like you said, maybe she doesn't want to be found. I can't say I've given up on her. I would give anything to have her here with me, but I can't make her decisions for her. Whatever she's doing, though," Addy said, wiping her hands on her apron, "I've come to believe it's not foolishness. She really believes in it."

"Well she is stupid for being so...stupid!"

She enjoyed seeing someone as frustrated with Jeanette as she was. "Well, then let's hope she comes back from wherever she is safe and sound. And then we can both tell her how stupid she is."

Corwin laughed.

"Addy! Addy!," came a bellow from the kitchen. Tilly came around the corner. "Get back to work. This is no time to be fraternizing with the guards!"

"I better go," Corwin said, inching away from her. "Thanks for talking to me Addy. I really appreciate it."

"So you are just going back to the academy?"

"That's all I can do for now."

"How is..." Addy started, and thought twice.

"How is what?"

"How is Rendall doing?" she said, her cheeks flushing.

Corwin smiled. "When I left him he was fine. A little homesick, but he seemed okay."

"Tell him I said hello."

"Most certainly," he said, and then left.

Addy lingered in the hall. She had not thought of Rendall

for some time. It used to be every day. Dreaming about being at the castle while he fought in the war. She would get home before he did and make him the best cake ever. He would fall in love with her sensibility and quiet demeanor. She laughed, thinking of how she teased Jeanette constantly...

*Aunt Jeanette.*

Whispers down the hall caught Addy's attention. It sounded like Marah. Addy walked toward the sounds, quietly against the wall. When she saw them, she ducked behind a large statue of King Amarin, the first king of the land. Marah and Prince Braxton were talking.

"Why haven't you come sooner?" Marah was talking to the prince.

"I'm sorry, it's just been so crazy around here," the prince answered. "I promise I wanted to see you, but between my mother and Lorelei, every last second of my life is being sucked dry."

"I have missed you," Marah said, sweetly, intently.

*Marah and the prince?!*

"I know, I have missed you too."

Addy leaned farther back and found she had a small view from behind the statue. Braxton stood with his back against the wall. Marah was close to him. Very close to him. They weren't embracing, but they were not far from it.

"Why have you been so distant lately? You've changed since coming back from the festivals."

"Of course I've changed," Braxton said, frustrated. "My mother is bound and determined to get me married to someone I care nothing about."

"So you aren't going to marry her?" There was a look of honest hope in Marah's eyes.

"It's not that simple, you know that."

"What about us?"

"What about us?" Braxton replied, and moved from the

wall, to the side, away from Marah. "I have to go now. Just...I just need some space, okay." His words were cold, unfeeling.

"I love you," Marah said desperately.

He stood for a second and then walked away, not saying a word. Marah wiped her cheeks and then headed back to the kitchen.

*She doesn't know about his desire for Jeanette.*

"Where is Addy!" Tilly screamed. Addy ran back into the kitchen, wondering if life was every going to be peaceful again.

# CHAPTER 41

Jeanette rode into Norbrook barely able to keep her eyes open. The trip to see the soldier across the river had been in vain. With no clue of what direction to take next, all she wanted was sleep.

"Jeanette! Jeanette!" she heard when the hooves of her horse hit dry land.

Tristyn.

Her heart lifted and she leapt from the horse. He ran to her. "I didn't think I would ever see you again," Tristyn whispered in her ear.

Tears filled her eyes. "But here you are and it's all I care about right now." She squeezed him again, his embrace comforting. "I told you I would get you to Bandar, didn't I?" she said.

After a few seconds, reality set in. "How did you get here, Tristyn? Where is..." Jeanette asked, looking around. Larrick and Vanora were also nearby.

"Your father is not here, Jeanette," Larrick said. "He insisted on going to look for you." Her father had come for her? Mixed feelings of guilt and joy flowed in her.

"Corwin was with us, too," Tristyn added.

"What? How could he leave his post at the academy? Did he go with my father?"

"He was on assignment," Larrick answered. "He had orders to track you and report back to the castle."

Jeanette looked at Hermes. There was fear in his eyes again.

"What did you find?" Salinda interrupted. "Did you find the soldier you were looking for?"

Everyone stood still, excitement in their bright, blue eyes. She did not know what to say. Her answer would only let them down.

"It did not go as we would have expected," Hermes finally answered.

"No, it didn't," Jeanette confirmed.

"And what is your next move?" Salinda asked.

Jeanette looked at her through tired, sorry eyes. "Now it is time to wait."

"So you are giving up too?" Salinda scolded, anger in her eyes.

"Salinda, please," Vanora pleaded.

"Honestly, Salinda, I don't know what to do next," Jeanette said. "I can understand your frustration, but today did not turn out like I had hoped either. We will figure out what to do next, I promise. And Larrick," Jeanette said, "I won't be here much longer. If Corwin has reported to the castle, then they will come here to find me. I can't bring you into this more than I already have."

"But where will we go?" Tristyn asked.

"We are not going anywhere," she said. "If it's okay with Larrick and Vanora, you will stay here and wait for Jacob. I'm sorry, Tristyn." More than anything, she wanted Tristyn with her, but she knew it was not safe.

"Of course he can stay with us," Vanora said. Tristyn nodded, understanding. He looked deflated, but did not push back as much as Jeanette thought he would.

"Thank you. Right now I just need to rest and focus for a little while on where to go next; then Hermes and I will be gone." She didn't know what the next move should be, and now with Corwin returning to the castle, a decision would be needed soon.

"I'm sorry you have to leave, Jeanette," Larrick said. "But we understand and appreciate your concern for our village."

Jeanette nodded and started toward her tent. She had summoned the visions herself before, maybe she could do it again. Tristyn walked with her. "How has it been here in Norwood? Is it what you hoped it would be?" she asked.

"It's been," Tristyn started. He looked at Salinda and then back at Jeanette, "really good. I was certainly worried about you, but being here is like a dream come true."

Jeanette grinned. "I see. So I'm out trying to stop this war and you are falling in love with the very first blue eyed girl you see. Is that it?"

Tristyn blushed. They reached the tent and Tristyn opened the flap. "I don't understand everything, Jeanette. But I do believe in you. Whatever you are searching for, you will find. I know it," he said and left.

A few seconds later, Hermes appeared at the door.

"Did you hear what they said?" Jeanette asked. "Corwin has gone back to the castle. What do we do?"

"I don't know who Corwin is or why the castle has him looking for us, but can we trust him?" Jeanette wanted to say yes, more than anything she trusted Corwin. But he wouldn't understand why she was running. At least not at first.

"I think so," she answered unsure. "I know he wouldn't do anything to harm me."

"Well, we need to consider what our options are moving

forward. It is not safe here for us anymore. We have until mid-day tomorrow, at the latest, to be out of here before anyone from the castle arrives."

"Just give me some time to think," she said. He closed the flap and left her. Still fully dressed, she sunk into the blankets on the floor.

*Relax.*

*Focus.*

*Let it come to me.*

Around her, everything was quiet, her eyes heavy. She waited for direction, but her body took control.

*What am I supposed to do next?*

No answer came as she finally gave in to sleep.

\*\*\*

"Wake up Jeanette...wake up!" Tristyn was shaking her. She slowly woke, feeling overly dazed. Her body was telling her to close her eyes and go back to sleep.

"Get up!"

"What is it?"

Tristyn practically forced her on her feet. She rubbed her eyes and tried to get her balance. Slowly, the noise from outside resonated in her ear.

"What's going on?"

"John is here!"

She opened the tent flap and saw John standing next to his horse, talking with Larrick. Burleigh was standing beside him, holding the reigns.

"What is he doing here?"

"I don't know," Tristyn shrugged. "You are the one that went to see him. You should go out and talk to him. You look wonderful by the way."

She reached to hit him and he flinched. John walked

toward her tent and she walked out to meet him. They were exchanging looks, almost like a wrestle. John ran his fingers through his hair and slowly made his way toward her. They stopped near each other.

"I'm sorry I didn't believe you before," he said, humbly.

Relief rushed through her. He wasn't there to pick a fight or turn her in; he had listened. "Thank you," she replied. "Did your men battle the Brown Eyes?"

"Yes, we did. It was a glorious sight, you should have seen it."

"When I walked out of camp, it didn't seem like you wanted my help and that I would not see you again."

"When you left, that's exactly how I felt. But..." he paused, searching for the words, "you were right. The things you said...you knew things you shouldn't. I decided to trust you.

"When the people of Brighton found out their city was spared, you should have seen their faces. I bet any of the citizens would have fought for us...for you."

"How many men did you lose?"

"None."

She had a purpose. Everything in her visions had led her in the right direction. Whatever this gift was, her green eyes could make a difference. She was supposed to help John win the war.

"I'm so glad to hear that. You had no reason to believe me and yet you did. That took a lot of faith. Thank you."

"You are welcome. You saved my men."

"How many are with you?"

"I brought enough, not knowing what to expect. The rest are still camped at Brighton."

"So...what do we do now?" Jeanette said, excitedly.

John's mood quickly changed. His eyebrows dropped. "What do you mean?"

"Well I assume you have come so that I can help. I want to do whatever I can to help with whatever is planned." In an instant, there was tension. The same tension she had felt the first time she spoke with him.

"Whatever is planned?" he said, abruptly. "I don't have a plan." He held out his hands towards Jeanette. "YOU are the plan!"

"I am the plan?" she repeated, unconvinced. "You are the captain! You must have some plan as to what is next...how to beat Tamir."

"Jeanette, everything that happened yesterday was because of you and what you said to me. For a long time I have struggled with following orders from the castle that I do not believe in. You changed that. What I did yesterday, even though technically a win for our side, will probably get the attention of the castle. I disobeyed orders and put my men and Brighton at risk. You have started a chain of events that..."

"*I* have started a chain of events?"

"Yes, you! The only reason my men believed in me, the only reason I believed in myself, was because of you. I don't know where this is going but for the first time in a long time...I feel like we can win."

Jeanette looked around. Larrick, Hermes and Burleigh stood close by, taking it all in.

She threw up her hands. "Well I don't know," she said. She turned to Hermes. "What does he expect me to do? I don't have all the answers." The visions had come and she had followed them.

Don't go to the castle.

Find Hermes.

Find John.

She had done what she was asked.

John turned and started to walk away. "I knew this was a joke. I don't know why I ever believed it in the first place," John said. He then turned to Burleigh. "We need to get back as soon as possible and see what we can do to help the castle understand why we did not follow orders."

Burleigh reached out and put his hands on John's shoulders, "Would you slow down? Crunch, we just got here."

Hermes walked over to Jeanette. "Why do you think he's so frustrated?"

"How am I supposed to know?!" Jeanette yelled. She was pacing now. What did he want from her? What else could she do?

"You do realize that he took your advice, right?' Hermes said. "Isn't that what you were worried about?"

"Yes, but...now he expects me to change everything."

"I don't think he expects you to change everything, Jeanette. That day when you were in the tent with him, you were able to give him something he had not had in a long time. It wasn't just direction," Hermes said, prodding her to the answer.

She already knew the answer. "The only reason I could give him confidence at that time is because I knew what he was supposed to do. Thankfully he listened!" she said bluntly, voice rising slightly, hoping John would hear. "I don't know what's next!"

Hermes was shaking his head at her, "You don't understand yet, do you? There doesn't have to be a plan...not yet. That will come. Do you remember how those soldiers reacted when you rode into camp? Do you remember how the people in this village gasped when they laid eyes upon you?"

She started to pull away. He grabbed her arm and pulled her back. "Look at me, Jeanette. Do you know why I am standing here with you today? Because you gave me something I had not had for a very long time," Hermes said softly, voice cracking. "You gave me hope."

She looked at him; past the age, past the scar and heard what he was saying.

"Jeanette, after hope, everything else is secondary. I know

you would rather not be here, dealing with this. But you are...you are the only one that can deal with it."

Hermes words sank in. She had no doubt she was needed, that she could help. She needed to be patient. She turned back to John. "I'm sorry, John. I didn't mean to get so flustered."

"I didn't either," he said. "There are just decisions that need to be made, and I don't know exactly what they are."

Jeanette understood. "I think if we work together the answers will come."

"All I know, from what I've seen, is it will not be possible without you and your...your," he said, motioning toward her eyes.

The eyes changed everything. As much as she didn't want them to affect her, to be a part of the equation, they were. She looked at John, past the boy she knew, past the soldier, and saw in his eyes desire. Desire to fight. Desire to win. A desire to work with whoever would help put an end to the fighting. It was a desire she now shared.

# CHAPTER 42

"How are you feeling this morning?" Addy asked, not looking directly at Marah. It had been two days since she heard her talking to Braxton in the hall. Addy had not said anything, but she knew the discussion affected Marah. Usually fun and vibrant, Marah had been aloof. Addy had been walking on eggshells.

Marah sat up in her bed, the covers pulled up to her chest. She thought for a moment and said, "Addy, have you ever loved anyone?"

"You mean...like a boy."

"Yes. Have you ever loved a boy."

"A boy?" Addy said. "You mean, like the prince?"

Shock came across Marah's face. "Why would say that?"

"I don't want you to be upset with me, but I heard you two talking the other night in the hall by the kitchen."

Marah's face turned sour. "You were spying on me!?"

"No, no, nothing like that, Marah. Honest. Remember how I said Corwin had come. We talked in the hallway for a minute and I...I heard you two talking."

In an instant Marah's eyes teared up and her guard came down. "He is the best thing that has ever happened to me, Addy. He's the only thing that gave me joy in this place."

Addy listened carefully, understanding coming to her a little at a time.

"I don't know if I thought we would run away or if he would ever *really* have me," Marah continued, "but it was nice believing that we could be more than just friends. It was a nice dream to hold on to.

"Before the festivals, he was so down, so frustrated about having to be involved. He did not want anybody's eyes to change. Every time he talked negative about the festival, or about his mother and her stupid plan to get him married, it made me feel so..."

Addy's heart ached.

"But now, you should hear the way he talks about Jeanette. I didn't understand what he was saying until the other night when you heard us. I realized that the reason he was in a bad mood was not just because he doesn't want Lorelei, but because he really wants Jeanette." Marah took a long breath and wiped her eyes. "He didn't say it, but he didn't need to."

"Maybe he's just confused," Addy said. "If he didn't want the festivals, I can only imagine how much pressure that must be on him."

"The hardest part is I think he has come to the conclusion that he has to be king one day; that there is no other choice for him," Marah said, her anger building again. "I was supposed to be his choice. He was supposed to run away with me," Marah said, "not go after a girl who was running away from him."

It was a lot to take in. Addy's mind was cluttered with what she could say to help Marah. It sounded like Jeanette had caused both of them pain, just in different ways.

The door flew open.

Marah, still in her night wear, pulled the covers up more. Addy stood to find the king barging through her door. Brandy came in directly behind him.

"Have you seen my toad flute?" the king asked peeking around the room, great concern on his face.

"Get out of the room at once!" Brandy screamed, grabbing the king by the arm. She was out of breath.

"Brandy, be gentle," Addy said. Since recovering from her illness, Brandy had found a useful job at the castle as an assistant the king's nurse, Fetima. Brandy was very excited about the opportunity at first, but over time realized that 'nurse's assistant' was a fancy title for babysitter.

"Sorry," she said, trying to pull the king back out the door, "he got loose." The king was hanging on for dear life, reaching for the hand mirror that was glimmering on Marah's desk. Marah reached over from the bed and grabbed it.

Brandy eventually pried the king off the door and back into the hall.

Addy shook her head, her adrenaline still pumping from the startle "Has the king always been like that?"

"Ever since I've been here."

The feeling in the room had changed. Addy wanted to help but did not want to pry. Marah seemed more content than before.

"Do you have someone?" Marah asked.

"No. There was a boy, Rendall, back home that I like...that I liked. But he's off at the academy now." Addy thought back to all the times she had spent imaging what might have been. Why did she like Rendall? Did she ever think anything would happen? "But it was just a silly crush."

"Do you miss anybody?"

The knot clambered up Addy's throat. "I miss my nephew, Drury. Sweet, innocent, cuddly...loud," she laughed.

Marah smiled. "It would be nice to have little ones around.

It's just me in my family; I guess that's why it was so easy to leave," she said, reaching over and picking up the mirror off the table.

"Did the prince give that to you?" Addy asked.

Marah nodded.

Addy felt, for the first time, that maybe there was a reason she was at the castle. A reason for something other than cooking.

"Don't lose hope. Maybe Jeanette will stay as far away from him as possible," Addy started, trying to lighten the mood, "and Lorelei will get a very nasty, contagious disease and get exiled."

Marah laughed. Addy could tell she was hitting the right notes. But there was one question she still needed to ask.

"Does Cadmus know about you and the prince? He seems to be very close to Braxton."

"Braxton has never said, but I think he does. Queen Devony would be furious if she found out, but Cadmus is like a father to him. Braxton loves him and trusts him implicitly."

*Trust.*

Even though she disagreed with Jeanette on almost everything, Addy had always felt that she could trust Jeanette. It brought comfort to feel that her relationship with Marah had the makings for something similar.

# CHAPTER 43

Jeanette lay in her hut. It was afternoon, and she was awake, but still contemplating closing her eyes again. What else could she do? She did not have any answers for John, or for herself.

She finally sat up, stretching. Tristyn came to the door.

"Dinner is going to be ready in a few minutes," Tristyn said, peeking his head through the door. "It will be good if you eat something.'

"Thank you."

"For what?"

"For everything. For believing in me and not giving up on me."

He nodded. "I've always believed in you, even before you had fancy eyes."

She laughed. He *had* always believed in her. Other than Addy, he was the best friend she ever had.

*Addy.*

She missed Addy. Would they ever see each other again? Was she handling Lorelei okay? Did she enjoy the castle life she always wanted?

Jeanette stood and walked with Tristyn to find the others around the fire. Hermes, Larrick, Vanora and Salinda were discussing John and his men.

Jeanette sat down next to Hermes. Tristyn sat down next to Salinda, a positioning that was not lost on Jeanette. She had never seen her cousin smile so much.

"How long do you think they will stay," Vanora asked.

"I don't know," Larrick answered.

"How long will we let them stay?"

"I did not get the impression that they would be here long. This is a complicated situation, Vanora," he said. "Things are...different."

Jeanette knew Vanora did not like John being here, and she had noticed the change in Larrick's usual hospitable attitude as well.

"They are only different if we let them be different," Vanora replied. "If they stay here, what kind of door are we opening?"

"My dear, I fear the door has already been opened. The only way we might be able to close it again is to give our help, to some extent or another."

Vanora shook her head.

Hermes responded, "Vanora, I know I am the one that started this whole series of events. If you need somebody to blame, please blame me."

"Oh Hermes," she sighed, "I don't wish to feel ill will. It's just..."

"It's just we've been sitting here idly while the rest of the world is at war and it's time to change," Salinda injected, looking at her aunt. She then turned to Larrick. "I'm glad that your eyes are finally opening uncle."

Frustrated, Vanora dropped the food basket she had been carrying and went back into the hut. Salinda had a guilty smile on her face.

"Larrick, when the time comes, assuming it does, are you and your people ready to help," Hermes asked. "How much influence do you have with the other villages? Are they ready to take on Tamir?"

Salinda stared at her uncle, encouragement in her eyes.

"I can't speak for the other villages or their leaders. We do not have much contact with them. But I believe the circumstances are too much for me and my people to ignore. There have been too many signs – Hermes returning, Jeanette, John – it is time for something to be done."

"Where are John and his men now?" Jeanette asked.

"They are camped on the outskirts of the village," Larrick answered. "There is plenty of room and they are close to the river without being fully in the open."

"Larrick! Larrick!"

A small band of Bandar soldiers came running into the village. Vanora came out of her hut at the commotion.

"There is a group of men coming over the river, heading this way," one of the soldiers said, taking a breath. "They are flying Amarin colors."

Vanora clutched her robe at the chest and walked closer to Larrick, grabbing his hand.

"How many?"

"Roughly twenty or so."

"Salinda, go and tell John and his men to come quickly. Go, now!" Larrick barked. Salinda caught a glimpse of Tristyn as she turned. He gave her a confirming glance and she sprinted off.

"Cadmus has sent them. They are part of the Royal Guard. They are coming for Jeanette," Hermes said. They had come quicker than estimated.

*Corwin!*

Corwin was the one that had led them here, to find her.

How could he not understand that she had no desire to be at the castle? Why would he turn her in?

"Quickly my dear, we must hide you," Vanora said, reaching for Jeanette's shoulders to lead her to safety.

Jeanette took a step back and avoided her. "I will not hide. That will only do more harm for your people. I am not here to do harm to anyone. What needs to be done needs to be done out in the open. No more hiding."

Vanora gave a look of uncertainty to Larrick. "Let her be my dear," Larrick instructed. "It's not our fight...not yet anyway."

The sound of hooves pounded through the forest opening onto the main path of the village. Larrick's men formed a line between the oncoming party and the small village. The horses drew closer, like thunder rolling into the village.

Hermes turned back to Jeanette. "Please do not stay out in the open. You must hide!" he said. There was fear in his voice, but she did not move. "If they take you it is over before it has begun."

The assembly of horses came to a halt in front of Larrick's warriors. As soon as the dust settled, Jeanette saw Cadmus.

He made the trip himself.

He sat in his saddle, high above the Bandar soldiers, who stood no chance against the Royal Guard in their breastplates and helmets.

Cadmus called out, "Who is the one they call Larrick?"

Larrick stepped forward.

"Good Larrick, I am terribly sorry to ride into your village in such a manner, but it appears," he said, looking at Jeanette, "that you have a young lady in your midst that the kingdom has been much worried about."

Larrick took another step forward. "If you are the one they call Cadmus, know that we have no fight with you. This young lady has sought refuge here, along with her friend. If she has no desire to go with you today, then I must ask that you leave our village, and our kingdom, in peace."

"That's where the problem lies," Cadmus said with an air of diplomacy. He dismounted. The lead guard on the horse behind him started to follow but Cadmus held up his hand telling him to wait. Cadmus, without any apparent fear or worry walked right up to the blue eyed wall that was separating him from Jeanette. Larrick's men tensed, hands grasping their spears.

"If you don't mind," he said, loud enough for Larrick to hear. "I mean you no harm, I only wish to talk."

Larrick looked at Vanora and then to Hermes.

"We can't trust him," Hermes whispered.

"Let him pass," Jeanette added. "I have plenty to talk to him about."

"Let him pass!" Larrick shouted.

The wall of men parted and Cadmus walked through. As he got closer, his eyes fixed on Jeanette. Two of the blue eyed soldiers walked behind him.

"Jeanette, I have not come to mix words," he started, a cold, sober look on his face. "I can appreciate that this is not how you wanted things to turn out. You got scared after the change and you fled. I can understand that, but my dear you must realize how your gift is of precious concern to the kingdom. We cannot have you running around unsecured. Your place is at the castle."

"Why did you lie to me?" Jeanette asked. The words felt so good coming out. "Why did you plant Auryn to spy on me?"

"She wasn't spying on you Jeanette; she was there to protect you. I have made it my business in life to try and understand people, and after your eyes changed, I have to admit, I was concerned about you. Put yourself in my position; if the chance had presented itself to place a loyal servant like Auryn at your side, to watch out for you, would you not have done the same?"

Jeanette could not help but agree with the argument. She was emotional and insecure with the change. He made a strong case. "But why can't you just leave me alone...just let me be?" she asked, desperate.

"I wish it was that simple, I truly do," Cadmus replied, taking a few more steps closer. "Maybe if we had talked it through, or if you had been honest with me about your aversion to going to the castle, we could have worked something out. But from what I hear, you have turned your escape into some sort of quest. You have been trying to find yourself at the expense of this gift Jeanette. That changes the situation."

"I have been perfectly safe without the kingdoms help," she said, stepping forward to stand by Hermes.

"You must be the one they call Hermes?" Cadmus asked.

"I am."

"And what is your interest in this young lady. I have heard that you have been quite the help to our friend. What is in it for you?"

Jeanette glanced at Hermes. He was shaking. "She will be able to finish what I never started," Hermes said in a loud, but hollow voice. One of pain and regret.

Cadmus titled his head in recognition. Hermes kept eye contact.

"Asa?" he said slowly, unbelieving.

*Asa?*

"Not anymore," Hermes said. "That man is long dead."

Cadmus' mouth sharpened and his eyes bent in disgust. "So Jeanette, this is the man you have been following...who will keep you safe? And you trust him?" Hermes continued to tremble. Jeanette reached out her hand and grabbed his arm to give him strength.

"This is a man who lives a lie. This is a man who killed his own wife and - apparently - faked his own death to avoid justice! Jeanette, this is who you put your trust in?" Cadmus asked, glaring at Hermes. "Jeanette, he has ruined his own life and he will ruin yours."

Tears were streaming down Hermes' cheeks.

"What is he talking about?" Jeanette asked Hermes.

"It's not like that, Jeanette," he said. In his face she once again saw the scared, lonely man she had first met back at the shop in Enzion. "It was an accident, and I have spent every day of my life since then with the pain of it," he confessed, the words aching in his throat.

Cadmus continued, "Jeanette, you are following an old, sorrowful man living in the past, searching for something he can't have. This old man is chasing a dream. Jeanette, the gift you have...I can help you. You were given it for a reason and together we can figure out what that is."

Tristyn reached over and grabbed her hand. Jeanette did not know what to think. The look on Hermes' face told her that there was truth to what Cadmus was saying. What had happened? Could she still trust him? Regardless, she knew she had no desire to go with Cadmus.

"All this talk is touching, but I'm afraid we must be moving along," Cadmus said, his tone impatient. "Guards!" he shouted, "I want the girl and the old man, they are coming back with us," he stated flatly, moving off to the side so his men could advance.

The guards advanced on the blue eyed warriors. Spears raised, the Bandar soldiers tried to barricade the Amarin horses from advancing. Swords drawn, the Royal Guard swiftly went through the blue eyed line. Jeanette watched in horror as some of the Bandar soldiers whelped in pain, falling to the ground, blood splattering.

Dead.

"Hermes, Jeanette, run!" Larrick called out.

Tristyn was pulling at Jeanette's hand for her to get off the road, but both her and Hermes stood their ground.

"Jeanette, come on!" Tristyn yelled, continuing to pull with no luck.

Jeanette seemed overly calm as the horsemen advanced to come and take her away. "Everything will be okay," she reassured.

Behind her, she heard thunder. The approaching horses sounded like a storm, ready to engulf them. Jeanette closed her eyes and could feel a rush of warm air go past her. John and his men had arrived.

Cadmus retreated behind his line of men. John's troops rode straight for them, battling their brothers. Jeanette watched as steel sparked, horses shuffled, and screams filled the chaos.

A moment later, it was over, Cadmus' troops retreated. John's men held the line. Both groups of soldiers had men off of horses, wounded. Nearby three Bandar soldiers lay dead.

Cadmus peered at John with his dark green eyes were half shock, half rage. "What is your name soldier? I look forward to telling the prince who it is that is raising a rebellion against the kingdom."

"My name is not your concern and we do not fight against the crown. We fight for Amarin and her citizens. That includes this young lady who you have tried to take against her will. You need to turn around and go back the way you came. Nobody is going with you today." Strength filled Jeanette at John's words, his desire to protect her.

"Let me tell you something," Cadmus said through clinched teeth, "whatever you are planning, it will not come to pass. You and your followers will not last, I will see to it. This is blatant heresy against the crown and you and your men will all hang."

Jeanette watched in awe as the peaceful, reserved man she knew transformed into a monster. Cadmus pointed toward her,

"And this citizen that you are protecting, she belongs to Amarin," he said, setting his jaw. "She belongs to me."

"You will leave, now!" John ordered. "Of your own accord or we will be forced to make you leave."

Cadmus hesitated to consider the options. He was outnumbered. How bad did he want to fight? Why was he so desperate to have her and Hermes?

"This is not the end," Cadmus promised and with a kick, he started down path he had rode in on, his men following behind.

Everyone was still until Cadmus and the Royal Guard were out of sight. Larrick and his soldiers ran to his fallen men. John dismounted, surveying the scene and attending to his wounded soldiers. Hermes looked like he had aged decades in a matter of minutes.

Jeanette tried to make eye contact with him, but he would not look at her. There was a shame in his face that she had never seen before, and it hurt.

John called to Larrick. "I think it best if you find a safe place to relocate. He will be back, and with more men."

Larrick nodded, as if he had already come to the same conclusion. Vanora walked over to him and took his hand. "Everything has changed...just like you said," she whispered to him and put her head on his shoulder.

"And we will be fine, just as we have been in the past," Larrick said.

John turned to Jeanette. "Do you know where we should go?"

"I don't."

"There is a place," Salinda called out. Jeanette saw the fight in her eyes.

"She is right," Larrick confirmed. "We know of a place, it is the only safe place...for all of us. What we have, Captain, consider it yours."

John acknowledged Larrick's offer and then called out, "Everyone needs to gather their things and then try to get some rest. We leave at first light."

The crowd dispersed. Jeanette looked around, trying to make sense of everything that had just happened. She turned to Hermes. "Why didn't you tell me?"

"It all happened so long ago, Jeanette. I didn't think it mattered."

"Was it true what Cadmus said?"

Hermes silence answered her question. She felt lost. She wanted to understand, but she didn't.

John approached her. "Are you okay?"

"What have we started, John?"

"I don't know, but it looks like there is no stopping it."

He was right. Jeanette was completely invested in the path she had taken.

There was no turning back. Instead of ending a war with an enemy, they were starting a war with their own kingdom.

# CHAPTER 44

Devony and Braxton gathered quickly in the council room upon hearing the news that Cadmus had returned.

"He better have come back with her!" Braxton declared. She was his salvation. A breath of fresh air. Jeanette was beautiful, energetic, and independent. He had fallen for her quickly. Over the past days he doubted his feelings. Was it really just to spite his mother? Probably; at least some. But the further Jeanette ran the more he wanted her. Lorelei had already overstayed her welcome in his mind. She was shrill, immature, and petty.

*Maybe she is a little like you.*

"And if he doesn't, everything will be okay," Devony reassured, trying to stay positive. His mother had picked up on his avoidance of Lorelei and had been trying to prod him, lovingly.

Cadmus walked through the door. "She is not with you, is she?" Braxton barked.

"No, my lord," Cadmus said, hanging his head. "I am so sorry I have failed you."

"Why did you take off in such a hurry to get her? We could have offered more support. You did not even say where you were going?" Braxton scolded.

"My Prince, I have considered this our number one priority since the girl first ventured from the caravan. All things told, I am the one responsible for losing her. Hindsight, I should have been more communicative, but I was desirous to right my wrong and help make sure that she was brought back unharmed."

Braxton felt the guilt in Cadmus' tone.

"Well, what happened?" Devony asked.

"Among other things, there is an uprising. One of our army captains is leading a group of men in direct disobedience to the crown."

"Can you be sure?" Devony asked.

"Make no doubt about it my queen," Cadmus answered. "I would not believe such news if I had not seen it with my own eyes. Not only is there a green eyed girl with fantasies of grandeur, but she has now led others, even our own captains, to believe that they can fight against the kingdom's wishes. They were all there before me. Our guards had to engage."

She shook her head worriedly. "I knew all along it would have been better if she would have just disappeared. We should have left her alone."

"Are you serious, mother?" Braxton asked. She had never talked so openly before.

"Well, Braxton what did you think I wanted to happen? Have two girls here that would be fawning over you and kissing up to me...no thank you. It's bad enough with just one," she said. "No, it's much easier to keep it simple. If she didn't have the desire to be here, as long as she wasn't making trouble, I would have wished her a good day and been done with it, but..."

"But I am afraid that is not possible now, my queen,"

Cadmus said.

It looked like his mother had been right all along. As much as he wanted to know more about Jeanette, to be close to her, to consider a relationship, it would not be. His opportunity to have a choice had come to an end. Not only had she run away from the castle - from him - she now wanted to go to war.

Braxton was left with no other reality than that of marrying Lorelei. In an instant, his interest in Jeanette went from one of desire and curiosity, to one of loathing and disgust. She was the one who brought this on him. She was the one that would chain him to the blonde temptress down the hall for the rest of his life. Because she did not have the faith to give him a chance, to at least come to the kingdom and see what he had to offer.

He couldn't have Marah because his mother would never approve.

He couldn't have Jeanette because she wouldn't stay still long enough for him to find her.

He did not want Lorelei, but it appeared he would have to settle. His life was over.

"Whatever you need, Cadmus, it is yours," Braxton stated boldly.

"Of course your majesty. I have just the man in mind to help," Cadmus said.

Braxton walked over and sat down in his chair. This was a new feeling. He knew what selfishness felt like, but this was more. This was the feeling that came with land and servants and edicts. It was the feeling he had been trying to avoid, but could no longer deny. He had a right to this feeling and was willing to let it grow within him.

Power.

With a cold, horrible look on his face and wall around his heart, he said, "I want them all taken care of."

# CHAPTER 45

"For those fallen, but not forgotten," Larrick said. "As your bodies sink below, may your spirit rise above." The members of Larrick's clan all lowered their head unison and the bodies of the three slain soldiers were set adrift on the river.

Jeanette watched in awe of the peace and reverence on display. The mourners eventually raised their head, one by one, and then slowly started for the village. There were no words to speak. Their last act before leaving their temporary home was to bury their own. It wasn't fair, but it was real. The consequences of her actions were more real than Jeanette had ever imagined they could be.

Back in the village, everyone started gathering, ready for the exodus into hiding. "What are we supposed to do when we get there?" Jeanette asked. Jeanette, John, Larrick and Hermes had gathered for a final discussion before departing.

"I don't know, but now the objective is getting to safety before Cadmus gets back," Hermes said.

Jeanette did not want to run. Just when it seemed like

everything was coming together, she didn't want to go back to being unsure.

"When will the rest of your men come?" Larrick asked.

"I don't know," John said. "We will travel with you until we make camp and then I will have to return to my unit and see where they stand. After last night and the confrontation with Cadmus, I fear retribution from the castle. But Hermes is right; getting out of here is the number one priority. Cadmus has every intention of coming back for you and Hermes, or Asa...or whatever his name is."

"What are we going to do?" Jeanette asked. "I thought I was just supposed to give you and the soldier's courage. I didn't think we would be starting a civil war. We cannot fight the castle and Tamir. How is that going to help anything?"

"Hopefully, Cadmus is acting alone in his crazy quest for you. After we get into hiding, we will need to build support for an offensive. Maybe if enough citizens understand the circumstances, they will rally and force the castle's hand." He then looked at Jeanette. "That's why we have you."

"I'm not going to be much help if Cadmus captures me and drags me back to the kingdom."

John stepped a little closer and said, "I'll make sure that doesn't happen." She paused at his sincerity. She had been too quick to unfairly judge him.

"Jeanette, I was wondering if..." John started. He seemed to be debating whether to ask what was on his tongue.

"It's okay, what is it?"

"I was thinking about you last night, and..." he said, pausing again. "And I wonder if you will have more guidance, or visions, to help us know what to do?"

She held her breath briefly as her mind turned, looking for answers. She had three visions that had guided her, but their purpose was complete. Would there be more? Could she make them come?

"I don't know," she answered honestly.

John nodded. He had a pleasant smile. It added a peace to his mature, stiff demeanor. A tinge of guilt built in her for the negative thoughts she had of him, most of which hinged on the fact that he was related to Lorelei. But he was not anything like Lorelei.

*Lorelei.*

How was she adjusting to the castle? Was Addy holding her own? So much had happened in such a short period of time, yet she felt worlds away from her best friend.

Jeanette *was* different. What about the rest of the kingdom? Would they be able to see, to understand what she was doing? Some already had. Would others? Would John continue to trust her and be by her side?

She thought finding the soldier across the river would be the end of her journey, but it seemed to be just the beginning.

"We need to go. Is everything ready?" John asked, climbing up on Cheswin. Jeanette took a step closer and Cheswin nestled his nose on Jeanette's arm.

"Hey, Cheswin," Jeanette said, low.

"I think he likes you," John said, with a look of surprise on his face. "He doesn't usually take to people so well."

Jeanette closed her eyes and ran her hands up and down Cheswin's mane. She took a deep breath, enjoying the peace. Little by little, her surroundings continued to interact with her.

"Larrick...Larrick!" came a yell. Bandar scouts were running towards the group. "Someone is coming across the river."

"That was fast," John said. "Everyone get back!" he commanded, leading his troops to forge a protective line.

Jeanette had confronted Cadmus last night and it had given her renewed faith and confidence. She walked to the front of the group, standing next to John.

He gave her a worried glance. But then his expression

changed to one of assurance, and he put his hand on his hilt.

"Everything's going to be okay," he said.

"I know."

Out of the clearing came a group of soldiers, some walking, and some riding, led by a lone figure on a horse. They did not seem to be advancing for battle.

"Jeanette!" the man in the front yelled.

A feeling of disbelief came over her. She put her hand to her mouth in wonderful surprise.

"Do you know who it is?" John asked.

"It's my father," she said, and started to run. It was the first time that she could remember wanting to run to her father.

When they met a relief came over him, she felt it. She had caused him so much grief, more than he already had to deal with, and she was sorry. She wrapped her arms around him. He did the same.

"Thank you," Jeanette said.

"I'm just glad you are all right."

She stepped back, breaking the hug. "Father, I am..."

He shook his head. "It's okay. All that matters is that you are safe."

"What about..." Jeanette started. She couldn't believe what she was about to ask. "What about mom?" More than anything, she couldn't believe her father would leave her mother's side.

"Rhilynne is looking in on her. She will be okay."

Jeanette looked behind him at the mass of soldiers. "Who are they?"

"They are the rest of my men," John said. "But why are they with you?"

"Because they were getting antsy without their leader," Jacob said with a grin. "You told them you would send for them if needed...I figured I would save somebody the trip."

John smiled. "You have no idea how much trouble you have saved us. Cadmus was here last night and would have come after them. Thank you for leading them here."

"Cadmus was here? Last night?"

"Yes. He says he will do everything he can to bring me in," Jeanette answered. "He is not the same man he was on the caravan."

Jacob shook his head. "I should have made Corwin stay."

"We can't worry about that right now," John said. "Larrick knows of a safe place we can hide and regroup."

"I don't know what you've started, Jeanette," Jacob said looking around, "but whatever it is, you certainly are not alone."

She was not alone. All she ever thought she wanted was to get away from Emerleigh, to be alone. To make her own decisions and to be who she wanted to be. To be free.

"It's time to go, we cannot waste any more time," Larrick shouted to the group. John started barking orders to his men while Tristyn and Jacob shared a short reunion.

Jeanette walked over to Hermes. He was the one that had been willing to give her a chance. "Should I call you Asa or Hermes?"

Years of emotion welled in his face. "I would appreciate it if you call me Hermes."

She nodded. There was more to his story and she would need to know it, but not now. "Okay, Hermes. Thank you, for everything."

Hermes gave her a stern look. "How many times do I have to tell you? You need to stop thanking me."

He was right, Jeanette had no idea what awaited her - awaited them - as they left Norbrook.

# EPILOGUE

It had been months since Cadmus rode the speckled shoreline on the banks of Lake Jezreel. Sitting in the heart of the continent, it was the natural barrier that touched all four kingdoms. Cadmus stopped his horse and dismounted, his boots hitting the sand.

He hated sand. It was too unpredictable, too soft. Unsteady. But he loved the view of the lake. Even in the pitch black of night, the moon hung a reflection that lighted the shore. It was calm, stable.

He walked toward a tent with four soldiers posted in front. The only light came from two torches in the ground. The guards stood, strong, tall. Their dark hair cropped and tight. Thick leather shirts and pants guarded them. With the dark of night surrounding them, their eyes looked black. The banner that hung from the tent was brown, with a golden arrow pointing up between the middle of two axes that crossed in the middle. No doubt, they arrived a short time before Cadmus with only a few minutes to prepare.

The brown eyed soldiers of Tamir were quick and

efficient.

Cadmus walked past the soldiers without saying anything and into the tent.

"Cadmus, it's good to see you."

"Sorry it's taken so long for us to meet again, General Raken."

"No problem. I trust you had a safe trip? I hope you got away undetected."

"Of course."

"And you traveled alone?"

"Yes, sir."

"What news do you bring?"

"We continue to have defense as our number one strategy. That seems to still be sitting well with the council."

"What of this upcoming wedding and the talk of new green eyed girls? This news has come to us and is most disturbing."

Cadmus hoped Raken would not have heard about the green eyed girls quite yet. "Nothing to worry about," Cadmus said, waving it off. "The queen is set on having her son married off. She wanted me to create a serum to see if green eyes could be brought back. I made a placebo, but it appears that there were two girls who changed...on their own."

"What do you mean 'on their own'?" Raken asked, with a hint of displeasure. Cadmus knew it was a stretch.

"It was destiny. I know that is not what you want to hear, but I can swear to you, my elixir had nothing to do with the change of those two girls," Cadmus said, lying...mostly. His elixir had everything to do with the change of Lorelei. She had been hand-picked even before the festivals. Cadmus knew Lorelei was the right girl to help tame Braxton.

But Jeanette, she was special. Her eyes changed on their own. There had been only one other person he ever knew whose eyes changed on their own.

Asa.

Raken did not look pleased. "What about the possibility of ending the six still living that have the true color? You said that was a top priority."

Cadmus postured an apology. "I know, Raken, I know. Things have been...complicated. The serum, and the festivals, everything is taking longer than planned."

"I don't say this lightly, Cadmus, but your actions make me question your loyalty to Tamir."

"Do not doubt my loyalty, General!" Cadmus exclaimed. He needed there to be no doubt in Tamir that his loyalty was still intact. He reached up to his left eye and with his fingers, and a little effort, he pulled out a small circlet. He laid it on the table.

Looking at Raken with one green eye and one brown eye, he said, back straight, "My true eyes are brown and always will be."

"You mean one true eye is brown. What is the color of the other one, again," Raken asked, condescending. Rage built in Cadmus. For now, he kept calm and cowering, just the way he was supposed to be.

Cadmus removed the ringlet from the other eye. "That's right," Raken teased, "purple. You are a half-caste and lucky to be alive Cadmus, don't ever forget that. You serve willingly under the King of Tamir."

He had never forgotten it. It drove him, obsessed him. Everything he did was because of the status and degradation that came from being born with two eye colors.

"Yes, of course," Cadmus said, feigning forgiveness.

"Good," Raken said. "You were sent to keep the kingdom from regaining their color. The prince cannot marry a girl with green eyes. Do you understand?"

"Of course," Cadmus said, picking up the circlets and putting them back in his eyes. They returned to their green color.

"You are dismissed."

Cadmus left, feeling the weight of the meeting off his shoulders. He felt positive, though he needed more time.

He needed time to keep Tamir off his back, more time for Braxton to be convinced of Lorelei, and more time to find Jeanette.

*Jeanette.*

She was the secret. He had hoped the sample Auryn brought him would be sufficient; it was not. He needed her and once he had her, there would be no more worry about loyalty, or war, or trust.

He would make everything right.

As he transitioned from sand to hard earth, the light from Raken's tent disappeared into the night sky.

"How did your meeting go?" Barrett said, appearing as if out of nowhere.

"As good as can be expected." Cadmus answered. He hated having someone involved as deep as Barrett was, but things had become desperate.

"Our kingdom needs a leader, Master Cadmus. You are doing the right thing," Barrett said. "Just give me the word...I will happily put down John and the girl and whatever rebellion they think they are leading."

"The time will come, Barrett. Of that you can be sure."

As they rode back to the castle, Cadmus' mind turned to the future. There was no need to dwell on the past; the future was all that mattered.

No more separate kingdoms, no more war. No more inequality and heartache, as he knew as a boy in Tamir. All of the people across all the kingdoms would have everything in common.

Including their eye color.

If you enjoyed MAIDEN, you are encouraged to rate and review the book on Amazon and Goodreads.

Please visit
www.maidentrilogy.com
for news and updates regarding...

# DAMSEL

## BOOK TWO IN THE MAIDEN TRILOGY

# MY SINCERE APPRECIATION GOES...

To Amanda, my wife and editor-in-chief. She has put up with me fretting, stressing, laughing, crying and all around obsessing over this story for seven years. It would have been impossible without your love, support, and input. And hey, if nothing else, at least I didn't kill you in this story.

To Michael, Alex, Andi, Jordan and Isaac, my children. For not giving me a hard time when I could have been home before 5pm, but wasn't. Each of you inspire me to be better. I hope you enjoy my stories and that they motivate you to come up with stories of your own.

To my parents, my biggest fans. Everything I am is because of you. Thanks for always being there.

To Justin, my numero uno storytelling companion. For your constant pushing and encouraging for me to do gooder. Your thoughts and insight were game changers. My characters nodding will never be the same.

To Lana Krumwiede, my writing mentor and friend. It is no accident we met when we did. You gave me a chance and put your arms around me and helped me understand truly what was possible. I will never be able to repay you.

To Richmond Children's Writer Group, my local comrades in storytelling. For the time, attention, and care you gave in your critiques. I learned more than I ever thought possible.

To David Estes, my digital pen pal. Your sincere love and energy of writing is infectious (in a good way). Because you never gave up on your dream, I didn't give up on mine.

To Trey G. and Kaitlyn S., my snowblitz buddies. For all the hot summer hours helping me shave ice and create Jeanette's world.

To Courtney S., one of my first beta readers. For not being afraid to give me a different perspective. Your humble encouragement always seem to come at just the right time.

To Kristin P., my greatest cheerleader. For always, well, being my greatest cheerleader. Never has anyone liked my Facebook posts with such speed. It is appreciated!

To Brooke 'The Cover Contessa', my educator of all things blog-ish. For not telling me no when you could have. Your positive influence kept me taking it one step at a time. Thank you!

To Molly Jaffa, for taking the time to get to know me at that conference so many years ago. You showed me by example that the more you give, the more you get. I sincerely hope you are on the receiving end of all the success you deserve.

To Kristi Tuck Austin, for everything you do for all the writers in Richmond. I have no idea how many hours went into all the programs you have planned, coordinated, and led, but please know that they changed my life.

To Enya, my muse. Yes, *that* Enya. If you ever happen to read this, know that if there was ever an award for the person who has listened to the album *Amarantine* the most, it would be me. Those songs stirred my soul and whispered to me. They are the spirit of MAIDEN. Thank you for sharing your gift.

# ABOUT THE AUTHOR

Chris Sorensen is a native of Richmond, Virginia, and a high school counselor by profession, but his passion is stories. He also loves naps, ice cream, watching cartoons with his kids, and making a fool of himself in public (according to his wife).

He has two adult, inspirational novels in publication. *The Greatest Discovery* was a regional favorite and won Book-of-the-Year for the Virginia College Stores Association (2003). The prequel, *The Greatest Choice*, followed in 2007. Both are available in print and ebook format on Amazon.com.

MAIDEN is his first young adult novel.

Chris loves to discuss anything to do with writing, books and publishing. He would love to hear from you.

www.csorensenwrite.com

chris@csorensenwrite.com

Made in the USA
Middletown, DE
28 May 2019